Conflicted

LISA SUZANNE

Heather-
Choose happiness.
XO,
Lisa Suzanne

CONFLICTED

Published in the United States of America by Lisa Suzanne.

ISBN-13: 978-1537100562
ISBN-10: 1537100564

Cover Art by Amy Queau at Q Design

Conflicted

BOOKS BY LISA SUZANNE

Not Just Another Romance Novel

Vintage Volume One

Vintage Volume Two

How He Really Feels (He Feels, Book 1)

What He Really Feels (He Feels, Book 2)

Since He Really Feels (He Feels, Book 3)

Separation Anxiety

Side Effects

Second Opinion

DEDICATION

To my husband, who always puts our family first,
and to our sweet little boy.

Chapter One

"Ladies and gentlemen, please welcome the brand new CEO of Benson Industries, my son and one hell of a man, Mr. Cole Benson."

The man who was about to become my new boss stepped up to the podium. "Thank you, Dad, and congratulations on your retirement." He smiled at his father, and then he turned toward the crowd of employees who had gathered in the lecture room. "I'm thrilled to take over the role of CEO from my father, who built Benson Industries on a dime and a dream, as he always says. Together, we will continue to drive products from design to market."

He started outlining some four-point plan, but my mind drifted. I couldn't help it.

I'd never met Cole in person. He'd been running the New York office, but he was relocating to Los Angeles to take on his new role.

I was sad to see Jack retire. He'd been a fair and kind boss, really like a second father to me. But as sad as I was to see him go, looking at his son was certainly much better than dear old dad.

I was sitting near the back of the lecture room, so my view was partially obstructed. I couldn't wait to get a good, clean look at him. I knew he was attractive—I'd been in the office as his father Skyped him, and I'd spoken to him on the phone several times.

I thought back to just about a month earlier when Jack had shown me some photos from a family trip to Hawaii. Cole Benson wearing just swim trunks had taken my breath away. The man was chiseled everywhere, and I just wished I'd had the chance to forward a picture to myself so I could really give it a good inspection. I Facebook stalked him—justifying my actions in my mind with the fact that he was my boss's son—but all his public photos were from business events.

I didn't know what to expect other than the daily temptation I'd face working for a man whose face rivaled a model and whose body rivaled a Greek god.

After Cole's speech ended and I realized that I hadn't heard a word aside from his first three sentences, I returned to my desk with the hope I'd meet the man I'd be assistant to. Unfortunately, though, Jack ushered him out to lunch to introduce him to some clients, and they didn't return by the time the clock struck five.

I glanced at my husband as the alarm clock sounded the next morning. He was snoring away. I couldn't help the feeling of resentment that came with the fact that he'd gotten home after I'd already gone to bed the night before. Sometimes I felt like he loved his job more than me.

I shook it off. Non-communication with John was nothing new, but what awaited me at work that morning was. I wanted to make the very best impression I could on Cole, so I woke up early and put a little extra effort into my morning routine.

I chose a professional fitted navy shift dress and matching heels. I dried and straightened my hair and polished off the look with a chunky necklace and matching earrings. I felt pretty and ready to meet my new boss.

Until I stepped outside.

Cole's first official day was a rare rainy Tuesday morning in LA.

I cursed the rain that turned my sleek hair into a frizzy mess. I ran across the apartment parking lot to our assigned space that was nowhere near where we lived as I wished for the umbrella that was stored in—you guessed it—my car.

I barely sidestepped a muddy puddle and patted down my hair. Normally, the apartment I shared with John was only a ten minute drive from work, fifteen if there was traffic. Unfortunately, though, with rain came accidents. So my fifteen minute drive turned into thirty.

It was five after nine when I finally arrived at my desk.

The man I'd drooled over in photos towered imposingly over my desk. Irritation glazed his handsome face as he turned toward me, and I froze for one brief moment as our eyes met.

The photos hadn't done him justice.

This man flew right past handsome on the hunk meter with his black hair and dark eyes that were fixated on me. A perfectly manicured scruff outlined his strong jaw, and my eyes stopped for the briefest of moments on his full, ripe lips.

He was pulled together, professional, and effortless, and I couldn't remember another time when just looking at a man had actually taken my breath away.

The attraction was instant and insane. My heart started racing as I thought about that picture Jack had shown me.

I reached up to wipe my mouth to make sure I wasn't drooling. The only thought in my mind was what he had hidden under that suit.

"You're late, Ms. Cleary. I expect you to be on time."

Those were the first words ever directed at me in person from the mouth of the god.

I rushed toward my desk, and I caught a hint of his scent. Fresh, clean, and masculine. "My apologies, sir. Traffic was—"

He cut me off. "Account for traffic in your commute. You'll stay late to make up your tardiness."

"Yes, sir."

I would *not* cry thirty seconds after meeting my new boss.

But he was right. I'd been late. I'd gotten up early to make a good impression, yet I still managed to make a bad one.

I got my computer up and running as I considered my options. I didn't want to bother him on his first day, but I wanted to let him know that I was available for whatever he needed.

I stood and knocked on his door.

"Yes?"

I peeked my head in. He was staring at his computer. "Cole, is there anything I can do for you this morning?"

He didn't look up from his screen. "Come back in twenty minutes and we will discuss your tasks."

"Okay," I said, turning to leave.

"And Ms. Cleary?"

I turned back toward him, loving the view of him behind his desk as he finally ripped his eyes from his computer to look at me. "Yes?"

"It's Mr. Benson."

I was about to object that his father had always insisted I refer to him as "Jack," but I didn't want to make things worse. Besides, he wasn't his father.

And it was clear that he was going to prove it.

I glanced through the calendar appointments for the next two weeks as I waited for our meeting. As the transitioning CEO, Cole had a ton of engagements with clients in the area. He needed to meet with the heavy hitters to assure them their accounts were safe and nothing would change unless it was for the better. That was where I came in—at least, that's what Jack had told me.

Since I'd been with the company for six years, I had quite the handle on clients, accounts, and data. Jack trusted me with everything after I'd worked my way up from an intern to his executive assistant. He had depended on me to keep him on schedule and informed about each client. I wondered how Cole's expectations would differ from his father's.

I printed the schedule and brought it with me nineteen minutes later to Cole's office. I knocked on the door.

"What?" he snapped.

"Mr. Benson? I think it's time for our meeting."

He looked up from his computer at me and raised an eyebrow. My heart leapt in my chest.

God, I couldn't seem to get past how handsome he was.

"You think?"

"It's been twenty minutes."

He sighed. "Sit."

I sat. "Here's a list of your appointments for the next two weeks," I said, handing over the papers I'd printed.

He took them and tossed them in the trash can beside his desk. "Send me digital appointments for each. Set up two reminders—one twenty-four hours in advance and one two hours in advance."

I hadn't thought that I might need to take notes during our meeting. I'd never had to do that with Jack. I glanced around for a pen and paper.

He sighed in annoyance. "What now?"

"Can I have paper and a pen?" I felt like a child asking.

"Never come to a meeting unprepared," he said, tossing a pad of paper and a pen across the desk toward me.

"I'm sorry." I scribbled down his request for the meeting reminders.

"My father left me a list of what you did for him. It's extensive. He trusted you with a lot of confidential information, but you'll need to earn my trust. Thus far, you're not off to a strong start."

"My apologies."

"It seems like you've done an awful lot of apologizing this morning. Instead, just get it right."

"Yes, sir." I took a shuddering breath, refusing to get upset. I needed to grow a thicker skin if I planned to get past the first day with my new boss.

"For now, you'll retain schedule and office management, some data analysis, and most client communication. You'll continue to prepare information and research as needed. You'll create client presentations, draft contracts, and manage some records. Once you've proven yourself, I'll give you additional duties with more confidential client information."

"Won't the contracts have confidential information?"

He gave me a look like I was stupid. "You'll leave those sections blank and I'll fill them in."

I nodded. "I promise to do all I can to earn your trust."

"This isn't a presidential election, Ms. Cleary. You'll earn my trust by arriving on time and prepared."

"Anything else, sir?" I asked.

"Did you take notes on my four-point plan yesterday?"

I shook my head as I felt the heat creep up into my cheeks. I hadn't even been paying attention since I'd been caught up in daydreams of Cole Benson wearing swim trunks.

He sighed and looked up toward the ceiling. I pretended he wasn't rolling his eyes.

"The document with the plan is in the shared folder. Draft an email to the staff that outlines the major points. Send it to me for approval."

"Will do." I tried my hardest to sound enthusiastic and cheerful.

"And get me a reservation for two tonight at Chamonix."

"How do you spell that?"

"If only there was some sort of device that you could use to find the answer."

I stared at him in shock as his eyes returned to whatever he was working on.

"Don't ever ask me something you could google."

I glared at him since he wasn't looking at me anyway.

"That's all for now," he said, effectively dismissing me. I headed back to my desk to start on the tasks he'd given me, feeling like I was the one starting a new job instead of him.

Chapter Two

I stood in front of my husband, waiting for him to look up and acknowledge that I was in the same room. Finally, I cleared my throat. He raised his eyebrows at me as if to say that I was interrupting him and could I please hurry it up.

"We need to leave in ten minutes." I glanced at his unkempt bedhead and sweatpants.

"Do we have to go?" John whined.

"Yes. Madi will only turn five once."

"Just go without me."

"They're expecting both of us."

He turned his attention back to his iPad. "Make something up, then."

Make something up? I wasn't going to lie to my family, especially not my sister. Kaylee and I shared everything. Well, almost everything.

I'd left out some of the details about my marriage.

"John, I'm not going to lie for you."

He sighed dramatically and set his iPad down, looking up at me again. "Tell them I had to work."

"Our goddaughter is expecting you," I said, trying to play on his soft spot for our niece, the girl who we'd agreed to raise should anything ever happen to her parents. I glanced at the iPad screen. He had some game going. "That doesn't look like work."

"Will you give me a goddamn break? I'm developing video game software, okay?"

"I don't have time for this." I still needed to wrap the present, so I left it at that.

And those were the last words I spoke to him that entire day.

Before I'd gotten married, I'd always lived by the rule that you should never leave the house mad or go to bed angry.

But dammit, I was mad. I wasn't going to be the one to back down this time. John was missing a precious five-year-old's birthday party—a five-year-old who adored him, by the way—so he could play video games. Or maybe so he wouldn't have to spend time with my family.

The drive to my sister's house in Santa Clarita took nearly an hour, giving me plenty of time to reflect on my marriage.

John and I had drifted apart in the three years we'd been married. Maybe we'd jumped the gun and gotten married too quickly, but we'd dated for almost two years before the big day. And after the big day, we settled into complacency. We'd become one of those boring, old, married couples I always dreaded being a part of.

It wasn't me who changed, though.

John had become virtually unrecognizable.

He used to bike all the time to stay in shape. In fact, he'd once trained for and competed in a hundred mile race. Now his bike was gathering dust in our storage closet.

He used to love sampling craft beer. He'd find a brewery within driving distance and we'd go spend the afternoon tasting beer and laughing together. The last time we'd done that had been for his birthday the year before.

We didn't take vacations because John didn't want to take time off work. We didn't go out on weeknights because one or both of us was usually working late. We didn't even have date nights anymore except for our obligatory last Friday of the month date.

I didn't feel like I had much in common with him anymore.

We got married because we loved one another. We had a small wedding and exchanged simple bands to save money for our future. We didn't need flashy diamonds or a big wedding, even if a small part in the back of my mind wanted those things just like almost every girl did.

Shortly after we'd gotten married, though, I started wondering if I'd said yes because I'd wanted the wedding rather than the relationship.

Something needed to change, but I didn't know how to get through to a man who cared more about his job than his wife.

"Where's John?"

I must've been asked that question ten different times at Madi's party. My mother, my father, my sister, my brother-in-law, my aunts, my cousins, my grandma, and, of course, the birthday girl herself.

Each time I answered the same: "Working." I feigned a sad face, but truth be told, I was kind of happy to be away from him for the day. It gave me the space to think that our small apartment didn't seem to offer.

It wasn't until the party was nearing its end that my sister cornered me. We were washing dishes when she started asking questions.

"Where is he, really?" she asked.

I shrugged. "Working."

"Lucy, it's me."

I glanced up from the soapy water to meet my sister's concerned eyes. She was my opposite with her blonde hair and big blue eyes. She was a replica of my mom, and Madi was her mini-me. I'd been graced with my dad's dark brown hair and caramel-colored eyes.

I handed her a plate to dry and refocused my attention on the dishes. "He said to say he's working. I don't know what he's doing. Sitting at home playing video games."

"Why didn't he come?"

"I have no idea."

She paused and looked up at me. "Do you think he's…never mind."

"What?" I scrubbed the dish in my hands a little harder.

"Do you think he's cheating?"

"John?" I shook my head. I hadn't thought he might have been until she brought it up. "No. He wouldn't."

"Okay. If you say so."

"I do," I said, trying to convince myself more than her.

"But it is a bit of a red flag."

"What is?"

"Not showing up for family events. Working all the time."

I nodded, not wanting to get into it with my sister—especially not at a family party.

"Are you still happy with him?"

My sister always knew how to ask the hard questions. She'd been one of the few people to ask me if marrying John was what I'd really wanted back before the wedding.

I rinsed the last dish and washed my hands before answering. "I don't know if I've ever really been happy with him. Not since before the wedding, anyway."

She nodded once, as if she'd known that all along. She stepped toward me, pulling me into a hug. "Thank God you finally admitted it."

"You knew?"

"Lucy, I know you better than anyone. Don't you think I could tell?"

I sighed and looked out the window above her sink. "So now what?"

"You either fix it or you move on."

Her words replayed in my mind for the rest of the day. I was never one to just give up, and our conversation gave me a boost of determination.

I was going to fix my marriage. I was going to be happy with John again. I just had to figure out how to battle against the first love in his life…his job.

Chapter Three

After two weeks under the tyrannical rule of Cole Benson, I missed feeling appreciated.

Saying goodbye to the boss I actually liked played in my mind often, but never so often as when Cole was acting like an asshole.

"Ms. Cleary, I need the Hinkley presentation by three o'clock."

"Yes, sir." I sighed heavily, thinking that his *father* never would've treated me like that.

I needed to stop thinking that way. Jack had retired. He wasn't coming back. Cole was my new reality.

The Hinkley presentation wasn't anywhere near finished, but if I didn't finalize it by three, my ass would be handed to me.

I'd managed to earn his trust in just a few days. I hadn't been a minute late since that first day. In fact, I was usually a half an hour early and stayed late because he seemed to need me even more than his father had.

But I was pretty sure the real reason he gave me his trust so quickly was that he didn't want to do the work. It was easier for him to dictate numbers to me—or better yet, forward me an email—than it was for him to open the contract and find the right spot to place them.

I dropped what I was doing and opened the PowerPoint, thinking how much I wanted to quit my job and do something—anything—else. Cole Benson was a slave driver, and I was slave to whatever he needed.

So why didn't I quit?

I liked the company, and I cared about the clients.

I needed the money. I had rent and credit card bills.

Plus, I was in the running for Assistant of the Year. It was a competition Jack had started before he left. If I won, it meant a ten thousand dollar bonus check. I was up against two other women—Mary, assistant to the head of marketing, and Jasmine, assistant to the director of human resources.

All three of us were deserving of the award, although Jack had often told me that I handled the biggest workload as the assistant to the CEO of the entire company.

But more than all that, I stayed at my job because I really didn't think Cole could get by without me.

It was crazy to admit it, but even though I hated him pretty much all the time, I wanted to work hard to impress him. The meaner he was to me, the more I saw it as a challenge to do something—anything—right just to hear a single word of praise pass from his gorgeous lips.

And so there I was, setting aside the mounds of paperwork that had somehow stacked up on my desk. I didn't have a choice. I had to appease the asshole in the large corner office with the big walnut desk I had the distinct displeasure of sitting beside every weekday.

I huffed my way through my work, thankful at least for my creative skills and PowerPoint knowhow. I was pissed once again at Mr. Benson, who I called "Cole" in my head simply because I could, but there was little I could do about it.

My cell phone started buzzing. "Hey," I answered when I saw it was my sister calling.

"Did you talk to John yet?"

I loved her bluntness. No greeting, no pleasantries. Just right down to business.

I cradled my phone against my shoulder as I multi-tasked, setting transitions to each slide while chatting. "Not yet."

"It's been over two weeks! What are you waiting for?"

"A time when I don't feel like I'm interrupting him just by talking to him."

"Bullshit. Do it over dinner. Get it done."

"Kaylee, it's not that easy. Every time I try—"

"Ms. Cleary," Cole's voice interrupted me mid-sentence. "I'm not paying you for personal calls. I'll expect your phone to be stored away during business hours."

"I have to go. I'll call you later." I hung up on my sister and raised my eyes timidly to look at my boss. "I didn't, um…your dad allowed it."

He narrowed his eyes at me. "I'm not my father."

"No shit," is what I wanted to say, but instead, I actually said, "I'm sorry, sir."

I finished the PowerPoint with about twenty seconds to spare, saving the file where Cole could access it. I dialed into his office.

"Yes?" he answered. It was better than the "What?" he snapped at me most days.

"I finished the Hinkley presentation, Mr. Benson. It's in the shared folder."

"Cutting it close, Ms. Cleary. I'll check it and get back to you."

He ended the call, and I dug back into the contracts I'd set aside to work on the Hinkley presentation.

I nearly jumped out of my skin when his voice cut into my thoughts as he stood in front of my desk a few minutes later. "Ms. Cleary, the presentation is missing a transition between slides seven and eight, and you need to double check the final numbers on the last slide. Perhaps if you hadn't been so busy on your personal call, you might've paid better attention to detail."

I couldn't decide if I wanted to smack his condescending mouth or feel it dragging along the skin on my neck.

I bit my lip to keep myself from responding with something snarky and silently counted to three. It was a technique I'd learned when researching how to deal with an awful boss.

"Yes, sir," I said, looking up at him and conjuring my sweetest smile.

He towered over my desk, all clean, hard lines in a navy suit as his milk chocolate eyes pinned me to my seat. He ran a hand over his wavy, black hair and then scrubbed a hand down the scruff on his cheek.

I couldn't help but wonder what that scruff would feel like under my fingertips.

Okay, fine. I had to admit it.

I hated my boss's guts, but I also had a tiny crush on him.

And by tiny, I meant massive.

It was a good thing he was such a dick, because if he was a likable guy, he'd tempt me every single day. This way was better, though. I could admire the outside of the package without getting into any real trouble.

And speaking of package, my eyes drifted down to his pants for a split second before I caught myself. "I'm sorry it wasn't up to your standard."

"Just fix it," he said thickly, and then he disappeared into his office. He *hated* when I apologized.

I watched his firm ass retreat back into his office, and then I finalized the file before calling to notify him that I was finished.

"What?" he snapped.

I wondered if he ever had a good day. Ever.

"The Hinkley file is done. Let me know what else I can do."

"Finally," he said, and then he ended the call. I sighed. It would be nice to hear a "thanks" once in a while, but Cole just wasn't that kind of boss.

I didn't dare leave a moment before five as I didn't want to endure his wrath, but once my day ended twenty minutes after everyone else had left the office—except Cole—I headed home.

The dread I felt as I headed into the office each morning sort of matched the dread I felt as I headed home each evening.

I walked into an empty apartment as usual. I went to the bedroom to change as I contemplated what happened between John and me. When we first got together, we used to have long talks that lasted well into the night. But now our talks consisted of conversational civilities rather than meaningful discussions.

I slipped off my shoes in my walk-in closet and pulled my dress over my head. I stopped and stared at the girl in the full-length mirror in my closet.

I couldn't help but wonder if it was me that was driving my husband to work so much. I didn't look much different than I had when we'd gotten married. My straight, dark hair that tumbled over my shoulders just to the top of my breasts was maybe a bit longer than it had been three years ago. As I gazed into my own caramel brown eyes, I didn't see anything different. I studied the light smattering of freckles across my nose that deepened in the summer months. They were exactly the same as they'd always been.

I unhooked my bra and slid my panties down my legs.

My body was essentially the same, too. I'd worked out a little harder closer to the wedding, so I'd been in better shape at the time. I hadn't put on weight in the years since we'd gotten married, though—I'd just lost some muscle tone. I pinched the skin around my belly. I was blessed with good genes that allowed me to stay fit as long as I watched my diet and exercised a few times a week. I used to consider marathon nights with John exercise, but it had been a long time since we'd had one of those.

As I stared at my naked reflection, my hands began to wander. I might not have been getting physical with my husband, but a girl still had needs. The stress of my job and my lackluster marriage left me with pent-up anxiety that needed a release.

I cupped my breasts in my hands. It felt good, and I knew it was because they'd gone untouched by my husband for so long. My fingers found my nipples and I squeezed them. My stomach clenched as the familiar strains of anticipation raced through me.

If John wasn't going to take care of my sexual needs, I was going to have to take care of myself.

I slowed my movements, allowing the tantalizing pleasure of my own touch to cultivate the ache between my legs. Eventually I allowed my fingers to trail down my body until I inserted one and then two into my wet heat.

I pushed them in as far as they would go and held them there for a few beats. I worked them out slowly, almost agonizingly so, until the need for friction compelled me to plunge them back in.

I moved leisurely, knowing I had all the time in the world since I was home alone—and probably would be for at least a few more hours.

I opened my eyes and watched the girl in the mirror. I watched as my fingers moved in and out of me. I watched as my breasts bounced with my movements. I watched as my lips contorted in pleasure.

I drove my fingers in and out until I felt everything down low tighten deliciously, and then I pulled them out and rubbed my clit furiously, the ache spurring me on toward my climax.

As the wave of bliss finally washed over me, it wasn't my husband whose face flashed through my mind. It wasn't Bradley Cooper, or Tom Brady, or Adam Levine.

It wasn't any of my favorite fantasies.

It was my dick of a boss.

I saw Cole.

It stopped me short for a fleeting second, but then it drove me to an even harder climax, my body clenching everywhere as pleasure pulsed erratically through me.

Chapter Four

I'll be at work until at least eight. Go ahead and eat without me.

I stared at the text on my phone, not sure how to respond. What was there to say? I'd be going home to an empty house and eating dinner alone. Again. I thought having a husband meant that I'd no longer feel lonely.

Wrong.

I'd never felt more lonely than I had since John and I had drifted apart.

"Ms. Cleary, I'll need you back at your desk in five minutes." Cole's voice broke into my silent seething as I stared at my phone.

I glanced up at him, and I felt uncomfortable as I thought about my closet climax the day before. Why had I come so damn hard when he popped into my head? I wondered if he was as dominating in the bedroom as he was in the office. I wondered what kind of kisser he was. What kind of lover he was.

He was rocking another suit, and my eyes drifted to his broad shoulders before I snapped myself out of my fantasies.

It was ridiculous. Cole was an asshole. I saw the kinds of ladies he took to work functions when I'd Facebook stalked him. They were leggy, blonde, and scorching hot. Even if I was single, he would never want me.

Even if there was some small chance in hell he had any interest, he'd never cross the line with his married assistant—especially not when he'd just taken over as CEO.

And I'd never cheat on John even if the offer was on the table.

"Yes, sir," I said, setting my phone down and focusing on shoveling the rest of my lunch into my mouth. His cap on my lunchbreak gave me a total of fourteen minutes, but arguing the point was futile. I didn't want to be accused of talking back to the boss, so I shut my mouth and did what he said.

I wouldn't win Assistant of the Year if I spent my time arguing with him, and he and the other company bigwigs were finalizing their decision within the next month or two.

I headed back to my desk. Mr. Benson sat in one of the chairs across from my desk. His elbows rested on his knees, and his hands were folded in front of him as he stared down at a spot on the floor. I took a moment to enjoy the view.

When his dark eyes met mine, a surge of anticipation bounced up my spine. I couldn't help but wonder if he felt it, too.

"I need you to book me a trip to New York. Flight and hotel." He stood. "I emailed you the details. I'm taking a last-minute opening for a presentation spot at a conference, and I'll need an assistant. It's partially over a weekend, so check your calendar." He headed back into his office without waiting for my reply.

Was that his way of inviting me on a trip to New York? Or was that his way of demanding I attend the conference with him?

Either way, with Assistant of the Year on the line and the strong desire to get away from John for a few days, I was in.

And I was just a little bit interested in what Cole might be like outside of the office.

I opened his email, a forward of the conference details. It was less than two weeks away, which meant that we had a lot of work to do in a short amount of time.

I supposed I had an obligation to check a five night trip with my husband, so I finally responded to the text he'd sent me earlier.

My boss asked if I can accompany him on a trip to New York a week from Wednesday through the following Monday. Do you have any reasons why I shouldn't go?

I could've been a little nicer, I supposed. But it took two to tango, and he hadn't exactly been full of pleasantries lately.

As I glanced at the calendar, I realized that the trip would take place over the last weekend of the month—over our monthly date night. I wondered if he'd even notice, let alone tell me not to go.

In the old days, he would've responded with something sweet—something to let me know that he didn't want me to go because he was going to miss me, or that he didn't want us to miss out on our important date night.

But it wasn't the old days anymore, and I wasn't sure he actually would miss me. I was pretty sure I wouldn't miss him, either. Maybe this trip was exactly what the two of us needed. Maybe it would help us get back on track and feel something for each other aside from irritation.

A reply came quickly. *Go ahead.*

I dialed into Cole's office.

"Yes?"

"I checked my calendar and I'll be able to accompany you on the trip."

"Fine. Start the travel arrangements."

His *fine* echoed around my head.

What was worse? Being buried in indifference at home? Or traveling with my son of a bitch boss for six days?

It wasn't like I had someone eagerly waiting for me to come home, anyway. John was always working late, and I would be, too, as I prepared for the conference.

The conference ran Thursday through Sunday, and Cole wanted to get there the day before it started. He chose to leave Monday in case he had additional business while we were in New York. I hoped we'd have time to sightsee—or, rather, I hoped that *I* would have time to sightsee as I didn't really picture myself tooling around town with Cole.

I wanted to see the Empire State Building and the 911 Memorial and take in a show on Broadway. I wanted to eat a hot dog from a street vendor and walk into one of those teeny-tiny restaurants where you could order your slice of New York style pizza and get it at the end of the counter.

I pictured myself doing all of that alone while Cole did whatever he did.

But it wouldn't be the worst thing in the world to have a travel companion.

Cole was presenting a segment on how to build a successful client base using technology. He dictated the things he wanted included in the presentation as I typed it and set it up. He sent me facts and figures and tables to include, and I set to work on creating a stunning visual presentation.

My phone rang, and I saw that it was Cole calling from his office. "Hi, Mr. Benson."

"Ms. Cleary, I was just informed of a working dinner tonight. Are you available for notes?"

"Yes, sir."

"Fine." He ended our call.

I'd gone to two other working dinners with Cole in the short time he'd been my boss, and the food had been spectacular. But the best part was that he paid me overtime. So I got a free dinner at a nice restaurant plus extra pay, and all I had to do was memorize whatever was discussed, type up some notes, and send them to him by morning.

I rushed home at five o'clock to change and freshen up. A kind boss might've let me go early so I had time to change, but not Cole. I rushed around, throwing on deodorant over a sweaty body and brushing my hair so fast I ripped painfully through a knot.

I picked out a new dress I'd bought, a springy white one with yellow flowers and a white belt around the waist. My favorite feature was that it even had pockets, the perfect place for my cell phone and keys.

I applied some shiny lip gloss and headed back toward the office. Cole had asked me to be back no later than half past six, and I rolled in with two minutes to spare, arriving at my desk right on time.

He was waiting outside his office door, standing with his arms folded as he leaned against the frame. He looked like a damn book cover standing there. He gazed at me for a moment, his eyes roving over my dress and down to my heels. I braced myself for some comment from him, wishing I could read him better. I wanted him to see me the way I saw him. I wanted him to think I was pretty. I wanted him to want me.

Wait. Where had that thought come from?

I hated that I had a crush on him.

Sure, John and I had our problems. Sure, I may have had a tiny (huge) crush on my boss. Sure, I thought about him constantly and wondered what it would be like to run my fingers through his wavy black hair.

But I was a faithful wife.

Just because I found Cole sexy didn't mean I would act on it.

But having that thought—that thought that I wanted him to do something about it, to touch me, to tell me how beautiful I was, to want me…that felt like cheating.

An immediate wave of guilt washed over me.

I wasn't sure where these feelings were coming from, but I thought maybe it was for wanting something I couldn't have. Or maybe because I'd been ignored at home for so long.

He glanced at the expensive watch he wore on his wrist and then his eyes met mine. "Cutting it close as usual, Ms. Cleary. I can't be late tonight."

"My apologies, sir." Why the hell was I *apologizing* when I was on time? I hadn't done anything wrong.

He sighed and turned toward the door. "Let's go." He started walking and his arm brushed mine on his way by. He never touched me in any way, so the accidental contact sent a spike of adrenaline through my stomach.

I grabbed my iPad off my desk and then followed behind him. We took the elevator down, my legs silently thanking him for taking the elevator instead of the stairs. I blew out a breath, grateful that I'd made it on time and hadn't had to endure too much wrath.

A black Ford Expedition was waiting at the curb for us. Cole opened the door and ushered me in before getting in behind me.

He tapped away on his phone and barked orders at me as the car moved toward our destination. "We'll be meeting with Lincoln Mathers from MTC Industries, his wife Alexis, and two other executives from the company. Pay attention when they introduce themselves because I don't know their names and I'll need you to draft a follow up tomorrow. Questions?"

I shook my head, ready to be the very best assistant he could ever ask for. I was still thinking of the Assistant of the Year bonus, and events like these were my time to shine.

We pulled up to Vine, a fancy restaurant where I'd always dreamed of eating but could never afford on my own. It was one of those places I only read about in the celebrity gossip magazines.

A hostess led us to a table, checking out Cole on the way. I didn't blame her. His ass was on point in that suit. She sat us in a cozy, round corner booth, and Cole slid in, leaving the end for me. He wasn't doing it to be nice, though—he wanted to be closer to the client. I just hoped I'd be able to hear the conversation from where I sat.

As I slid in beside him, I accidentally bumped my knee against his. He glanced over at me, and where I expected annoyance, I found something else when our eyes met.

Okay, my imagination was working overtime. There was no way Cole Benson was giving me the eye.

But would it really be so bad if he was?

And holy shit, he still hadn't moved his knee. I broke our eye contact first, and then I moved my knee. I wasn't sure if he was subtly flirting with me or if he was asserting his dominance over me.

It had to be dominance. Cole would never flirt with his lowly assistant. He usually looked at me like I was barely good enough to serve him coffee.

I focused all my attention on the menu rather than the fact that my knee had touched Cole's and he hadn't moved his. I opted for a chicken dish and a glass of white wine while Cole studied his phone.

I couldn't wait for my wine to arrive. Truthfully, I worked better after a glass took the edge off. I'd remember the details of the night better because I wouldn't be feeling self-conscious as I sat next to my sex-god of a boss and his sexy knee.

The hostess led four more people to our table, and introductions began. I scooted out so Cole could stand to introduce himself. Lincoln Mathers was an attractive older man, and his wife was much younger than him. She could've passed for a Victoria's Secret model. The two others were company executives named Dean Humphry and Nathan Leonard. I stared at their faces, trying mnemonic devices to remember their names. I wished I could write this shit down.

Once our orders were placed and the drinks began to flow, I focused on the conversation. Mainly Cole and Lincoln were talking, which was helpful so I didn't have to remember what five different people were saying. Dean and Nathan observed as Cole gave Lincoln the hard sell.

Cole's hard sell sounded the same as usual, so I focused on Lincoln's responses. He seemed receptive, but Cole didn't pay me to give my opinions on his client's disposition.

Apart from the knee incident, I had basically no other interaction with Cole. I noticed Alexis staring my way with sympathy more than once, but I didn't want her pity. I forced a bright smile and moved my attention back to the conversation.

"Get me numbers first thing in the morning, Benson. Your company has great talent, but as you know, money talks. If your bid comes in below your competitors, you've got yourself a deal."

When I heard Lincoln speak those words at the end of the meal, I knew I had a long night ahead of me. Cole would need me to draft a contract while he calculated the costs and tried to pinpoint a lower number than his competitors.

When Cole needed to calculate costs, it always took longer than it should. I'd already started mentally adding and subtracting. I didn't know the money side of the business the way my boss did, but I had a fairly good grasp on it from working with contracts. I was confident that together we could come up with a number that would be fair and competitive.

Once Cole took care of the check and we sat in the back of the Expedition, I took out the iPad to notate the evening. Cole's attention was glued to his phone until I looked up and his eyes were on me.

I smiled awkwardly, surprised at his attention. He'd become fairly prone to ignoring my existence except when he needed me to do something for him, so seeing him gaze at me with no context was quite out of the ordinary.

He didn't smile back, and something in his expression changed. It had to be the darkness in the backseat of the Expedition. I was crazy to think I may have caught a hint of heat in his gaze, but then he turned his head and stared out the window with a heavy sigh, breaking the moment between us.

"I thought tonight went well," I said, trying to cut into the tension he'd created.

"Just have to figure out that magic number now." He said it quietly and without turning his head from the window.

"I can help in the morning."

"I need it tonight."

I glanced at the clock on the top of my iPad. It was getting late. Dinner ran longer than I'd expected.

But what did I have waiting for me at home? Maybe a husband—if he was home—who wouldn't bother saying more than two words to me if he was so inclined to rip his eyes away from whatever device he was working on?

"Then I'll help you tonight."

"Shouldn't you go home to your husband?"

The mention of my husband sent an icy regret down my spine.

"He's fine. I want to help you. The details from the night are fresh in my mind now. They'll fade by morning."

He finally turned from the window, but only in order to glare at me. "I pay you to make sure they don't fade."

I held up my iPad. "That's what this is for." I smiled, hoping to lighten the mood. It was futile. Despite the success of the evening, Cole was in as bad a mood as ever.

The Expedition pulled up to the front of our building, and Cole got out. He stood beside the door while I scooted out the same door he'd used.

"It's late. Go home," he said tiredly. "I'll see you in the morning."

"I just need to pop upstairs to finish my notes and drop off my iPad."

"Fine."

I followed as he strode toward the elevator. He pressed the button and we waited in silence for it to arrive.

I tried to think of something—anything—to say, some piece of trivial conversation to try to break into the awkward wall between us, but I came up short.

My biggest problem when I felt uncomfortable was my tendency to ramble. Cole Benson did something different to me. I was struck speechless in his presence. I was too busy dreaming of what he kept hidden under his expensive suits to figure out something to say.

The elevator arrived and the doors opened. We walked in together, and as soon as the doors closed, the air shifted. The tight, enclosed space grew warm with a new kind of tension between us, and I found myself thinking about his lips. His full, velvety lips.

I wondered what sorts of talented things he could do with those lips.

And the tongue that he kept hidden behind those lips. I wondered where on my body I would like the feel of his tongue best.

Over the weeks I'd been working for him, I'd noticed Cole's tongue several times. When he was deep in concentration pouring over contracts, reading emails, or pondering a specific campaign, his tongue peeked out from between his lips.

Every single time I caught a glimpse of that tongue, I couldn't help but put it to use in my mind's fantasies. I imagined his tongue dancing against mine. I imagined it licking its way from my ankle to my knee to my thigh to my center. I imagined it caressing my ear, whispering across my nipple, grazing my hipbone.

The elevator felt suddenly too small. I waved my hand in front of my face, fanning myself as I tried to cool down.

Cole's eyes were on me. I could feel them, but I refused to acknowledge them.

I wanted to look at him. I wanted to see his eyes on me. I wanted to feel like he didn't hate me. I wanted to feel like he wanted me as much as I wanted him.

I couldn't want him.

I didn't want him.

I hated him.

I was married.

I snuck a peek at him in the mirrored reflection of the elevator doors. His body was turned in my direction, but his head faced forward. Body language spoke loudly, though. The way he was turned in toward me suggested that maybe he didn't dislike me as much as he acted like he did.

Our eyes met in the reflection as a soft sheen of perspiration broke out on my forehead.

I shouldn't have been in an elevator on my way up to the office alone with my hot boss. I should've just taken my iPad home with me, typed up my notes, and gotten in bed beside the man I married.

Instead, I found myself wanting Cole to kiss me and touch me in a tiny elevator too late at night.

I broke our eye contact.

Being attracted to somebody was one thing, but in that moment on the elevator, I wanted to act on it. I wanted to feel that tongue I'd been fantasizing about moving against my body.

I wanted something to make me feel alive again.

If I acted on it, though, I'd not be just potentially ruining my career. I'd also be potentially ruining my marriage.

Chapter Five

As we exited the elevator, I had no idea what to expect. I saw several potential outcomes. In one scenario, Cole swept all the papers and office supplies off my desk in a dramatic movie-inspired moment and took me right there in the empty office. In another scenario, he had me pressed up against the windows overlooking the skyscrapers of Los Angeles.

The thought that he wouldn't act on that random, steamy moment in the elevator never crossed my mind.

And the scenario that actually happened also never entered my mind.

"What the fuck are you doing here?" Cole said to an unreasonably gorgeous blonde woman sitting in one of the chairs across from my desk. She wore a tight, black dress that left very little to the imagination, and I suddenly felt very juvenile in my sundress with flowers all over it.

"You said you'd be coming back to the office after your dinner," she said, her voice low and sultry.

He gave her an irritated look before glancing back over at me. I noticed he looked at her with a different irritation than he reserved for me on a daily basis. "Get in my office," he growled at her.

I had to wonder if he was going to use the blonde to dispel the sexual tension that had thickened the air of the elevator around us.

I had no business wondering it, and I should've been relieved that an obstacle had presented itself. Whoever she was, she'd stopped me from making a mistake, one that I certainly had never even considered making before.

He followed her into his office and slammed the door. I sat at my desk, shoved my disappointment out of my mind, and typed my notes from the evening. I did a few basic calculations, emailed my notes and my numbers to Cole, and bolted out of there before I had a chance to hear what might go on between the two of them.

Except for the days Cole was a total tyrant, I actually liked my job. I was good at it, and it wasn't something that came easily overnight. I'd worked hard to get where I was, and I wasn't going to let some dumb crush ruin it.

I'd put Cole out of my mind. I'd force myself to get over my attraction to him, I'd talk to John, and I'd get everything back on track.

Besides, I was being totally silly. I didn't know why I thought just because he'd been looking at me in the elevator reflection that he suddenly wanted me. It was ridiculous.

I saw John's car in the parking lot. I assumed he'd be home since it was after eleven, and when my mind drifted to Cole and that blonde, I immediately banished the thought and the jealousy that paired with it.

I'd read somewhere once that it took two weeks to make something a habit, so if I forced myself to think of John every time Cole entered my mind for two weeks, then maybe I wouldn't think of Cole anymore. Maybe all this time I was to blame for the rift between John and me. Our marriage might not be such a mess if I'd put more focus on the two of us and less focus on work.

John was in front of the television when I walked in.

"Hey," I said, setting my purse down on the counter.

"Hey."

I sauntered into the kitchen and poured myself a large glass of wine. I sat down on the couch beside him, taking a few gulps of wine before turning to study him. "How was your day?"

He glanced over at me. His green eyes seemed surprised to see me sitting beside him. He ran a hand through his short, dirty blond hair. "Fine."

I sighed. "Mine was fine, too." My voice came out a touch more annoyed than I'd planned it to, but for God's sake, it was a common courtesy to ask someone how her day was in return.

Another look of surprise met me.

"John, we need to talk."

He didn't say anything.

"What's going on between us?"

"What do you mean?" he asked.

"I mean things have changed. We used to talk and do things. We used to love each other. Now it's like we're roommates who don't even like each other."

"You don't like me anymore?"

I refrained from rolling my eyes. "That's your takeaway?"

"We're fine."

"Fine. We're fine. My day was fine. Everything's always *fine*, John."

"Yeah, it is. Where is this coming from?"

"It's coming from months of frustration. From you ignoring me when I walk in the door. From me not caring to ask about your day beyond your '*fine*.'" From me having a really strong attraction to another man.

I left that last part out, but it probably needed to be said. Maybe then he'd realize the gravity of the situation and he'd say more than one word to me, because our marriage certainly wasn't *fine*.

"Do you really want to hear about my day?" he asked.

I nodded. That wasn't what this was about, necessarily, but we had to start somewhere.

"I went on a call to an office this morning. Their server crashed, and I spent a couple of hours fixing the problem. I went to Burger King for lunch, where I had a Whopper and a Coke. No fries. I went back to the office and logged my work, got to work on a new website, had a meeting with two managers, and worked on the video game software I've been developing. Then I came home."

The television blared in the background, but we'd made a tiny step in the right direction. We'd at least gotten the ball rolling on conversation. I knew if I told him to turn it off, he'd just think I was nagging him.

I waited for him to ask me how my day was or why I was so late. I waited for him to tell me I looked pretty or that he'd missed me.

But it never came. After he told me about his day, he turned his attention back to the television.

Fine. If words weren't going to work on him, maybe some action would.

I gulped down the rest of my wine and set my glass on the table in front of me. I scooted a little closer and leaned in to nuzzle his neck.

He wasn't taking the hint. His eyes were still focused on his show.

I dragged my lips up to his earlobe and sucked. A soft sigh escaped him, so at least I knew I had his attention.

"Lucy, what are you doing?" His voice sounded annoyed.

Why would he possibly be annoyed when his wife wanted a little intimacy?

"Isn't it obvious?" I whispered.

He shook me off. "I'm tired."

"You just sit back and let me do the work." I thought that maybe once I got started, he wouldn't be able to resist. Maybe a little fun on the couch would help spark things back up between us.

I moved off the couch and knelt between his knees. He wore a pair of basketball shorts and a t-shirt. I ran my hands along his firm thighs and then cupped him on the outside of his shorts, expecting some reaction. Instead, when I looked up at him, his face was unreadable as he continued to stare at the television.

Whatever.

I had all this pent up sexual tension inside of me, and I needed to do something to get rid of it. I lifted his shirt up just a little and dropped kisses on his stomach. He wasn't muscular, but he was slim.

I pulled him out of his shorts, and he didn't stop me. He was only semi-hard, but I knew what to do to get him there. I shoved him right into my mouth without preamble.

A small groan escaped him. It had been a while since I'd done this, but it was like riding a bike. I took him to the back of my throat and slowly sucked my way up to the tip. I wasn't surprised when he squeezed my shoulder after what seemed like only a few bobs of my head. It was his signal that he was about to lose it. I didn't move my head, and his warm fluid shot to the back of my throat.

And as my husband basked in the glow of a fabulous blow job from his wife, I couldn't help the thought nagging in the back of my mind despite my promise to myself that I would stop.

What did Cole taste like?

I sat back on the couch, shaking my head slightly to clear Cole out of it. I sighed triumphantly and waited for John to make his move and return the favor.

Instead, he tucked himself back into his pants, shot me a quick smile, and turned his attention back to his show.

Chapter Six

One of the highlights of my job was the annual Benson Industries Benefit. It was a first class event that took place at the Ritz every year, and even though the price tag was astronomical, the event was always pure class and raised a ton of money for charity. I was always given a ticket plus one guest, and every year was better than the one before. The benefit had an amazing silent auction and a fantastic dinner in addition to a night of drinking and dancing.

Plus, as an added benefit, I'd get to stare at Cole in a tux.

I was still a little pissed at John that he'd taken a blow job and didn't even think of reciprocating, but it was in the past. This benefit could be our night to reconnect, to have a fun night out drinking and dancing.

The benefit was on a Saturday night, and I spent the majority of the Friday before making sure Cole was ready. I had a handful of responsibilities handed down to me from the Public Relations department since my direct boss had to approve every last detail of the benefit. Excitement always abounded through the whole office, but Cole managed to dampen that with his foul mood on Friday. I tried to ignore it, but it was difficult given his proximity.

I almost asked him why he was so crabby, but I had a good idea why. Jack Benson had created excellent relationships within the community, and it would be interesting to watch his son at the helm this year. Cole had to give a speech the following night, and it was his first time officially hosting the benefit.

He'd sent me a rough draft of what he planned to say, and he'd requested a copy of his father's speech from the year before. He'd never even so much as attended one of these benefits—at least not here in California—so I imagined he was anxious to ensure the event lived up to the high standards his father had set.

Not to mention, his dad would be in attendance. I was certain Cole was intent on impressing his parents.

"Mr. Benson?" I asked, knocking lightly on his door.

"What?" he snapped.

I walked partway through the door and stopped. He glanced up from some paperwork on his desk, and I couldn't help but think how achingly handsome he was, even with all that irritation on his face. "Sorry to bother you, but I just wanted to tell you that I thought your speech was perfect. I sent you some notes over email, and I'd be happy to go over it with you if you want to read it to me."

"I don't have time for that shit. I'll look over your notes." His eyes lingered on me for a few short beats, and then he looked back down at his paperwork. "I need you to pick up my tux before lunch today."

"Yes, sir." I returned to my desk with a heavy sigh, wishing he could be just a little nicer to me.

But if he was, I'd be in real trouble. If he gave me any glimmer of hope that he might be a likable person, I wasn't sure I'd be able to suppress my attraction to him.

As the warm California air blew in through my lowered window, I couldn't help but think how nice it was to get out of the office. Even if it was because I was running around as my boss's bitch. After I picked up his tux, I grabbed him a Venti Vanilla Latte from Starbucks as a special treat. I hoped it would cheer him up a little and maybe calm his nerves.

On second thought, caffeine probably wasn't the answer.

When I got back to the office, I stood in Cole's doorway with his tux. "Sir, I have your tux. Where would you like it?"

He pointed toward the door in his office that led to a private restroom, and I opened the door and found a hook to hang his tux on. When I emerged, I set the coffee on his desk. "I also brought you a little treat," I said sweetly.

He glanced at the coffee. I expected his eyes to soften as he looked up at me gratefully, or even a word of thanks for the coffee and the tux, but instead, he looked back at his paperwork. "Thank God you didn't spill any on my tux."

I glared at the top of his head. What an asshole.

I hated him more and more every single day.

When I arrived home after work, the apartment was quiet as usual. I stepped into the closet and pulled my dress for the following night out of the garment bag. I sighed happily as I stared at the dress.

It was a dream dress, one I shouldn't have bought due to its price tag but did anyway. The top was a tight, sparkly, beaded champagne color. It looked strapless, but it had a beaded sweetheart neckline that doubled as a necklace, and the back had a gorgeous tie-up corset. The beads on the top faded as they moved all the way down to the floor. I'd found heels that matched the color of the dress perfectly, and the diamond studs John had given me on our first anniversary would complete the outfit.

I'd made an appointment to get my hair and make-up done. I was, after all, the assistant to the company's CEO, and it gave me a good excuse to pamper myself.

I couldn't wait for the next day. I'd told John about this date months ago, and I'd reminded him over and over so he wouldn't have to work or invent some other excuse.

When Saturday afternoon rolled around, I headed out to my hair and make-up appointment while John stayed behind, telling me he had some work to do but assuring me he'd get it done before we had to leave.

I didn't care if he didn't get it done. We were going together to the benefit, and he'd have a good time if I had to force him.

Or at least I wouldn't let him ruin my good time.

As my stylist curled my long, dark hair into sexy, loose waves, an image of Cole flashed through my mind and I suddenly had the strongest pull deep in my belly. The unwelcome thought that I wished I was getting ready to attend this benefit with him instead of with John wiggled its way into my consciousness.

I forced the thought away. I forced myself to focus on images from our wedding day. Smiles as we fed each other cake. His eyes looking down into mine as we shared our first dance. Nervous jitters as I walked down the aisle toward him.

I calmed my errant thoughts with those soothing images, pushing Cole away as I forced John back in.

I shouldn't have had to do that, but it was as if my brain had taken on an agenda all its own.

I continued to force Cole out of my mind the remainder of the afternoon, but he kept finding his way back in. That look he'd given me on the elevator. I had to have been imagining things, but what if that girl hadn't been in his office?

What had he done with her?

Had he fucked her over his desk?

Had he made love to her up against the windows?

Did he think of me the way I thought of him?

When I emerged from the closet and found John sitting on the couch in the tux I'd rented for him, I forced myself to hope tonight would be our new beginning.

He was on his iPad, tapping away furiously. I cleared my throat to get his attention.

"You look nice," he said, his eyes moving over my dress. *Nice?* I looked fucking amazing, and it would've been nice to hear it.

"Thank you. So do you."

I waited for him to get up, to come over to me and kiss me. To tell me he loved me and looked forward to our night together. Instead, his eyes returned to his iPad. "I'll be done in a second."

I sighed, forcing myself not to get angry. He was dressed and he was attending this event with me, and I wasn't going to let a little rocky start ruin our night.

We got into John's Volvo and headed toward the Ritz. It didn't go unnoticed that he'd tossed his iPad into the backseat. He sure as fuck wasn't bringing that damn thing into the ballroom with him.

I took a deep breath and silently repeated some mantra about not allowing myself to get mad.

We pulled up to the Ritz, and John dropped me off at the doors while he drove around to park. As I waited in the lobby, I waved to some coworkers.

Once John made his way in, we headed into the ballroom. He still hadn't touched me. He was obviously preoccupied with whatever was going on at his work, but he didn't care to share it with me. I let it go.

Our PR team had thought of everything, and when we entered the ballroom, we were given our table numbers. Dinner was set to start in just under an hour, and that was also when Cole would deliver his speech.

We perused the auction items, and John pointed out some football players he recognized while I pointed out an actress I'd seen on television just the day before. We stopped at the bar where I picked up a glass of wine and John got himself a beer.

I spotted Cole across the room. He was too far away for me to catch a really good look, but he was handsome even from the distance. A gorgeous blonde in a tight, red dress had her arm looped through his. She was a different blonde from the one I'd seen in his office after the MTC meeting. I wondered how many blondes he had in his contact list. He laughed at something she said, and she smiled easily along with him.

I decided I immediately hated her for no good reason other than the fact that she'd made Cole smile. Well, that and the fact that she was practically glued to him.

I wanted to go say hi to him, but I felt so awkward.

All throughout that first hour, I could physically feel the distance that spanned between my husband and me. I'd been trying to reach him, but he insisted everything was fine. When one person doesn't think there's a problem, it's difficult to move forward.

We finally headed toward our assigned table a few minutes before dinner was set to begin, and I found Jack Benson already sitting there with his wife, Arlene.

"Jack!" I exclaimed, and he stood and gave me a hug.

"Lucy," he said warmly. God, I missed him. He'd always told me I was the daughter he'd never had. He'd been such a nice boss, and once again I had a hard time believing he had fathered the evil Cole.

"Arlene, it's so good to see you again," I said, and she stood and gave me a hug.

"Good to see you, too, dear."

We all took our seats, and I sat in the one next to Jack so we could catch up.

"How was your vacation?" I asked, referring to the cruise he'd taken immediately after retiring.

He launched into a story about Arlene's sunburn that had me giggling. He kept sipping from a tumbler with amber liquid in it, and it struck me that I'd never really seen him drink before. I supposed since he was retired now, he didn't have to worry about giving the speech and he could cut loose and have a good time.

"How's Cole treating you so far?" Jack asked.

Did he want the truth? I opened my mouth to respond, but I was cut off before I had the chance.

"She's lucky to have such a great boss." I turned to see the source of those words, and Cole himself stood behind his father.

Holy. Fucking. Hell.

He was gorgeous in the tuxedo I'd picked up for him. He was freshly shaven and his hair was neatly groomed, as if he'd gone for a haircut that morning. His dark eyes burned into mine, and his date possessively clutched his arm a little tighter.

I pressed my lips together. "Mr. Benson, I'd like to introduce you to my husband, John." I motioned to John, who stood to shake Cole's hand.

My husband shaking the hand of the man who I lusted after struck me as incredibly odd.

"Good to meet you," Cole said, and then he ushered the blonde to an empty seat across the table from us and he sat beside her. Interesting that he hadn't taken the time to introduce her to me.

The emcee, who happened to be professional baseball player Cody Moretti, took the microphone. "Good evening, ladies and gentlemen," he said. "Thank you for your attendance tonight. Please take your seats as dinner will be served shortly. During the dessert course, we'll hear from Benson Industries' new CEO, Cole Benson. I'd like to take this opportunity to congratulate Mr. Jack Benson on his retirement. Jack, where are you?"

Jack stood beside me, and the room exploded in applause. "Jack, tonight's about charity, but it's also about having a good time. So everyone, raise your drinks high in the air. Every time someone says 'congratulations' tonight, Jack has to take a drink. So, Jack, congratulations."

Jack smiled and waved, and then he took a sip from his tumbler.

"Congratulations on a long and successful career, and congratulations on your retirement."

Jack took two more drinks and then held up his hands in surrender, causing a smattering of laughter in the room.

Cody laughed. "I'll stop, but I'm sure you'll hear it a few more times tonight. Enjoy your dinner and your evening, everyone, and please remember that the silent auction tonight benefits One Heart One Way of Los Angeles. Open those pocketbooks and show us your generosity. Have a great night." Cody stepped down to applause, and the servers placed our salad plates down immediately.

Jack entertained us with stories about his years at the wheel of Benson Industries, and I couldn't help shooting quick glances across the table at Cole. Jack was hilarious, and the laughter at our table was raucous. I kept looking at Cole because I wasn't used to seeing him smile. I wasn't used to seeing him have a good time.

I was used to being treated like shit because he was in a perpetual sour mood.

But I caught him smiling as he listened to his father, and then I caught him looking back at me. His smile faded when our eyes met. He looked away first, back toward his father, but I couldn't help but wonder about that little moment.

I tried to avoid looking in his direction, but it was nearly impossible. My eyes were drawn to him involuntarily.

After the dinner course, Jack excused himself and moved across the room toward the microphone.

"Ladies and gentlemen, thank you. Thank you for your support of Benson Industries and of One Heart One Way. Thank you for your continued charity and for celebrating here with us tonight. Each year, I've given a speech at this event where I discuss both Benson and One Heart, but tonight, I'm handing over the reins to someone else. I'm so proud of my son. He's managed to make a smooth transition so far, and I know he's going to revitalize the company and create more success than I ever could have imagined. Please welcome the new Chief Executive Officer of Benson Industries, Mr. Cole Benson."

I clapped along with the rest of the attendees in the room. Cole's eyes met mine for the briefest of seconds before he stood and strode confidently toward his father. "Thanks, Dad," he said, and the two men hugged. I almost felt a tear in my eye at his tender display of affection for his father.

Tender. Now there's a word I never would've thought I'd use to describe Cole.

He launched into the speech he'd sent me and I'd reviewed. He'd memorized it, and it was perfect…he was perfect. He was assured and confident throughout his discussion of Benson's current state, and he explained how the money raised at the benefit would help One Heart One Way, a children's charity. He ended with a plea for attendees to dig deeply into their pockets before telling everyone to have a good time.

I couldn't help my fantasies about this man. I'd never do anything about it, but I was drawn to him for some inexplicable reason beyond my attraction to him.

I wanted to see his tender side again.

I wanted to be the one who could make him smile. Instead, more often than not, I was the one who made him scowl.

I glanced over at John at some point during Cole's speech, and he was engrossed in reading something on his phone. I smacked him on the shoulder and gestured toward Cole on the stage with my head, as if to tell him to pay attention. It was flat out rude to sit on his phone while Cole gave his speech—especially considering he was my boss and we were sitting at the same table as him. I fumed in silence, but I forgot about it quickly as I found myself enraptured by the man on the stage.

Cole stepped down to a standing ovation and made his way back to our table. He sat, and everyone congratulated him on an excellent speech as he blew out a deep breath.

I caught his eyes, and I smiled at him. He held my gaze for a few beats before pressing his lips together and looking away.

His hot gaze on mine had sent a tremor of lust down my spine.

I shook it off. My husband was right beside me. I was imagining things.

The music started back up and the wine flowed. I'd had just enough that I wasn't drunk—I refused to make a fool out of myself at a work function—but I felt light and happy.

The speech was over, and the auction would close in another hour. Until then, it was time to dance.

"Dance with me," I said to John, looping my arm through his.

He gave me his "do I have to" face, and I met his expression with my best "yes, it's your obligation as my husband" face.

"I'm really tired from work this week," he whined.

"Come on. It'll be fun." I stood and pulled on his arm. We headed out to the dance floor as Justin Timberlake's "Can't Stop the Feeling" started playing. I shimmied around to the beat, giving him some of my best moves, but he wasn't having it.

He was being a giant stick in the mud, but I refused to let him ruin my good time.

Jack and Arlene started dancing beside us, and it was clear that Jack had been following Cody's rule of taking a drink every time someone congratulated him. He was dancing like an old man, shaking it and boogying on down beside us, and I couldn't help but laugh every time he bumped clumsily into John, who just kept rolling his eyes. The whole situation struck me as incredibly funny—especially the more annoyed John became.

A group of women stole Arlene away to chat just as John excused himself to the restroom. So I danced with my old boss as the song switched from dance music to a slower ballad.

Jack looked at me with raised eyebrows and held out his hand, and I smiled and took his hand in mine. He twirled me around the floor to the slow song, and I giggled. I caught Cole's gaze from across the room, and my smile faded as he held my eyes captive with his.

"So, Lucy, tell me how things are going with Cole," he said, making a bit of a slurred conversation as we danced. He bumped into the couple next to us.

"It's fine. We miss you around the office."

"He can be hard to handle sometimes. I'm sorry I didn't warn you about him."

I didn't have a chance to respond before he continued talking.

"He was a funny kid. Stubborn as hell and a pain in the ass. He'd do the dumbest things. He'd go out back and touch our cactus and then come inside crying because it hurt. Arlene would calm him down and then he'd go do it again."

I giggled. I could imagine Cole as an adorable little boy just learning how to be the stubborn man he eventually grew into.

"When he was little, he used to take off his clothes all the time. It started when we'd gone to a deserted beach and he was wearing jeans. He didn't have his swim trunks, so we told him to go in the water naked. Well then he thought it was okay to do it whenever he wanted. Once he even took off his clothes in the middle of a department store."

My giggles turned into full on laughs.

"I'll save myself from further embarrassment by cutting in." His voice was deep, and I caught his scent before I saw him. Jack smiled at me and made a face like he'd gotten in trouble.

"I'm off to get Arlene some more wine." He elbowed Cole in the ribs. "She gets a little randy after she's had a few." He laughed and scampered away to find his wife while Cole rolled his eyes in disgust.

He took my small hand in his big one, and my entire body flushed with heat at his proximity. Our hands had never touched before. If anything, he did his best to avoid any sort of contact with me.

His skin against mine was electric.

Just our hands touched, but it felt as if he was touching me everywhere.

He laced one arm around my waist as the notes of another ballad filled the room. We were dancing like old people, my hand in his, his arm around my waist, and my other hand resting on his shoulder.

That big, broad shoulder hidden behind his tuxedo coat.

My fingers flexed involuntarily, and I couldn't help but notice how hard his entire body was beneath that sexy tux. My mind wandered and my mouth watered as I thought back to that picture I'd seen of him wearing just his swim trunks. That mental image mixed with the man in the flesh sent an aching need right to my core.

He pulled me just a bit closer to him, surprising the hell out of me, and I felt something rigid pressing against my hip.

Holy. Shit.

Was he as hot for me as I was for him?

No way. There was no possible way.

But his erection digging into me told a completely different story.

"What was my father telling you?" he asked in a deep rumble. I looked up into his eyes.

God, he was handsome. His milk chocolate irises had golden flecks in them that I'd never been close enough to notice before, and his breath smelled of peppermint.

I couldn't think when I was this close to him. Words caught in my throat.

"That bad?" he asked. I sensed his nervousness.

I cleared my throat and broke our eye contact so I could think. "Just a proud father bragging about the time his son took off his clothes in a department store."

"God. He tells everybody that stupid story. I'm surprised this is the first time you've heard it."

I smiled. "It's not so bad."

"I was ten."

I choked on my laugh as I tried to hold it in.

"It's okay. You can laugh."

I didn't hold back, and even Cole chuckled along with me. I couldn't help the joy that filled my heart in hearing even a small chuckle out of the man who was in a perpetual bad mood.

I made the mistake of looking up at him as we both laughed. When he smiled, adorable little crinkles outlined his eyes and he had a tiny dimple in just his left cheek. He looked carefree and young, ten times more beautiful than he had just moments earlier.

But when our eyes met, the mood instantly changed.

Neither of us was laughing anymore. Instead, an intense heat passed between us and the air around us filled with a raw and savage tension.

Cole cleared his throat and looked away first.

"Your speech went really well," I said softly.

He nodded once to acknowledge my words, but the wall that had so briefly come down was firmly back in place.

The song ended. "I should get back to my date," he said, still avoiding eye contact with me.

Of course. I supposed I should go find my husband, too.

He let go of my hand and dropped his arm from around my waist. "Thanks for the dance," I said.

He didn't reply. Instead, he walked away from me, and I stood in my place for a few beats as I allowed the disappointment to wash over me.

His date. He hadn't been turned on because he was dancing with me. He'd just been thinking of his gorgeous date.

I headed back to the table and found my husband drinking another beer and messing around on his phone again.

"I thought you went to the restroom," I said.

He set his phone down with a sigh. "I did. When I came back, you were dancing with Jack, so I figured you were fine."

I had been fine. Better than fine, actually. I'd had a better time in the three songs I'd danced with Jack and Cole than I'd had with my husband the entire night.

I went off in search of one more glass of wine before the auction winners and the grand totals for the charity were announced.

I needed the wine to calm my nerves after my encounter with Cole, but instead, I found him at the bar ordering some bourbon.

"We meet again," I said stupidly.

"It's not that big of a room."

"Well, plus I'm following you."

He gave me an odd look.

I smiled. "I'm teasing."

He raised his brows and then walked off with his bourbon. God, could that have been more awkward?

The benefit had been a huge success—even more successful than the year before, and I knew Cole would be proud of that fact considering it was his first benefit as the CEO.

I stared out the passenger window of John's Volvo as we drove home, but I wasn't thinking about my husband.

All I could think about was Cole.

He'd shown me a different side, even if it had only been for a split second. I'd been using the excuse that he was an asshole to keep myself from feeling more than a crush for him. Now that I knew there was a human being with real feelings behind that nearly impenetrable wall, everything had changed.

Everything.

"I have to go into work for a few hours tomorrow," John said, breaking into my thoughts. I'd nearly forgotten my husband was sitting beside me despite the fact that he was driving.

"Fine," I said, disappointed but not shocked that he was going into the office on a Sunday. Sundays used to be days for us to spend together. Not anymore, apparently. "Did you have a good time tonight?" I asked, trying to make conversation.

"It was alright. You?"

I thought back to Cole in his tux. "I had a great time." It was a lie. There was a handful of moments that night that I'd considered "great," but the rest of the night had been meaningless drivel that I was forced to endure to get to those moments.

Cole's speech. Cole's eyes meeting mine across the table. Cole's arm around me as we danced. Cole's erection pressing into me. Cole's smile. Cole's celebration at the end of the night when the final numbers raised were announced.

Those were all the great moments of the night. Those were the times that I'd remember.

But dancing with John for half a song? Sitting beside someone who couldn't even be bothered with small talk? Finding him scrolling on his phone instead of paying any attention to his wife—who, by the way, looked smoking hot?

None of those moments made the list.

John pulled into the parking lot and parked the Volvo, and we made our way to the apartment in silence. A heavy ache pressed between my legs. As much as my husband had been ignoring me lately, I was still a wife with needs.

And my husband had to have needs, too. If he wasn't getting it from me, where was he getting it from? I thought back to my conversation with Kaylee.

He wouldn't cheat.

So when we walked through the front door of the apartment and John locked the door behind us, I turned around and pushed him against the door. Shock flashed across his face as I pressed my body against his.

I was horny as hell. It may not have been because of John, but John was sure as hell going to be the one to take care of me.

I pressed my lips to his, and he slowly started to respond. I ran my hands from his shoulders down his chest, and I cupped him through his pants.

He was hard. He was ready for me, and even though we'd largely been ignoring each other for months, this was something natural for a husband and a wife to do.

He moaned softly, and I backed up and looked up at him. His eyes held a fire that I hadn't seen in a long time.

Silently, I took his hand and led him to the bedroom. I knew we'd both be more comfortable in our bed than on the floor in front of the door.

He started undressing, and I mirrored his movements as I pulled the dress over my head and set it gently over a chair.

He sat naked on the bed, and I walked over to him in my lace panties and matching bra. I took the set off in front of him. My dark hair tumbled around me as I straddled his lap and he pushed up into me. I was drenched, but it wasn't because of the man I was having sex with. He buried his face between my breasts as I used his shoulders to push myself up and down.

After a few pumps, he lay back and allowed me to do the work. I bounced up and down over him, trying not to feel insulted that he didn't want to kiss me or even touch me as I fucked him.

He leaned back up after a few moments and let out a long, low groan before pushing his hips up into me. I knew he'd found his release, but I still had a ways to go. I reached down and stroked my fingers across the bundle of nerves, hoping to get closer to my own climax. It wasn't working.

Until my mind betrayed me with the image of Cole laughing as we danced together. Those sexy crinkles around his eyes. The way his erection dug into my hip.

My body shattered in a soul-crushing orgasm.

As I lifted off of my husband and made my way to the bathroom to clean up, I pushed away the guilt I felt. I hadn't done anything wrong.

I didn't mean to think of him, and I hated that I'd been able to get off so easily the second he entered my mind.

As I climbed into bed beside my already-sleeping husband who hadn't even bothered to kiss me goodnight, I couldn't help but think what a night with Cole might be like. Just one night. From the way his body moved as the two of us had danced, I had a feeling it would be incredible.

Too bad I'd never find out.

Chapter Seven

A little over a week later, I found myself on an airplane in the coach section while my boss sat several rows ahead of me in first class.

I stuck my purse under the seat in front of me, ready to catch up on my reading during the long flight. I had a romance novel I'd been meaning to get to for a while, but between my late nights working and worrying about my marriage (definitely not thinking about Cole), I found my mind too overwhelmed to concentrate.

I had to admit that I was totally nervous to be traveling with Cole. My plan to think of my husband every time my boss entered my mind wasn't really working. I thought of Cole far more often than I should have. Especially his lips.

His full, ripe, juicy lips.

I forced myself to think of John, but all that did was make me think back to that morning.

I didn't even get so much as a proper kiss when I left for the airport. He'd been running late for work, so he pecked my cheek on his way out the door. It was another one of those obligations husbands and wives had, and he barely fulfilled it. He didn't wish me safe travels or a good trip. He was too wrapped up in his own little world.

So I headed to the airport via the car I'd arranged rather than even suggest to my husband that he take me.

After the night of the benefit, I'd tried three more times to start a conversation about the state of our marriage, but each time, John brushed off my concerns and refused to admit we had a problem.

I didn't see Cole until I boarded the plane. First class had the privilege of early boarding, and apparently Cole had taken advantage of the first class lounge rather than wait for the flight with the rest of us peasants.

I stared at him as I passed by, trying to get him to look up from his phone and acknowledge that I'd boarded, but he was engrossed in what he was doing. I could always feel eyes on me when someone was looking at me, but apparently he didn't have that same sixth sense.

I pulled out my earbuds, flipping through iTunes for a good playlist to accompany my reading when the flight attendant stopped by my row. I assumed she was going to start the in-flight emergency exit talk that I typically ignored since I'd been on a plane before, but instead she stared me down with a smile until I took out my earbuds.

"Ma'am, your seat has been moved. Can you grab your belongings and come with me?"

I looked around as if she might be mistaken. "Me?"

"Are you Lucy Cleary?" she asked. I nodded. "Follow me."

I sighed, pulling my purse out from beneath the seat and tossing in my earbuds and phone as I expected her to lead me somewhere even further back.

Instead, though, she surprised me as we started walking to the front of the plane. She passed through the curtain separating coach from first class, and she led me to the open seat beside Mr. Cole Benson.

He smiled at me. It was rare that he looked at me with anything other than total exasperation, and it looked good on him. His eyes crinkled in that adorable way they had at the benefit when he smiled. He looked relaxed—more his age instead of his usual stiff demeanor.

It was the first time I realized how hard it must have been to take over for his father. He probably felt the need to prove himself.

"Welcome to First Class."

I grinned back like an idiot, suddenly excited at the prospect of traveling with him. Maybe this wouldn't be so bad. Maybe he'd loosen up a little and stop acting like a tyrannical asshole. I hoped to see more of the nicer side I'd seen when we'd danced at the benefit.

Or maybe this was the one good deed he'd planned and he'd be a total jackass the rest of the time. Only time would tell.

"This is so unexpected, Mr. Benson!" I gushed. "Thank you so much!" I slid into the seat next to him. He'd taken the aisle, so I had to shimmy past his legs to get to the window. I didn't hate the way his legs felt against mine as I crossed in front of him.

I slid my purse under the seat in front of me, grateful for the extra legroom, the comfortable seat, and the man sitting beside me even though he was hogging the armrest. I couldn't really fault him for that. He'd been about to sit by himself when he'd offered me the seat.

"Good news, Ms. Cleary," he said once I settled in. I looked over at him with curiosity. "We got the MTC Industries account."

"We did?" I shrieked.

He smiled again. "We did. I used the numbers you drafted, and it was the magic number Lincoln Mathers was looking for. He sat on his decision for nearly two weeks, but he called me late last night to let me know."

"Congratulations, Mr. Benson."

"There's more. You've really proven yourself in the month I've been here, and I'd like to give you more responsibility. I'm putting you on the MTC account."

"What?" I sputtered in shock.

"It's only if you're interested, and you'll be working side-by-side with me. I'll make the final calls, but you'll have a hand in market research, product development, creating campaigns, data analysis, the whole nine yards. It's a big jump from assistant, but I believe you have the skills and determination to handle it in addition to your current responsibilities."

"May I ask what brought this on?" I asked, shocked that he'd want me so involved with such an important account.

"Two things, actually. I've been considering giving you more responsibility for some time now. But it was Mathers who really convinced me."

"Mathers?"

"Lincoln Mathers," he clarified. "He said he was impressed with your attention to detail."

"How would he know about that?"

He smiled sheepishly. "He asked me how I remembered so much about our dinner meeting. I was honest and told him you were my memory."

"Thank you for the credit," I said, shocked that he'd given it to me.

"He told me, and I quote, 'Don't let that one out of your sight. She's a valuable asset.' When I told him I'd consider putting you on the account, he said he was all in. He sees something in you, Ms. Cleary. And I have to admit, I see it, too."

"Are you kidding me?" I asked incredulously.

"I never kid about business, Ms. Cleary." His voice was stern, but I detected a definite note of pride. I couldn't have imagined this trip getting off to a better start.

The flight attendant started her speech about airplane safety, effectively ending our conversation.

My mind raced with possibilities. If I thought I was putting in long hours before, I couldn't imagine what this new challenge would bring. And I'd be working alongside Cole, which was both a blessing and a curse. He was an expert at what he did, and it would be an honor to work with him on the actual creative side of the business instead of just as his assistant.

But it would also present additional obstacles. Just when I hoped I might be able to overcome my crush, I was going to be spending a lot more time with him.

And with him being so nice to me as to move me up to first class and essentially give me a promotion, the crush was back in full force.

Maybe even a little stronger than before.

Or maybe a lot stronger.

Chapter Eight

My plans of reading were shot to hell when I woke with a start.

I hadn't realized I'd fallen asleep, and as I lifted my head and looked around, I saw my boss smirking at me. I rubbed my eyes, careful not to smear my make-up.

I looked out the window. We were on the ground.

I was immensely confused, but the pieces started to fit slowly together.

We'd celebrated with mimosas, and the champagne had knocked me out. The jostling of the landing gear hitting the ground woke me. I'd slept for the entire flight.

On my boss's shoulder.

I glanced down, thanking God that at least I hadn't left drool behind. "I'm sorry," I said, blushing furiously.

"You were so adorably peaceful, I couldn't wake you."

Did he just call me adorable?

I couldn't decide if his playful personality shift was going to make this trip fun or dreadful. If he was going to completely change and start being a decent human being, I was screwed.

We stood when the flight attendant opened the door, and Cole grabbed his luggage down from the overhead bin. He glanced over at me as if he was waiting for me to say where my bag was. "I checked my luggage," I explained.

He rolled his eyes, the old irritation back. I liked sweet Cole, but I was pretty sure I preferred irritated Cole. It was the beast I was most used to, and it provided a tiny shield of defense against my attraction to him.

A man holding a sign that said "Benson" greeted us outside the terminal. Apparently he was the ride I had arranged for us. "Don Henderson," he introduced himself.

Cole jerked his thumb toward me and rolled his eyes again rather than introducing himself. "She checked."

The man nodded. "I'll get her bags, sir," he said.

"It's okay," I said. "I'll get it. I'm Lucy, by the way." Cole shot me a warning look, as if I shouldn't fraternize with the help—or, at the very least, I should demand he call me Mrs. Cleary—but I ignored him and chatted with Don as we walked toward baggage claim.

My bag tumbled down the carousel a few minutes later, and then Don led us to the big, black GMC Yukon we'd be traveling in for the next five days. We were quiet in the backseat, the pleasantries from the plane long forgotten as the nice Cole burrowed back into his hole and the mean one emerged again. He studied his phone as usual, and I sat and stared out the window at New York City. I didn't want to miss a second of scenery as it passed by my window.

I probably should've texted my husband to let him know I'd arrived safely, but the childish part of me wanted him to worry about me. It would be nice to know he still felt *something* for me—even if it was concern for my well-being.

So I waited it out, hoping he'd text me first as I stared out at the magic that made up New York. Traffic was horrid, drivers were crazy, and pedestrians took unnecessary risks in their rush to get wherever they were going, but I was in love with this city.

"I'm meeting with a client tonight, and tomorrow we'll attend the conference during the day and dinner at night. There's a mixer, but we should skip it to finalize Friday's presentation. The conference ends early Sunday, and I've blocked out some time Sunday night to meet up with friends.

You're free to do what you want Sunday night and Monday morning, and then we head home. Any questions?"

I shook my head. At least I'd have some free time while I was there, provided Cole didn't change plans last minute and schedule additional business meetings.

We pulled in front of the hotel, and Don got out to open Cole's door first and then mine. "Mr. Henderson, we'll need you back for an eight o'clock dinner at Brighton. We'll be down at half past seven."

"Yes, sir."

Cole nodded once, and then Don took our bags out of the back of the Yukon. He handed them to the bellhop, and Cole and I headed inside to check in.

I'd booked our rooms at the hotel where the conference was being held. We walked to the check-in counter, a long slab of white quartz that sparkled in the light. Crystal chandeliers hung down from the ceiling, casting a glow over the lobby. The place was chic, modern, and expensive—perfect for someone like Cole, but a bit upscale for someone like me.

Thank goodness he was footing the bill, because I'd never have been able to afford a place like this.

"Reservation for Benson," Cole said, handing over his license and credit card.

"Yes, sir," the woman behind the counter said as her eyes lingered on Cole a bit longer than necessary. I glanced at her nametag: Gretchen.

"I have a suite with a view of Times Square and a king bed."

"The reservation should be for two rooms," Cole said.

"I'm only showing one."

Cole shot me a look. "Did you book two rooms?"

"Yes, I booked two." I pulled up the reservation in the reminder email I'd received just two days earlier. I swore I'd booked two rooms, but I felt suddenly nervous as heat crawled up my spine.

1 King Suite – nonsmoking – Times Square view

How the hell had this happened? One king suite? I definitely booked two rooms. I knew I had, but it was right there in black and white.

I pulled up the email confirmation I received right after I'd booked the room almost two weeks earlier. That one said two rooms, but the more recent one showed just one suite.

What the hell?

"Sorry, it appears my assistant made a mistake. Put a second room on the card," Cole said.

"I can check, but we might be full," Gretchen said, tapping on her keyboard. Her eyebrows knit together in concentration. "I'm so sorry," she said after a few moments. "We are completely booked."

"Shit," Cole muttered under his breath.

"It's fine," I said. "It was my mistake. I'll just find another hotel nearby."

"I'll make some calls for you," Gretchen said.

"Go ahead," Cole said.

We waited in silence while Gretchen worked.

After his compliments earlier that day regarding my attention to detail, I couldn't believe I'd made such a rookie mistake.

A tiny, horrendous thought crept into my mind that my subconscious had done this on purpose.

I brushed it away.

But would it really be so bad to have to stay in the same room with Cole?

Yes, it would be. It would be temptation and it would go directly against my initiative to eliminate my crush on him and focus on John.

It would lead me down a path that I couldn't come back from, even if nothing happened between us. It didn't matter, anyway, since it was an unrequited crush.

Was having feelings for someone else just as bad as acting on it? Were feelings considered cheating?

At what point was I crossing the line?

If having feelings for someone else meant cheating, then I'd been cheating for a while. I'd chalked it up to a crush, but it was time to be honest with myself.

Crushes came and went, but my heart fluttered every time Cole walked into the room. He treated me like shit half the time, but it was better than the indifference my husband treated me with. I dressed every morning with the intention of impressing a man who wasn't my husband. I did my hair and make-up thinking about him. I went to the office, working hard and staying late with the hope I'd have more time to talk to him.

It had grown into more than a crush despite my best efforts to suppress it.

"I'm so sorry, but the closest hotel with vacancy is about five miles away. Would you like me to book that for you?" Gretchen looked directly at Cole, not me.

Cole sighed. "With traffic that'll be a nightmare. Just give me two keys."

She printed our keys and gave us directions to our room, and then we headed toward the elevators.

I thought back to the night on the elevator when I'd wanted him to kiss me after the MTC dinner. I wondered how different this elevator ride would be.

He remained silent as we boarded the small car alone. I chanced a glance in his direction, and he was scowling as he stared at the floor numbers on the electronic panel of the elevator.

"I'm so sorry, Mr. Benson."

He ignored me, which felt an awful lot like being at home.

We entered our room, and I was glad I'd at least booked a suite. It had two rooms—one with the king bed in it, and another that was a living area with a couch, some recliner chairs, a television, and a wet bar—in addition to the large and luxurious bathroom complete with a soaker tub.

"Take the bedroom," he said.

"No, you should have it. You need good sleep for your presentation."

"I insist. I'll take the couch."

"I'm sorry again," I said, surprised that he was being such a gentleman after I'd made such an idiotic mistake.

"You know how I feel about apologies."

I nodded, because I did know. He expected me to work efficiently and never make mistakes.

A knock sounded at the door, and the bellhop dropped off our luggage. He put my suitcase in the bedroom.

"Be ready for dinner around seven," Cole said, pulling his laptop out of his suitcase. "I'll need to prep you on a few things before we go."

"Yes, sir." I went in the bedroom and shut the door to freshen up after our long flight. I didn't have much time to kill.

I shot off a quick text to John. *Landed and safe at the hotel.*

I waited for a response while I brushed my hair, and I still didn't have one after I'd applied my make-up, changed clothes, and spritzed on some perfume.

I wanted to give Cole as much privacy as I could, so I stayed in my room until about five minutes before he'd requested me to meet him. I found him sitting on the couch, a tumbler in his hand filled with ice and some amber liquid. He took a sip as he stared out the window. He was lost in thought, and he hadn't heard me. I indulged in a few seconds of shameless staring. He'd freshened up, too, and he looked spectacular in black pants paired with a charcoal shirt. He was the picture of professionalism. And beauty.

Allure.

Masculinity.

Sex.

I cleared my throat at that thought, and he snapped out of his reverie and turned his attention toward me. I couldn't help but notice the slight appreciation in his eyes as he looked me up and down. I'd settled on a turquoise dress that was low cut enough to be fun in case we went out anywhere but could also pass for professional.

I swore I wasn't just imagining things. I wanted him to take notice, and he was.

I just wasn't sure if he'd act on it.

I wanted him to.

More than ever.

But I would never be the one to make the move. If he did, that was one thing. Then I could say yes or no. I *should* say no, but I wasn't convinced I would.

I waited for a compliment because I knew I looked good, but he didn't give me one. He shook his head slightly and took another sip of his amber liquid, averting his eyes to the window.

"Tonight we're meeting with the CEO of GeoTech. It's an account I secured a few years ago, just a follow up while I'm in town. I'm good friends with him, so it'll be sort of a boy's night. Will you be uncomfortable with that?"

"What does that mean, exactly?" I asked.

"It means swearing and cigars and I can't say we haven't ended up at a strip club before." He said it in a rush, like he was embarrassed to admit it, while he stared down at the floor.

It sounded like a whole lot of fun to me.

"I can handle it," I said.

"Are you sure?"

I nodded.

"Are you easily offended? Because if you are, I need to know now."

I shook my head, and he pulled some paperwork out of his suitcase and set it on the desk. He handed me a pen.

"Can I get that in writing?" His voice held a tinge of nervousness that I hadn't expected to hear from him.

I giggled. I couldn't help it. I glanced through the paragraph that basically said I wouldn't sue him if sexual comments were made in my presence. I signed with a flourish and handed him back the papers.

"Thanks," he mumbled.

"You don't have to be embarrassed."

"I'm not." He totally was.

I held back another giggle, and he eyed my outfit again.

"Is what I'm wearing okay?" I asked, glancing down self-consciously.

He paused, his eyes flicking to my breasts for just a moment that I was certain I hadn't imagined.

"Yeah. It's…uh…it's fine."

Don was waiting for us exactly where he'd dropped us off only a few hours earlier. Cole ushered me into the back of the Yukon. My phone buzzed in my purse, likely with a text from my husband finally replying to mine from earlier…but I ignored it. I was officially on business time as we made our way to dinner, despite what the paper I'd signed may have implied.

Don expertly darted from lane to lane, and we made it to Brighton ten minutes early—just the way Cole liked to arrive. "You never want to be the last to arrive to a business meeting," he'd explained to me a couple of weeks earlier. When I'd asked why, he said, "Because you might miss any business that takes place before your arrival."

A hostess led us to our table, a round affair with seating for six.

After I ordered my standard glass of white wine and Cole ordered some fancy bourbon I'd never even heard of, he said, "You'll be my eyes and ears tonight, Ms. Cleary. I don't plan on remembering too much."

"Yes, sir." I chuckled. So *that* was why he'd brought me with? So he could get drunk?

A man with a small entourage made his way to our table. The leader of the pack was probably around Cole's age—late twenties, I guessed. He was attractive and rugged and definitely fit all the qualities of my type. Not that it mattered.

Cole stood and gave one of the men one of those bro-handshake-half-hug things. "Good to see you, man. This is my assistant, Lucy Cleary." It was the first time I'd heard Cole actually use my first name, and I loved the way it sounded. I imagined him saying it in the throes of a heated moment.

I snapped out of it as the man extended his arm toward me. I took his hand in a firm grip.

"Vince Hanover," he said.

"Nice to meet you." I smiled, trying not to blush as his dark eyes bored into mine.

"Assistant my ass," he said to Cole after he broke his gaze with me.

The whole "trying not to blush" thing was shot to hell with that comment as I waited for Cole's reaction.

"Give me a break," Cole said. "She's married."

I let out a disappointed breath, but he was absolutely right. I was married. I was off limits to all men, no matter what sort of attraction I found myself having.

Cole's words sent an icy chill down my spine. He'd just confirmed that even if there was an attraction between the two of us, nothing ever could or would happen. He wasn't going to get involved with a married woman, and he probably assumed that I wouldn't get involved with him.

I wished I could say he was right.

But he wasn't.

"These assholes came along for a free dinner," Vince said, motioning to his "entourage" of three other men. He introduced them as Brock, Tanner, and Aaron.

We placed our orders as I stared at the men and memorized their names. All four of them ordered the same bourbon Cole was drinking. I wondered for a moment if that was why Cole had ordered it in the first place—did he know his clients that well and wanted to make them feel comfortable? Or was he drinking it because he actually liked it?

Cole and Vince seemed to go way back, but the other men appeared to be new acquaintances, which I assumed was why Cole had dragged me along.

"Tell me how the campaigns are performing in your eyes," Cole said once the drinks had been served.

Vince smiled wickedly. "Getting business out of the way early?"

Cole shrugged. "If you want me to expense this meal, we have to touch on it."

Vince nodded his head toward Aaron. "Aaron can fill you in. Or maybe I should have him talk directly to your assistant since you won't remember any of this."

"Fuck you, Vinnie," Cole said. It was a clear joke and banter between friends, but it surprised me nonetheless to hear that sort of language fall from Cole's lips at a business dinner.

The little shudder than ran down my spine told me I kind of liked it.

Why was I so attracted to him? He was such a douchebag.

Vince nodded in Aaron's direction, who started in with a summary of our services. "Overall we've experienced a lot of success with your campaigns. Your market research was on point. We have four underperforming ads that we want your team to take a look at and revise."

"Email the details to Ms. Cleary," Cole said. "She will get it to the right people, and we will ensure those four ads are revised immediately."

"Ms. Cleary?" Vince teased Cole. Cole looked away while Vince turned toward me. "I've known this asshole for a lot of years, and the only time he calls his assistants by their last names is when he's attracted to them."

Cole rolled his eyes. "I apologize, Ms. Cleary. Vince is drunk already and it was a mistake to bring you tonight. I'll call you a cab."

"Nonsense," Vince boomed. "She's staying. And we're going to show her one hell of a good time." He winked at me and raised his glass in the air.

Vince and Cole talked business through the meal, and the drinks kept coming for the men.

By the time Cole paid the bill, I had five semi-drunk and very loud men on my hands, and the one glass of white wine I'd guzzled at the beginning of the meal was doing nothing to help me control them—or their volume.

As unprofessional as their raucous laughter and totally inappropriate language were, I couldn't help but think how fun and unexpected it was to see Cole let loose. I always saw him in his professional role as the hard-ass, demeaning boss, so seeing him as a normal guy who could act like an immature idiot with his friends was oddly comforting.

Vince continued to make suggestive comments about Cole and me throughout dinner, and Cole continued to ignore those comments. I, however, ate them up. It was all in good fun.

Because, as Cole had mentioned earlier, I was married. And he wasn't interested.

After dinner, Don drove the six of us to a bar Vince recommended. The music was pumping, and there was no way I was going to be able to hear any of the discussion. So I had two choices: sit around bored or participate in the fun.

When they all ordered another round of bourbon, Vince looked in my direction. I nodded, and the waitress donning little more than a bikini brought me my very own tumbler filled halfway with amber liquid. I watched Cole's eyes flick toward her ass as she walked away, and I felt a wave of envy.

I took a sip from my tumbler. The bold and spicy flavor warmed my throat as I swallowed it down. I'd never had straight bourbon before, so this was a brand new experience for me.

It didn't take long for the alcohol to hit me. I was used to drinking wine, and the alcohol content of bourbon was much higher, thus making me a total lightweight.

And tipsy Lucy plus sloshed Cole equaled what could have become one hell of a hot mess.

Vince ordered me another on the second round, but I nursed it. I kept an eye on Cole because I suddenly felt responsible for him. I wanted to take care of him. I wanted to make sure he got back to the hotel room safely.

I watched as he got louder and louder with his buddies. I watched while he exclaimed that he was the CEO of Benson Industries, as if that made him untouchable and indestructible. I watched while his eyes kept sneaking glances in my direction as he fended off gorgeous, drunk women and waitresses in bikinis.

And as Don pulled up to the hotel at the end of the night, I watched as Cole's lips moved toward mine.

Chapter Nine

"Cole, we can't," I whispered, pressing my hand to his chest to halt his forward progress toward my lips.

What the hell?

Why was I stopping him?

This was what I wanted, wasn't it?

While it was definitely what I wanted, this wasn't *how* I wanted it. I wanted sober Cole to kiss sober me because he wanted to kiss me, not because he was drunk and stupid and ready to make a mistake.

If I was going to put my entire life in jeopardy by kissing a man who wasn't my husband, it wasn't going to be because one of us was drunk.

He stared at me for a beat, and then he backed off. "Sorry," he muttered, and then Don opened the door beside me and I slid out of my seat while Cole took a moment to himself in the back of the car.

He got out and we headed together to our room. I slid the keycard into the door and opened it, and then I walked Cole to the couch—his bed. I went to the bathroom, and when I came out, Cole was asleep…but not on the couch.

He was asleep in the bed. The bed that I was supposed to be sleeping in.

I weighed my options as I slipped into my tank top and shorts. I could take the couch, which would give me a stiff back and make me miserable for the next few days, or I could slip into bed beside my boss. The bed he'd insisted I take when we first checked in.

My husband snuck into my mind. He was at home, completely unaware that his wife was considering getting into bed with another man.

It was completely innocent. Well, mostly innocent. I wanted to be close to him in case he needed me. Cole was pretty wasted, and what if he got up in the middle of the night and needed something? If I was out on the couch, I wouldn't be able to help him.

It was a poorly constructed justification, but my tired mind bought it fairly easily.

I slid into bed beside Cole, who slept soundly.

And I lay awake, staring at the ceiling for the entire night.

I probably would've gotten more sleep on the couch, but I convinced myself that Cole shouldn't be alone.

I finally fell asleep when the first rays of sunlight started peeking through the sides of the heavy curtains.

"Ms. Cleary?"

The confused voice broke through my dreamless sleep, waking me.

I opened my eyes to Cole Benson's handsome face. In the morning after a drunken night, slightly hungover and still half-asleep, Cole managed to be totally swoon-worthy. His sleepy eyes were gorgeous, and I was sure I looked as frightening as usual first thing in the morning.

His eyes widened as he sat up quickly. Too quickly, apparently. His hand came up to his forehead and he massaged his temple.

"We didn't…" He trailed off, eyes cast down to the comforter.

I paused a beat, wondering what he would say if I told him that we *had*.

"No," I said, shaking my head.

"Thank God," he muttered, still refusing to look at me. He'd gone from rubbing his temple to holding his head in his hands. "Then why are we...?"

"You passed out in the bed. I stayed in case you needed help."

"Thanks. You didn't have to."

"Yes, I did. I'm here as your assistant, and I considered it part of my duties."

A frustrated chuckle slipped out from between his lips. He still hadn't looked at me. "It's not. I apologize."

"It's okay. What can I get you?"

He finally looked over at me. "Some ibuprofen and a big glass of water. Did you drink last night? Or are you always this perky when you wake up?"

I giggled as I got out of bed, checking the clock. We still had two hours before we needed to check in for the conference.

I headed toward my suitcase to grab ibuprofen. "I had a glass of wine and some bourbon."

"And I had somewhere around twenty or thirty glasses of bourbon."

"Maybe seven or eight."

"Fuck," he muttered. He glanced up at me. "Sorry."

"Don't apologize. It's fine."

"Why are you being so nice to me?"

I went into the bathroom to fill a cup with water. I handed it to him along with the pills before answering. "You had plenty of fun last night, but clearly you're paying for it this morning."

"Thanks." He took the pills and sipped the water slowly.

"I'm going to go type up what I remember from dinner before I forget. Go take a shower and I'll take care of ordering breakfast. What do you want?"

He stood and stretched, still wearing the black pants he'd been out in the night before. He'd managed to remove his shirt before passing out, and he wore just a white undershirt. As he stretched, the shirt rode up, offering me a peek of his stomach. I saw just a glimpse of that carved, tight abdomen I'd seen in Jack's photos, and I took in a sharp breath at the sight. I forced my eyes away, but that patch of skin was burned into my mind as I tried not to pant.

"Toast."

"Just toast?"

He thought for a moment. "Bacon, scrambled eggs, and orange juice. And some strong coffee." He started toward the bathroom to take his shower.

"Yes, sir," I said with a smile.

He smiled back, causing my heart to flutter before he turned and shut the door behind him.

I sighed for one dreamy moment as I stared after the door, and then I called room service to place our order for breakfast.

I dug through my suitcase to get everything I'd need to get ready for the day, and then the bathroom door opened.

I looked up, and my jaw dropped. I really hadn't expected to see what I saw when Cole emerged.

He'd just gotten out of the shower and barely toweled off. His hair was damp, and a few droplets of water glistened on his smooth, broad chest. He sported just the tiny hotel towel around his waist, and if I thought that little patch of skin from his abdomen a few minutes earlier was burned into my mind, this was a sight I'd surely never forget.

My mouth watered hungrily for him. He was gorgeous, but his body was spectacular. He was athletic without being hulking, all hard lines and smooth skin.

The abs in the picture had nothing on the abs in person.

Nothing.

They must've been carved from marble.

I was staring. And possibly drooling.

I couldn't help it, and I couldn't stop. He moved through the room past me, leaving a trail of his delicious scent behind. He stopped in front of his suitcase.

Apparently he'd forgotten fresh clothes in his quest for a shower. His forgetfulness was definitely my gain.

I cleared my throat. "Are you, uh, done in there?"

"You can use it. I'll finish when you're done."

I nodded as I clutched my clothes and stared at him. Finally, I spun around and ran into the bathroom. I shut the door behind me, got into the shower, and got right down to business.

And by "business," I didn't mean freshening up with a shower.

I meant relieving the ache that had been building between my legs since I'd first seen Cole sitting on that couch staring out the window the night before.

I hadn't felt real desire in a long time. But with Cole, everything was exciting and new.

Forbidden.

I shouldn't have been so attracted to him. I should have been fighting harder against it.

But each passing moment brought me closer to doing something that I wouldn't be able to come back from.

Maybe it was time for me to take a leap. To stop being so safe. To do something completely out of character.

Maybe it was time to let Cole know I was more than interested in him—that I wanted him. If he denied me, well, so be it. But if he didn't, maybe he could be the one who would finally relieve the ache of desire.

It was that final thought that pushed me over the edge, spiraling toward bliss as my own fingers gave me the release I'd been seeking.

But as soon as I came down from the high, the ache was present again. I was pretty sure that the only one who could alleviate it was currently in the next room wearing just a towel.

And my God, I bet he could *really* alleviate it. Over and over.

And over.

Before I turned off the water, I picked up one of the travel-sized bottles he'd left in the shower. I unscrewed the lid and breathed in deeply. It was the clean, fresh scent that followed him everywhere he went. It was his shower gel, and the scent was all sex and man and lust. I breathed it in a few more times, taking a moment to memorize it.

I wanted to smell like it—but not because I'd borrowed his shower gel. I wanted to smell like it because his body had been all over mine.

I dressed quickly, not wanting to be that girl who took forever to get ready. I did my make-up speed-style and dried my hair as fast as I could, opting to braid it and stick it in a bun.

I emerged from the bathroom to find that Cole had disappointingly put on clothes.

He wore khaki dress pants with a navy blue button down shirt, the sleeves rolled up to his elbows. I couldn't help but notice that we matched as I glanced down at my navy dress with a tan belt.

I had the sudden urge to stand beside him and look in a mirror to see what we'd look like as a couple.

It was a ridiculous thought that I immediately brushed off.

I needed to get a grip on reality.

And to make matters worse, I finally remembered that I never checked my text from the night before. I'd been so distracted by Cole that I hadn't even thought to look at my phone.

I went over to my purse and pulled it out. It was from John: *Glad you're safe.*

That was all it said.

Glad you're safe.

No *I miss you.* No *I love you.* Nothing to show it was a husband communicating with his wife. Nothing to show a relationship at all.

The text left me feeling empty, and as my eyes moved toward the man sitting on the couch tapping away at his laptop, I wondered if he could make me feel whole again.

I started toward him. I wanted him. I wanted his fingers between my legs, pumping in and out of me as he alleviated the ache that was just for him. I wanted his hard body that I'd glimpsed just a few minutes earlier writhing against mine. I wanted the mouth I'd stupidly stopped the night before hot on mine.

I wanted it all, and I wanted it now.

I was standing over him. I opened my mouth to speak, not sure what exactly I should say except to invite him back into bed with me.

And just as the first squeak of a syllable emerged from my mouth, a knock at the door stopped me.

"Room service!" the voice on the other side of the door said.

I shut my eyes and took a breath.

"Breakfast is here," Cole said, not looking up from his laptop.

Clearly he expected me to get the door. I was back to being the servant, the lowly assistant who was lucky to be on this trip in the first place.

I'd been about to seduce this man, and he was so engrossed in whatever he was doing that he couldn't even be bothered to stand and walk the ten feet to the door to open it.

It was why he'd brought me along.

I couldn't even begin to imagine what a relationship with him would be like. He'd constantly be treating me like I was beneath him, because that's how he viewed me. His simple words telling me that breakfast was here was a command in disguise, and he expected me to drop what I was doing to succumb to whatever he told me.

Maybe I was overthinking it.

Maybe he'd really just announced that breakfast was here.

But every time I turned a corner and thought I had the right answer, something else crashed over me to tell me I was wrong.

I opened the door and the server rolled in a cart with our food on it. He unloaded it onto the table, and once I'd signed the bill, charging the food to the room with an inordinately large tip since Cole was paying, he finally closed his laptop.

We ate in silence so loud it started to become uncomfortable. I wasn't used to spending this much time with Cole, let alone in such close quarters.

And I wasn't used to the pull between us constantly coming at me all day long.

It was taxing, but I'd signed up for it when I'd agreed to this trip—just not in one hotel room. I needed a space of my own to get away from him and my irrational feelings.

He glanced up from his plate, and our eyes locked. I looked away first, back at my plate of food. I poked my fork around, pretending to eat my omelet when really I was trying to find something—anything—to say to break the silence.

Cole spoke first. "We've got about a half hour before we need to head down. I've got some work I can do, and I'd like you to review the presentation for tomorrow."

I nodded, not trusting myself to speak. A half hour would be plenty of time to take care of what I really wanted to do, but this was Cole's show.

"I've got it on a flash drive."

I looked up at him blankly. My mind had wandered, and I had no idea what he was talking about.

"The presentation," he said with a hint of frustration. "Do you have a laptop?"

I shook my head. "No, but you can email it to me and I can review it on my iPad."

He nodded. "That'll be fine. Notate what changes need to be made and be specific."

"Can you upload it to Slides? Then I can just make the changes."

It was his turn to look at me blankly.

"Never mind," I said, not wanting him to feel incompetent when it was a presentation on *technology* that he was giving. I was baffled at the irony. "Email it to me whenever you can."

"I'll give the orders around here, Ms. Cleary."

I nodded. "Of course. I'm sorry, sir."

He sighed, and I remembered too late his feelings on the words.

Whatever. If he was going to be a dick, I was going to stick with saying things I knew pissed him off. In fact, I was going to do things I knew irritated him, too. Between my rabid thoughts and extreme arousal that no one was taking care of, I was in no mood for his moodiness. I had my own ways of dishing it, and this bastard better just get ready for what was coming.

While he emailed me the presentation, I sipped my coffee loudly with an exaggerated "ahh" after each sip because I knew he hated it. I caught his irritated glances in my direction, but I ignored them.

As I opened the presentation and began flipping through the slides, I hummed a tune to myself—another of his pet peeves. He preferred to work in complete silence, and frankly, I was tired of it.

I knew I was being immature, but that was hardly going to stop me from doing it.

"Can you stop?" he said sharply after a few minutes.

"What?" I asked innocently as I looked over at him.

"The humming. Stop it."

"Oh, I'm so sorry. I didn't even realize I was doing it."

Silence rolled back over us like a thick fog. I hated working in silence as much as he loved it.

I forced myself to focus on the presentation, and I was about halfway through reading the slides when we had to leave.

We headed down to the lobby and followed the signs to the conference center. I couldn't help but notice the women gazing at Cole as we made our way there. They looked at him the same way I did.

We received lanyards baring our names and company as well as a tote bag upon check-in. We were directed toward a large room, where we were told to take our seats because the first session would be starting shortly.

Cole found us two seats. He set his tote bag down and left. I watched his ass as he walked away, and I felt that strong tug of desire deep within me again. He stopped to talk to some people, and I couldn't help but notice the way he networked. He was self-assured as he spoke. His confidence oozed out of him, but somehow he didn't come across as arrogant.

It was a pleasure just to watch him. Something deeper than desire fluttered in my stomach. The feelings were familiar but long forgotten.

Butterflies.

They flew with zest around my belly. A tiny smile tugged at my lips.

Strong, intense feelings were strong and intense no matter how you sliced it. The strong hatred I'd felt for him had suddenly morphed into something else, something that caused butterflies and made me stare at him as he worked the room.

I wasn't just attracted to Cole. I was starting to develop real feelings for him.

As much as I sometimes hated him and the way he treated me, the line between hate and love was razor thin. And I was pretty sure I'd just sailed over that line.

He glanced my way, catching me staring.

I looked away in embarrassment as a blush crept into my cheeks. I forced myself to look through the tote bag, even though watching Cole was actually a lot more interesting than whatever was in the bag.

I pulled out a spiral-bound book. It was a schedule of events as well as notes for the main presentations. Cole's presentation the next day was a break-out session, one of several optional events for the conference. I found his name and saw that he'd be presenting at eleven o'clock in the morning.

We'd be ready by then.

And I wouldn't let him drink as much as the night before. He'd need his wits about him—although, as I glanced over at him again, he seemed to be doing just fine.

An emcee told everyone to take their seats, and then he introduced the president of VAYO, the company sponsoring the conference. Cole slid into the empty seat beside me, and I breathed in his scent.

I shook my head to clear him out of it.

I needed to focus on this damn conference, because as I glanced beside me, I saw that Cole was busy checking his email. If I didn't pay attention for him, he'd get nothing out of the time away from the office.

Every once in a while, his knee accidentally bumped mine or his elbow accidentally brushed against me. When it happened once or twice, it was easily forgivable, but when it happened for the third or fourth time, I started to wonder whether he was doing it on purpose.

When his knee bumped mine for a fifth time, he left it there. Neither of us moved. I didn't even breathe for a few seconds as I realized what was happening.

It took everything in my power not to look at him. I felt his eyes on me, but the idea of looking over terrified me. Whatever I saw in his eyes could mean the difference between remaining a faithful wife or doing something that would ruin my marriage. Perhaps the speaker who was droning on and on about the important and varying roles of consultants in today's marketplace wasn't holding his attention. Maybe I was Cole's entertainment.

I refused to just be "entertainment." The emotions that crept over me as I'd watched him work the room less than an hour earlier told me that my feelings ran deeper than I'd been willing to admit.

I had the sudden urge to talk to John, to tell him how strongly I was starting to feel for a man who wasn't him. The space between us wasn't just physical. Sure, we were an entire country away from each other, but the emotional distance between us was oceans wider than that. It had been for a long time, and I couldn't seem to find the answer to close that gap. I'd tried talking. I'd tried sex. I'd tried everything I could think of, and none of it had been enough.

I felt conflicted as I contemplated my options. To move my knee or not. To look over or not. To say something or not. To act on my feelings or not.

So I sat there, staring straight ahead at the speaker while I didn't listen because I was too lost in my thoughts to pay attention.

I finally turned my head to give into him. And as I looked at Cole, he was watching the speaker.

Had he even looked at me at all? Or had it been wishful thinking that he was looking in my direction, studying me and wanting me the same way I wanted him?

His knee was still pressed to mine. I finally moved mine over with a surge of disappointment.

The seats were small. His knee wasn't up against mine because he wanted me; no, his knee was there because we didn't have much room and he was tall. He needed the extra space, and I was in the way. He was asserting his dominance the same way someone would over an armrest on an airplane or at a movie theater.

I hated how I kept allowing my mind to betray me. I kept letting myself get caught up in the moment and think that there might actually be something between us.

I was stupid to think that he'd almost kissed me the night before because he wanted me. He'd been drunk. He probably would've tried to kiss Don, for heaven's sake.

I just had a crush on Cole, and I'd get over it. It certainly wasn't love. It wasn't anything that could ever possibly develop into something more than a boss and his assistant.

Chapter Ten

Lunchtime came, and it was another reminder that my boss was an asshole. We walked to the room where lunch was being served and found an open table. I sat, and then Cole sat—not next to me, but across the table from me.

I gave him an irritated glance, which he completely ignored.

I knew no one at this conference. The only reason I was here was to assist Cole. How was I supposed to do that if we weren't even involved in the same conversations?

It didn't take long for me to figure out why Cole didn't want to sit by me. One leggy blonde and one busty redhead took the seats on either side of him, and he had the audacity to look like a kid in a candy store.

An attractive man with friendly brown eyes and dark hair who introduced himself as Luke took the seat beside me. After shooting a glare across the table at Cole, who I couldn't help but notice was gazing in my direction, I settled into small talk.

"Where are you from?" he asked.

"Los Angeles. You?"

"Phoenix."

"How do you like the summers there?"

He grinned. "It's not bad if you like the sensation of sticking your head in the oven."

I giggled. "I have some family in the Phoenix area. We only visit in the winter."

"I don't blame you. So what do you do in LA?"

"I'm an executive assistant. What about you?"

"I'm a consultant for an engineering firm."

The salad course was served, and I found myself lost in conversation with the friendly Luke. I'd expected to be able to attend the sessions with my boss, but by the looks of things, he had his hands full. I had a feeling I was going to be responsible for taking good notes while he got busy in a hotel room with either Leggy or Busty. Or maybe both. I didn't know how he liked to swing things.

It was better this way. Seeing him in his natural habitat, flirting with other women and giving them his full attention, solidified my plan to get over him.

After the post-lunch sessions, we had a two-hour break before dinner and the mixer with cocktails to end the evening. I was looking forward to the cocktails.

I headed up to the hotel room, where, to my surprise, I found Cole. Alone and typing on his laptop.

I didn't bother greeting him. I was mad at him for choosing to sit with two women who clearly only wanted to get in his pants.

I headed straight into the bedroom and sat on the bed with my phone. I shot off a quick text to John. *Everything okay at home?* It was another attempt to reopen the blocked lines of communication.

"Did you get notes on that last session?"

I glanced up from my phone to see Cole standing in the doorway to the bedroom. He looked so painfully handsome in those khaki pants that fit him like a glove and just a shadow of scruff on his jaw.

What would that feel like against my skin? Under my fingertips? Brushing against my cheek? Rubbing on my thighs?

I looked back down at my phone just to have somewhere to look besides Cole.

"Yes."

"I missed the first couple of minutes."

I hadn't seen him come in late, but I'd been engrossed in my notes. "Well I got them."

I felt his eyes on me. "What's the matter with you?"

I sighed. I didn't want to do this. I didn't want to talk to him. I didn't want to be tempted by him.

"Nothing," I muttered. It was a total lie. For one, I was pissed that he abandoned me at lunch. Maybe it was petty, but I thought at least we could've gone over the morning session together and discussed where the information we'd learned could be useful.

Second, I was irritated that he was late to the session because he was busy entertaining those women.

And third, I was pissed that I even had a crush on the asshole in the first place.

He stepped into the room, invading my space. "Don't give me that bullshit."

The sharpness to his voice caused me to look up at him.

I sighed as I looked out the window in embarrassment. "I thought we could've talked about the morning session over lunch. That's all."

"You're acting like a child because I didn't sit by you?" He seemed genuinely surprised, but I supposed that was what it came down to.

My eyes landed on him again. I pressed my lips together. "You ditched me. I don't know anybody here, and I felt like an idiot sitting by myself."

"Let's be clear. I didn't *ditch* you. I'm not here to *entertain* you. The first rule of conferences is networking. Sitting with people you know isn't the road to making new contacts."

"And I suppose those two women who you sat with are new contacts?"

He rolled his eyes. "If I wanted a lecture, I'd have brought my mother along with me."

I looked down at my phone, not sure how to respond. He sat on the bed beside me.

"Not that I need to explain myself to you, but both women are from companies here in New York. I've worked with them for years. We were just catching up."

I raised my eyebrows, surprised at his explanation, but I kept my eyes down. "You're right. You don't need to explain yourself."

"Besides," he said, lowering his voice to a gritty husk, "if I would've sat next to you, I wouldn't have been able to look across the table at you."

My head whipped up. This time, I was absolutely certain I saw lust and heat in his eyes.

We were alone in a hotel room, and we had the next two hours free. The possibilities for the next one hundred twenty minutes were endless.

I opened my mouth to speak, but I was interrupted by the jarring ring of my phone.

Had he really just said that to me?

I looked at my phone again. "It's my husband," I blurted, holding up the screen.

He nodded once with clear disappointment and stood, and I watched his retreating back as he left the room, closing the door behind him.

I cleared my throat, shocked over Cole's words and then worried why John was calling. I immediately thought something was wrong. We rarely spoke on the phone, opting instead to communicate via text message. "Hey. Is everything okay?"

"The hot water heater broke. I've been taking cold showers."

It figured something would break while I was out of town. I was always the one who had to put in the order with our apartment manager whenever something broke. I wasn't even sure if John knew how to do that. "Did you call the super?"

"Where's his number?"

"I taped it on the inside of the medicine cabinet."

"I'll call tonight when I get home. How late can I call?"

"I don't know. Leave a message if he doesn't answer."

"What do I say?"

Sometimes he was beyond helpless. "Probably your name, apartment number, phone number, and the problem."

"If I text you the number, will you just call?"

I sighed. "Seriously, John?"

He was quiet.

"Fine. Text me the number and I'll call."

"Thanks."

It was my turn to be quiet. I was so tired of stupid shit like this. I was out of town on business, and he had the balls to ask me to call about the stupid fucking water heater?

"Well, I guess I'll talk to you later," John said.

"Okay," I hedged, waiting for an *I love you* or an *I miss you* that never came.

"Bye."

The call ended before I had a chance to even say goodbye.

It was moments like that—phone calls like that—that pushed me further and further away from John. Meanwhile Cole was telling me he wanted to sit across the table from me so he could look at me.

After his admission about his seating choice at lunch, I felt like Cole was now actively working to steal me away from my husband, and I was pretty sure that I didn't want to fight against that.

I tossed my phone down on the night table beside the bed. It was time to stop thinking, because all thinking did was bounce me back and forth like a ping pong ball.

I stood and walked to the door. I closed my eyes and drew in a deep breath.

I was really going to do this.

I turned the handle, and my eyes immediately found him. He was on his laptop again, but this time he looked up at me when I entered the room. Our eyes met and locked, and he set his laptop down and stood.

"Ms. Cleary?"

I took a step toward him, and he took a step toward me. We both moved toward each other until we met in the middle. His hand came up to cup my neck, and my eyes closed as I leaned into his warm touch.

I took a deep breath, that clean scent washing over me.

I opened my eyes, and he was a breath away from me. "I think it's time to start calling me Lucy."

He closed the final gap between us as he pulled me closer with the hand around my neck. He wrapped his other arm around my waist and hauled me against him. "Okay, Lucy," he said, and then he touched his lips to mine.

He stopped and looked at me as if thinking it through, but I didn't want to think. I just wanted to feel.

And then his lips collided with mine, firm and assured. He opened his mouth to allow our tongues to dance together in a slow tango.

Every feeling left my body except the desire that twisted through my veins and exploded everywhere. I thought of nothing other than how good it felt to finally kiss Cole Benson.

The way my body reacted to him was unfamiliar. I'd forgotten what true sexual excitement and craving felt like. It had been missing from my life for far too long, but Cole's kiss was the spark to reignite the passion I deserved out of life.

His hand around my neck moved up to grip my hair as he kissed me with arrogance and dominance. He took control, and my body begged for more as my hips involuntarily bucked toward his. My hands gripped his hard biceps, as if I might fall should I let go.

I felt movement, but I was so caught up in the kiss that I didn't realize he was moving us toward the bedroom.

Toward the bed.

I couldn't wait to get that navy blue shirt off of him, to run my fingertips along the smooth muscles I'd had the pleasure of seeing in the flesh that very morning.

As if he was reading my mind, he pulled away and started working the buttons on his shirt. His hooded eyes gazed at me just the way I'd dreamed they would, full of passion and lust.

He was on the third button and my stomach clenched with excitement when a knock at our door interrupted us.

"Fuck," Cole muttered, glancing at the door before looking at me again. His eyes rounded as if he'd just realized what we'd done.

"Fuck," he repeated, running a hand through his hair.

I'd never seen him so flustered. It might've been comical if I could get over the fact that I'd just kissed my boss.

The knocking became louder and more persistent. He buttoned his shirt hastily on his way to the door while I smoothed a hand through my hair, trying my best to appear like I hadn't been brought to my knees by that kiss.

I'd already started daydreaming about sex on my desk at the office. Or sex on his desk. Going out on a date with him. Holding hands in public. Being a couple. Leaving John.

John.

Oh my God.

What the hell was I doing?

Cole looked through the peephole and then glanced at me to make sure I was decent before opening the door.

"Hey, Nicki," he greeted the leggy blonde who he sat next to at lunch. Her eyes zeroed in on me.

"Oh, I didn't know you had company."

Cole glanced over at me. "She's not company. She's just my assistant."

Just my assistant.

Just *my assistant.*

I thought about his words with disappointment.

Just when I started to think that there could be something between us, I was put back in my place. Shoved back into place, really. I'd gotten carried away with the kiss, that was all. It hadn't meant to him what it might've meant to me.

I was relegated back to his assistant. Not the woman he kissed and would've taken to bed had we not been interrupted.

"Is now a good time?" Nicki asked.

"Let's chat in the hall."

He followed her out, closing the door behind him.

Guilt washed over me.

I'd been ready to do so much more than kiss Cole.

It wasn't fair to John, and it wasn't fair to me. But life wasn't fair, and I could stand in place all day thinking about how wrong it was or I could do something about it.

I wasn't sure exactly what to do about it, but the walls of the huge hotel suite were suddenly suffocating me. I needed to get out.

I grabbed my purse and my phone, made sure I had my key, and walked out the door.

Cole was standing too close to Nicki—or maybe Nicki was standing too close to Cole—but it wasn't my business. I was just his assistant. I brushed past the two of them, my legs carrying me toward the elevator as I struggled to catch my breath.

Maybe his eyes were on me, and maybe they weren't—but I didn't check to see. Either way, it didn't matter. Because I was *just his assistant.*

I was married, and I'd just kissed another man.

When the elevator doors opened, I practically ran through the lobby toward the hotel exit. "Lucy!" I heard a voice calling me. I stopped with my hand on the door.

"Is everything okay?" Luke asked, rushing through the lobby to get to me.

I shook my head. "No. Nothing is okay."

I pushed open the door, and Luke followed me out. I'd expected a breath of fresh air by stepping outside, and instead I was hit with humidity as I inhaled car exhaust.

I missed home. I missed California and balmy temperatures and warm breezes and fresh ocean air.

"Do you want to talk about it?" Luke asked, falling into step beside me.

"I really don't."

"Do you want a friend?"

I just wanted to be alone, but he seemed like he cared about my feelings…something I was currently missing from the men in my life.

I didn't answer.

"How about someone to walk beside you in silence?"

I allowed a tiny smile.

"I'll take that as a yes."

We walked a few blocks in silence before Luke spoke. "Okay, I can't take it anymore. What happened in the twenty minutes since I last saw you?"

I looked around at the tall buildings and the people rushing by me. I spotted a bench up ahead, so I beelined it there and sat. Luke sat beside me, concern etched on his brow.

"My husband asked me to call our building's maintenance guy because the water heater is out. I hate him sometimes."

"The maintenance guy?"

"My husband."

"So you're married?"

I nodded. "And I think I'm in love with my boss, but I hate his guts."

He chuckled. "Been there."

"Yeah?" I asked.

He nodded. "My ex-wife. I loved her so much, but sometimes I really hated her, too. When you feel so much passion for someone, it's easy for the lines between love and hate to blur. We got divorced when I realized that I didn't actually like her anymore. I could deal with loving and hating her, but I couldn't deal with not liking her."

I thought about my feelings for the two men who were currently starring in my love life. I'd been so sure that I loved John. I didn't hate him.

I disliked him.

He wasn't the same man I'd fallen in love with, and the new version of him was easy to dislike. I didn't feel the igniting spark of passion for him. I wasn't sure if I ever really did.

And then there was Cole.

Cole set my blood on fire—one minute I wanted to strip his clothes off and straddle him, and the next minute he made me so fucking angry that I wanted to slap him across the face.

It was soul-crushing passion that I felt for him, and even when I hated the hell out of him, I never really disliked him.

And that was the difference. It literally took two minutes of talking to a complete stranger for me to sort out my feelings.

But the feelings I had were absolutely terrifying. I was thousands of miles away from my husband, but the man who'd somehow stolen my heart was just blocks away. I was considering ending my marriage and throwing away five years of my life for someone who looked at me as nothing more than his assistant.

"What happened with your boss?"

"He kissed me and we were interrupted by a knock at the door. I think it would've gone a lot farther than kissing, but then he called me his assistant."

"Isn't that what you are?"

I sighed. He didn't get it. "It was the *way* he said it. I'm *just* his assistant."

"And you're married."

I nodded.

"Here's my advice. Take it or leave it. Tell your husband. I've been the guy who was left in the dark. Even if you don't think you deserve it right now, everyone deserves happiness. Your husband included. Let him in or let him go."

He was right. I sat in silence as I processed his words and these new revelations.

Finally, I said, "Thanks, Luke."

He shrugged. "I'm just a guy who found a pretty lady to sit next to at a conference."

"A pretty lady who is pretty screwed in the head at the moment."

"We've all been there. You'll get through it, and when you're on the other side, you'll look back and remember the sage advice of the dashing man from the conference."

I chuckled. "You're absolutely right."

We watched the people walk by us for a few minutes, and then I said, "I think I need to call my husband."

"Will I see you at dinner?"

I nodded. "Save me a seat."

He stood, and I watched as he melted into the crowd on the busy sidewalk. I pulled up John's contact information.

What was I going to say to him? I couldn't end our marriage over the phone. But he had to know that I was done.

"I'm in love with someone else." "I kissed my boss." "I don't love you anymore." "I'm not *your* assistant. Call the super yourself."

None of those sentences sounded exactly right to me, but maybe this wasn't something I could rehearse. I pressed the call button, and I waited with shaking hands.

I counted the rings. One, two, three…and that was it.

The call went to voicemail. Usually it took six rings before I heard his outgoing message. Today, though, it had only been three.

He'd sent the call to voicemail on purpose. He'd looked at his phone, saw it was me, and chose to ignore it. It was after five, so even if he was at work, he wasn't on company time anymore. He could've easily picked up.

All the late nights. The feeling like the spark had gone out. The disinterest. Maybe I wasn't the only one who'd developed feelings for someone outside of our marriage.

I left a vague message. "I need to talk to you. Call me when you can."

I hung up, realizing right away how stupid my message had been. It could've been about the water heater for all of the emotion I'd put into it.

And "call me when you can"? He might not call at all with a message like that, or he might call when I wasn't prepared to talk. It had taken a lot of effort to dial the phone, and I imagined it wouldn't be any easier the next time.

I took a deep breath as I slid the keycard into the hotel room door, not sure exactly what I was going to say to Cole. I was still offended by his reference to me as *just* his assistant, but the kiss we shared told me I was more than that.

My heart started beating faster as the nerves coursed through my blood and tingles rushed through my chest.

When I opened the door, I found an empty hotel room.

He was probably off fucking Nicki while I was contemplating the end of one relationship and the start of another.

I sat alone in the hotel room, in the very seat where I'd watched Cole stare out the window just the day before. I stared where he'd stared, looked over the same city and the same buildings he'd gazed over, lost in thoughts of my own.

I didn't have much time until dinner, so I freshened up. As I walked toward the door to head down, it opened.

Cole's eyes met mine, and I saw the remorse in his. I just wasn't sure if the remorse was because he kissed me or because of how he'd introduced me to his little friend.

Seeing him in the flesh only reignited my anger. He'd treated me like trash earlier, but that feeling of anger only reminded me of the conversation I'd had with Luke and the revelation that anything I felt for Cole was magnified because of the passion between us.

He came into the room and the door slammed shut behind him. I waited for him to speak first. I didn't trust what might come out my mouth given the emotions hitting me from every direction.

We stood for a long moment. I wanted to know what he was thinking, but his face was unreadable.

He finally asked, "Can we talk?"

I shook my head. "We need to head down for dinner."

"Dinner can wait."

"We can talk later." I brushed past him on my way out the door, and he grabbed my arm. He spun me around to face him.

"Or we can talk now."

Something about the intense way his eyes latched onto mine caused a penetrating heat to trickle down my spine. He let go of my arm and walked further into the room while I stood by the door.

"Then talk." My voice was filled with angst, and I was proud of myself for standing strong when I really wanted to collapse into his arms.

He gazed out the window when he spoke. "I'm sorry."

I was shocked to hear those two words fall from his lips. He couldn't even look at me when he said it. I supposed he was in the vulnerable seat for a change, but I wasn't going to make this easy on him.

"For what?"

He turned back toward me. "You know for what."

"No, actually, I really don't. I feel like there might be two things you need to apologize for."

He shot me a look. "Two things?"

"Why don't you tell me what you're sorry for first?" I supposed I was playing a game—a dangerous one at that—but his answer was going to tell me a lot. If he was sorry about the kiss, he'd spent time thinking about the implications of my marriage and was sorry that he might've overstepped a line. He'd be sorry for something that had nothing to do with my feelings.

But if he was sorry for calling me *just his assistant*, maybe he understood how much that hurt me. Maybe he felt something deeper than a physical pull to me. That apology would mean so much more.

I didn't want him to be sorry for the kiss. I wasn't.

"I'm sorry that I kissed you. I got carried away. It won't happen again."

"Why won't it happen again?" I challenged.

He sighed and looked away from me again. He was clearly uncomfortable with the direction of this conversation. "Because you're married."

"What if I wasn't?"

His head turned slowly back in my direction. His eyes filled with a carnal ferocity that nearly melted my panties right off my hips. "If you weren't?" His voice was low and gritty, and he spoke with an honesty that completely unnerved me. "I would've kissed you that first day when you walked in late in your pretty little dress."

I gasped, my jaw dropping at his confession, but he kept talking, his voice gaining in volume while his eyes turned from ferocious to sad. "I would've thrown you across your desk the night of the MTC dinner and fucked you hard and fast until you screamed. I would've fucked you slowly on the bed instead of sleeping alone on the couch the second I found out that we were sharing this room."

He walked over to me and ran his thumb across my bottom lip, a sly smile forming on his lips. "I would've crammed this pretty mouth full of my cock a long time ago." He lowered his voice again. "But you are married, and my apology is my way of respecting that regardless of how I feel about you."

It was his turn to brush past me, but I didn't grab his arm as he walked out the door. I didn't try to stop him. I was too stunned to do anything but stand and stare after him.

Chapter Eleven

I pulled myself together, lost in a daze over Cole's admission.

He had feelings for me.

If he had feelings for me all this time, why was he such a dick to me? I'd always figured he'd just been an ass because he had something to prove. He wanted the world to know that he wasn't his father, and treating his subordinates like shit was his way of proving that.

But now I wasn't so sure.

I headed down to dinner as I allowed myself to think about the time that had passed since Cole first started.

If things were going well with John, if I was in a happy marriage, this would be a totally different story.

But that wasn't my life.

Instead, I wasn't happy, and I pined away for something I thought I never could have. But maybe I *could* have it. I'd always just assumed that I wasn't good enough for someone like Cole Benson, but maybe I was. And maybe things would change now that he'd admitted his true feelings for me.

I looked around the banquet room. I spotted Luke with an open seat beside him. As I walked to his table, I spotted Cole sitting between Nicki and the brunette from lunch. His table was otherwise full.

He wasn't smiling, though, like he had been earlier that day. Far from it, actually. He wore a frown, his eyebrows turned down and his eyes full of sadness. He stared at a spot on the table in front of him, oblivious to my gaze as the two bimbos attempted to turn his frown upside down.

I stopped and stared for a moment, wishing I could hug him to make him feel better.

It was my fault he was full of all that unhappiness.

His gaze lifted, and we locked eyes. His frown deepened, and he turned toward Nicki and started engaging in conversation. He smiled at her, but even from my distance I could see how forced it was.

He was trying to make me jealous. And it was working.

I sighed, feeling the heavy weight of gloom settle in my chest. The only way we were going to move past this was for me to be honest about my feelings, too—that is, if he'd give me the chance to talk to him.

I plopped down in the seat next to Luke.

"What's wrong?" he asked.

"Don't ask."

"The boss or the husband?"

"Both, really." I took a sip of water from the glass in front of me.

"How did your talk with your husband go?"

"He sent me to voicemail."

"That asshole!" Luke said, feigning complete shock and eliciting a laugh from me along the way.

"Right?" I smiled, feeling just a little bit better.

"And the boss?"

"Just admitted his feelings for me."

"Damn," he muttered. "You really are one hot mess, aren't you?"

I shrugged. "Just lucky, I guess."

"How did this revelation come to be?"

"He said if I wasn't married, he would've kissed me the day he met me. And he said some other, dirtier stuff, too."

Luke chuckled. "I get it. Your husband is a lucky man that he captured you, but your boss is even luckier."

"Why's that?" I asked, playing along for the moment.

"Because he's the one you're obviously in love with."

"I love how a complete stranger could see in five seconds what it's taken me a month to figure out." I played absently with my napkin.

"It doesn't take a genius to figure it out."

"Oh?"

"You haven't gone more than five seconds without looking at him since you sat down."

Salad was served, and we moved away from the heavy subjects toward lighter conversation. I couldn't help my eyes as they darted constantly in Cole's direction, proving Luke's theory absolutely, one hundred percent correct.

We were treated to a speaker during the dessert course, and after that we were instructed to go to the lobby bar for the evening's mixer. I glanced over in Cole's direction, desperate to talk to him, but he was gone. And so was Nicki.

I hadn't seen him get up, but I assumed he'd gone to the lobby. Well, I hoped he'd gone to the lobby. The alternative was too heart-wrenching to consider.

I walked with Luke toward the mixer. My heart dropped when I realized Cole wasn't there.

I had two viable options. I could sit with Luke and drink my sorrows away, or I could head up to the hotel room and wait for Cole to get back from wherever he'd gone off to with Nicki.

Option two sounded like hell. I'd be sitting there, wondering while I waited. Wondering if he was with her, if he was naked, how deep his feelings for me ran, why he was such an asshole. Wondering when I'd be able to finally talk to John, really talk to him and tell him it was over.

So I sat with Luke. We drank whiskey sours, which turned into just whiskey, which turned into loads of laughing and a whole lot of fun. It was a night I'd needed badly after the strange couple of days…weeks…months I'd been having.

I was definitely drunk by the time he walked me up to my room and bid me goodnight.

To my surprise, Cole was sitting on the couch, his gaze over the city when I walked in. He looked handsome as always sitting there, and I wanted to freeze the moment and just stare at him.

He turned in my direction when the door shut behind me.

"Hi," he said softly, his expression unreadable.

"Hey," I said, stumbling on a snag in the carpet. I leaned on the wall with one arm to steady myself.

He stood. "You okay?"

"Yeah, fine. Just great." My words came out with a bit of a slur.

"You're drunk."

I held up my fingers in a pinch and squinted my eyes. "Maybe just a little."

"Let's get you into bed."

"Oh yeah, baby. Bed sounds real nice."

He chuckled as he put his arm around my waist to help steady me. "You smell like a bar."

"You smell like you should be on top of me."

"Christ," he muttered. "If only you weren't so wasted."

"If only," I repeated, kicking my shoes off and climbing into bed. "And if only you hadn't spent the night fucking Nicki."

And then everything went black.

Chapter Twelve

One ray of light fell across my face, and I squinted as I pried open my eyes. The curtains were drawn, but it was morning. I glanced down to find I was still wearing the dress I'd worn to dinner the night before. I didn't remember getting into bed or closing the curtains, but I must have. I just remembered drinking and giggling with Luke, and I vaguely remembered running into Cole before I fell asleep.

I turned and looked at the clock, and my stomach rolled. My head pounded, and I tried to make sense of the numbers on the clock. It was just before ten, and the sun peeking through the sides of the curtains told me it was morning.

Something important was nagging just under my conscience, but I couldn't piece together what it was.

Until it hit me.

"Fuck!" I yelled, hopping out of bed.

Bad idea.

The whiskey from the night before crept up my throat.

I ran to the bathroom and promptly threw up. I held my head in my hands for a split second, but I didn't have time to feel bad.

I flew into the other room of our hotel suite, but it was empty. Cole and his laptop were gone. He was probably getting ready for his presentation while the assistant he needed had the hangover from hell.

I'd been feeling so sorry for myself that I'd forgotten he'd needed my help finalizing the presentation. I'd stupidly jumped to conclusions and then got drunk with Luke.

I was a royal idiot.

And most definitely not Assistant of the Year material.

I hopped in the shower and got ready in record time. I grabbed my iPad and phone and practically flew down the hall to the elevator. I texted Cole on my way down.

Where are you?

I didn't have time for pleasantries, even though he certainly deserved more than that as well as my profuse apologies.

I was here for a job, and I'd let too much come between that. I'd worked hard to become an executive assistant, to have the opportunity to work on a new project alongside Cole, to travel to New York because he trusted me to help him with his presentation. And I was throwing it all away because I was allowing my personal feelings to come between me and the job I'd come to do.

His reply came quickly. *Conference Room B.*

I ran down the hallway as fast as my legs would carry me in a dress and heels, and I found Cole practicing his presentation in an empty room.

"I'm so, so sorry," I said, interrupting him as he rehearsed his speech.

He gazed at me for a long moment, but he didn't say anything. He turned to his laptop, typing something and essentially ignoring me.

"What can I do?" I asked.

"Be a good little assistant and go get me some coffee."

I shut my eyes for the briefest of moments.

I thought we'd had a breakthrough. I thought that once he'd admitted that he had feelings for me—that once we kissed—things would change.

I couldn't have been more wrong.

Instead, his words just stung that much more. All that hate I felt for him bubbled up as my feelings weren't just hurt—

instead, they were torn to shreds and pounded into the ground.

On some level, I supposed I deserved it this time. I'd gotten drunk when he'd been expecting me to help finalize the presentation, and that was my fault. But he didn't need to hurt me to get across the point that he was pissed at me.

I spun around on my heel and headed toward the coffee shop in the hotel. I placed an order for a large vanilla latte for Cole, and I splurged and ordered a coffee for myself, too. I certainly needed it after the night and subsequent morning I'd had.

As much as I just wanted to tell him to screw himself, I didn't. Instead I rushed to deliver his coffee.

And once again, he completely ignored me. I set his coffee on the podium beside him, and he didn't even have the decency to thank me. He didn't look up from his laptop.

I sat at a table and watched him for a moment before pulling up the presentation on my iPad. I couldn't help but stare at his lips, which moved silently to the words he was going to say with each of his slides.

I finally pulled my eyes away from him to focus on my iPad. I'd already been through the presentation what seemed like a hundred different times, but this was the final read-through.

I found a few minor details that needed editing, so I wrote them down and waited for Cole to address me.

And waited.

And waited some more.

I glanced at my watch. We only had about fifteen minutes before Cole needed to start his presentation. Finally I cleared my throat. Cole looked up at me, irritation clear on his handsome face.

"Um, Mr. Benson, I found three things that need to be changed."

"It's getting a bit late for changes, Ms. Cleary." Frustration thickened his voice.

"I know, and I'm so sorry."

I stood and hurried over to him to show him which slides needed the changes.

He stopped and looked at me, and I saw it all there in his eyes. He had to act like he hated me to cover up his feelings for me.

"I needed you last night," he said, his voice a harsh whisper.

"I'm sorry."

He glared at me. "I don't have time to deal with your shit right now, so we'll figure out the repercussions later. What needs to be changed?"

I showed him the three minor errors, two of which he'd already corrected on his own.

"Are you ready?" I asked once the presentation was finalized.

He glanced at the clock on his phone. "I guess I have to be."

"What can I do?"

"I need you to record the entire presentation. I'm considering creating a webinar with the information."

"That's a great idea."

He glared at me again. "I know it is. Stop kissing my ass and do your fucking job."

I nodded, my cheeks burning with embarrassment. I hated how easily he could hurt me, and I tried my hardest to just let it roll off of me. "Of course."

We headed to the room where Cole would be presenting. The previous presentation had just ended, and people filed out while others started to enter. The front row was filling up quickly. I reserved a chair by throwing my bag on it so I'd be able to film Cole as requested.

Cole stood at the front of the room on a small stage. He stared a bit helplessly at the wires sticking out of the podium. I took a deep breath and headed up to help.

"I got it," he said in a furious whisper, as if by having a woman help him he might somehow be emasculated.

I raised my eyebrows as if to tell him to go for it, and he fiddled with the obviously wrong wire. He looked all along the side of his laptop for a hole that matched the plug in his hand to no avail.

I watched as his hands shook ever so slightly. As someone who dealt with him every day, it was easy to see that he was flustered, but the people walking into the room would've never sensed it. Not with the cool demeanor he was doing his best to project.

"Cole, just let me do it," I finally said, pulling the wire out of his hand. "Go over your notes one more time and take a deep breath while I get you set up."

He shot me a grateful look that he immediately masked with the glare he'd saved just for me.

I inserted all the right plugs into all the right holes and pulled up his intro slide, projecting it onto the screen. "Anything else I can do?" I asked.

He shook his head without looking up at me.

"I'm turning on the mic now."

He nodded, still not looking at me. Before I clicked the button, I said, "Good luck. You'll be as amazing as you always are." And then I headed down to my seat.

A man in a suit who I didn't recognize rushed up toward Cole. His gray hair told me he was around Jack's age, and he bore a resemblance to the Benson men, but, unlike Cole, he wore a friendly smile. He and Cole shook hands vigorously and exchanged some words, and then the man took the microphone and I held up my phone to begin recording the presentation.

"Good morning. I'm Rob Benson, an executive of Benson Industries, and I'm here to introduce your next speaker. I worked with Cole here in New York for eight years before he made the decision to take over as acting CEO of Benson Industries in California, and from what I've heard, it's been a smooth transition because of Cole's professionalism, knowledge, and business savvy. You're in for a treat with this next speaker as I'm positive you will walk away with not just some new strategies, but a new way of thinking. And I'm not just trying to suck up to my boss. I'm also his proud uncle." His last line garnered a small chuckle from the crowd, and I turned around to see that the room was completely full…and the audience was comprised of almost exclusively women.

I rolled my eyes, but I didn't stop filming.

"Ladies and gentlemen, Mr. Cole Benson."

The crowd applauded for their presenter, and then I watched as Cole shook Rob's hand again. He took a deep breath, and his eyes locked ever so briefly onto mine. I gave him a huge smile of encouragement, and he nodded almost imperceptibly and then started the speech he'd rehearsed what seemed to be hundreds of times.

I watched as he delighted the crowd through the small screen on my phone.

I didn't have pictures of him on my phone. I relied on the mental images when I thought about him.

Instead, the album on my phone was filled with photos of my personal life.

The album was aptly titled "Moments," a title given by Apple, not by me, and it was a series of moments over the past few years, mostly moments I shared with my husband. Moments where we appeared to be happy. Moments appropriate for sharing on social media. Moments that made us seem like the perfect couple to anyone who was looking.

But they weren't real.

They were just photos snapped at perfect moments of two smiling people. They didn't show our struggles or our fears. They didn't show the dents in our armor or the cracks in our hearts. And they certainly didn't show the vast ocean of nothingness that had somehow wedged between us.

But now there was a new Moment on my phone.

As I watched Cole give his speech, starting out a bit nervous but easily and quickly gaining confidence, making the crowd laugh and swoon, I couldn't help the piece of my heart that fell a little harder for him.

At the very end of his speech, just after he gave his final thoughts, he said, "And one final thing. I have to thank my assistant, Lucy Cleary. She dedicated a lot of hours to putting together this presentation, and I hope you've all learned something new that you can take back with you. Thank you."

I was touched—and, frankly shocked—that he'd mentioned me with praise. He wasn't the praising type of boss. He was much more the insulting, demeaning, hurtful type of boss.

He received a standing ovation for his presentation, something I'd never seen happen at any work conference I'd attended. While the information he'd given was valuable, I had a feeling that the applause had more to do with how hot he looked in a suit than with the material.

After his presentation, which lasted a full hour and drained the battery on my phone, a line of women formed at the side of the stage. I was certain they wanted to ask him questions, but I highly doubted the questions had anything to do with what he'd just discussed.

It was lunch time, and I needed to charge my phone. I looked over at him after gathering my stuff. I wanted to ask if he needed me to do anything else, but I didn't want to interrupt him. He was so hard to read sometimes, and I didn't want to do the wrong thing and piss him off. Some blonde cougar held his attention, anyway, so I turned to leave.

Just as I turned, he glanced in my direction. We locked eyes for a split second again, and then he turned his attention back to the cougar.

Maybe I was just reading into it what I wanted to see, but I could've sworn that all of the anger was gone and all the heat was back.

Cole Benson wanted me, and I was pretty sure that he was done hiding it.

Chapter Thirteen

"Lucy! Over here!" I turned at the sound of my name, and Luke wore a huge smile.

I walked over with my boxed lunch and slid into the seat beside him. "You look awfully chipper considering our night out."

"I didn't drink half the amount you did."

I rolled my eyes and opened my box to find a sandwich, a bag of chips, and an apple. "Thanks so much for stopping me."

He chuckled. "You kept telling me you could handle it. And you were doing fine."

"Until I wasn't."

"Yeah, until you weren't."

We both laughed. "How mad was he?"

"On a scale of one to ten? Eleven. He said we will deal with the repercussions later."

Luke made a face. "Whatever that means."

"I mean, if he wants to spank me…"

He set down his burger. "God, Lucy. You are aware that I'm a single man, right?"

"I'm not."

"Like it matters."

Part of me wanted to be offended, but I laughed at his teasing. Sometimes laughter was the only way to deal with a serious situation.

Luke took a sip of his drink. "His presentation was outstanding, but I'm guessing it's because you did all the work on it."

"Shut up," I mumbled. "It was all his. I just put it together."

"You're too modest."

I shrugged. "I'm glad you were there."

"I heard him thank you."

"I was shocked. Like beyond shocked."

"So was I based on what you've told me about him."

"Speak of the devil," I said, my eyes glued to Cole as he walked into the banquet room. He wasn't alone; a flock of women followed him, but I watched as he glanced around the room with a bit of anxiety. I wondered what he was looking for, and then his eyes caught mine. His face smoothed over until his eyes darted to Luke beside me, and then his expression darkened ever so slightly.

He turned back to one of the women vying for his attention, and I wondered what that was all about.

"He wants you, Lucy. He wants you and he wants me away from you."

"How do you know that?"

"Because I see how he looks at you. He searched you out the second he walked into this room. And then he gave me a dirty look."

"That's ridiculous."

Luke shrugged. "Believe what you want."

After lunch, I headed back to the suite. I was relaxing on the couch, scrolling lazily through my phone to avoid reality. I'd just started thinking I should head back down for the next session when the door opened.

Cole walked in, and his hand went immediately to his throat to loosen his tie. I watched him tensely from where I sat. He ran so hot and cold—one minute he was telling me how he wanted me since the moment we met, and the next minute he was ordering me around and treating me like dirt. I wondered which version of him just walked through the door.

His eyes landed squarely on me. "We need to talk."

My phone started ringing in my purse. My eyes darted away from his and in the direction of the sound.

"Ignore it."

"But it could be—"

"I don't care who it is." He strode through the room until he was standing in front of me. He held out his hand. I took it, and he helped me up.

His eyes bored down into mine, and I sensed that I was getting the Cole that wanted me.

Badly.

"This is so fucking stupid, Lucy. I can't take it anymore."

"What is?" I asked, confused. My phone stopped ringing, and silence filled the room.

"This back and forth shit between us. I've tried to respect the fact that you're married, but I want you, and I know you want me, too. It's time to stop ignoring what's right in front of us and do something about it."

"What do you want to do about it?" My voice shook.

He leaned down toward me, and our lips met. His kiss was gentle, the opposite of what I'd expected from him based on his demeanor. His arms tightened around me, but his kiss remained tender.

My phone dinged with a notification.

"Dammit," he muttered, dropping his arms and backing away from me. He walked over to my purse and handed it to me.

I threw my purse down on the table. "Whoever it is can wait," I said, and I threw my arms around Cole's neck as my lips crashed onto his. Whoever it was *needed* to wait, because this thing between us couldn't wait any longer.

The tender kiss from seconds before was gone. This one was fiery and passionate as all the emotions I'd bottled up for Cole surfaced. Love and hate and *passion* and jealousy and irritation and admiration and everything in between flooded out of me and into our kiss.

And I felt it all back from him, too. The times we'd both held back, and the times we'd both wanted to do something but my marriage or our professional relationship or some other obstacle stopped us.

We weren't thinking anymore. We were just acting on the pure, animal magnetism that drew us together.

His arms tightened around my waist as our kiss deepened, tongue hurtling against tongue and lips attacking lips.

He pushed me down onto the couch and tumbled on top of me, and our bodies immediately started grinding in tune with our kiss. My nerves awakened and my blood heated as I knew that I was finally, finally going to get everything I'd wanted since the moment I'd first met this dangerous man.

Cole's hand made its way up my torso and had just reached the underside of my breast when the hotel room phone started ringing.

He paused, and his hand retracted slightly. He pulled away, and I blew out a frustrated breath. "Should we get that?" he asked.

I couldn't hide the disappointment I felt. "I guess. And I should probably check my messages."

Cole stood and looked down at me with fire in his eyes. "This isn't over."

I pulled my phone out of my purse while Cole answered the hotel room phone.

I had a missed call from John. I supposed he'd gotten my message and was calling me back.

"It's for you," Cole said. He wouldn't look at me. "It's your husband."

A sick feeling formed in the pit of my stomach. Why was John calling me at the hotel?

Something was wrong.

Really wrong.

He never would've tried to track me down at the hotel for something as simple as a broken water heater.

Which, I just remembered, I never actually called about.

Cole's eyes met mine, and the fire was gone. I took the phone from him.

"John?" I said, my voice shaky.

He didn't say hello. No greeting. No pleasantries. No questioning why Cole was answering the phone in my hotel room. Just right to the point.

"There's been an accident."

My heart stopped. I didn't speak as I waited for him to drop the bomb.

His hoarse voice shook as he started rambling an explanation. "Kevin was driving and a truck hit them. The driver had fallen asleep."

"Oh my God." My hand flew to my mouth as my stomach churned.

"Kevin and Kaylee are in critical condition."

"Madi?" I asked, the five-year-old face of my sweet niece popping into my head. Madi had to be okay.

"She was with your mom."

"Thank God."

"Come home. Madi needs you. Kaylee and Kevin need you. Your mom needs you."

I waited for him to say that he needed me, too. I needed him to tell me he loved me and that everything was going to be okay.

But he didn't.

And we didn't actually know if it was going to be okay.

My sister was hurt, and I'd ignored the call coming through to tell me what had happened so I could kiss someone who wasn't my husband.

"Of course," I said. I held the phone to my ear in shock, totally unsure what my next move was supposed to be.

"Hang up the phone and get to the airport. Come home."

"Okay." I hung up the phone and stood rooted to the spot. I took a breath that wasn't quite deep enough.

Cole walked over to me but didn't touch me. "What's going on?"

"My sister and her husband were in a bad car accident. They're both in critical condition." I spoke the words, but they didn't feel real. Not yet. The next few days would certainly make them feel real. Going home would make it all real.

But staying right here, holed up in this hotel room with Cole…that would forever pause the world outside. I could stay right here and never have to deal with reality.

"Oh my God," he said, wrapping his arms around me. I couldn't seem to lift my arms to wrap them around him. I couldn't seem to move. My body numbed from the inside out. "I'm so sorry."

"My brother-in-law was driving. My niece was with my mom."

"At least she's fine," Cole said, trying to point out the positive.

I pushed him away. "She's not fine," I said. "Her parents are in critical condition. She might never be fine again." I sat on the couch. I waited for this to be real, for the news to hit me, but everything around me felt so thick. Thick and fuzzy.

I looked right at Cole, but it was like he wasn't there. My chest felt so heavy, like I couldn't breathe deeply enough to get in a good, deep breath. I kept trying, but nothing seemed to satisfy the need for oxygen. I heaved another deep breath, but…nothing.

Panic set in as the feeling of suffocation took over.

I coughed as I tried drawing in another breath.

"Lucy, relax. Take a breath and hold it in until I tell you to let it go." I did what he said. His voice was so soothing. I'd never heard Cole take on a soothing tone before.

"Okay, let it go."

I did.

"Again, Lucy. Deeper this time."

I drew in a deeper breath.

"And let it go."

I did again. It still wasn't deep enough, and it still didn't alleviate any of the weight I felt pressing down on my chest, but at least it was something.

"I'm going to take care of this, and I'm not going to leave your side, okay?"

I nodded.

He laced his fingers through mine and pulled his phone out of his pocket. He pulled up his contact list and dialed a number. "Hey, Dad. I need your help."

I stared at him as he worked. I was just kissing him a few minutes ago. My biggest problem had been whether or not I should cheat on my husband and sleep with my boss. And now my sister's life was on the line and my niece might have to live her life without one or both of her parents.

"Oh my God," I whispered, a new realization dawning on me.

Cole looked at me with wide eyes. "What?"

"They want me to be her guardian if something happens to them."

"Lucy, it's okay. They're going to be okay."

"You don't know that."

"You're right. I don't. Let's get you home so we can figure this out."

He spoke again to his father, and I faded in and out of their conversation as I thought about Madi. Her world was about to change no matter what happened, and I was responsible for taking care of her until her parents were able to.

I was barely responsible enough to care for myself, and now I had to take care of a five-year-old?

Chapter Fourteen

It was strange sitting next to Cole on the flight home. So much had changed between us in just a few short days. I'd gone from thinking he was an asshole whose face I accidentally pictured while I fingered myself to developing real feelings for him.

I told him he didn't need to come with me and that I'd be fine, but he insisted. It shocked me to see this new side of him. Even in the few instances he'd shown me his nice side, he'd never been so tender and caring.

And it just made it all that much more difficult to consider the road ahead of me.

Kaylee and Kevin had sat John and me down just after we'd gotten engaged. They'd told us they wanted us to raise Madi in the event that something happened to the two of them. It was one of those morbid conversations that parents have to consider, but all four of us naively believed we'd never really have to do what they were asking us.

But here we were. I had no idea what condition my sister was in apart from *critical.* That could mean any number of things, and I wished I'd been coherent enough to ask John that when we'd spoken. I hadn't had time to call him back or even text him between packing, getting to the airport, and boarding the plane. It was all a blur, but at least each task had forced me to do something other than worry.

Cole had been by my side every step of the way. He hadn't lied earlier when he'd told me he wasn't going to leave me.

But now I had more than five hours of sitting on a plane with little else to do besides worry. I texted John before the flight attendants asked us to switch our devices to airplane mode, and I'd asked if he had any more details. I didn't hear back from him in time.

"I'm paying for the wifi if you need to use it for anything," Cole said, his voice breaking into my thoughts. He reached over and took my hand in his. "And if there's anything else I can do, please just ask." His dark eyes were a warm, milk chocolate. Sincere and genuine and concerned. He squeezed my hand and neither of us let go.

It may have been because he was offering me the comfort I hadn't gotten from my husband during our short conversation, but I didn't want to let go of Cole's hand.

I shifted in my seat. I crossed my leg, and then I uncrossed it. I tapped my nails on the armrest. I lowered the shade and then lifted it. I shifted again.

We'd only been in the air for three minutes and I was already restless, but Cole's hand firmly clutched mine.

"Does he have an iPhone?" Cole asked.

My head whipped over in his direction. "Who?"

"Your husband." His voice was quiet as he averted his eyes.

I shook my head. "Android."

Cole rolled his eyes.

"Why?"

"If he had an iPhone, you could still message him from your phone even in airplane mode."

"My mom has one."

"Why don't you try her? Maybe she can give you an update."

"Good idea," I said. I had to let go of his hand to use my phone, and his hand shifted down to my thigh.

He kept touching me, letting me know he was right there. And it was a bigger comfort than I could put into words. I hadn't realized how much I needed to feel loved until I felt it again.

I connected to the wifi and texted my mom. *In the air. Flight is 5 and 1/2 hours. Any news?*

I watched as my phone delivered the message, and I felt a bit of relief as the three little bubbles appeared to indicate she was typing a response. Soon I would know more.

Cole moved his hand from my leg to pull out his laptop from under the seat in front of him.

My mom's message came through. *Kaylee is out of surgery and upgraded to stable. Kevin is still in surgery for brain swelling.*

I breathed a quick sigh of relief that Kaylee was stable at least. But that still didn't tell me much. *Is she going to be okay? Is he?*

I waited with impatience for the reply as I watched Cole log onto his computer.

She'll be okay. Still out from the anesthesia. Broken ribs & arm plus concussion & whiplash. We won't know more about Kevin until he's out of surgery.

I felt a mix of emotions—relief that my sister was going to be okay but fear for her husband. Fear for what her life would be like without Kevin and what Madi's life would be like without her dad. Fear for the future of my family without Kevin. He was as much a part of our family as I was.

I shook my head, clearing out the negative thoughts. He needed every positive thought I could possibly muster while he was in surgery.

I texted my mom back. *Thanks for the update. Let me know if anything changes. I'll be praying.*

Fly safely. See you soon. Love you.

"Any updates?" Cole asked.

I showed him my mom's messages, not trusting myself to speak.

"Your sister is going to be fine," he said, a ghost of a smile forming on his lips.

"But Kevin…"

"He's going to be fine, too."

I nodded, hoping with all my might he was right.

The flight felt like the longest five and a half hours of my life. I watched as Cole emailed some people to let them know that he had to leave the conference early due to an emergency. I couldn't concentrate on anything long enough to take my mind off of the tragedy awaiting me back home, so I sat and stared at the clock on my phone, willing time to speed up to get me home faster.

When the landing gear finally touched down, I felt a wave of relief. Soon I'd be where I needed to be.

Cole threw his arm around my shoulder as we waited for my bag at the baggage claim, and I couldn't help but think of what almost happened between us. So much heavy shit had gone down in the past seven hours that I was having a hard time processing everything.

Maybe I didn't need to process anything. Maybe I just needed to feel what I felt and live in the moment.

Everything happens for a reason, and maybe this accident had to happen to remind me that we're only given one life. It was selfish to make this about me, but I had to take what little positive light I could find.

And the light in that moment was the learning experience. It was the fact that I was trapped in an unhappy marriage. It was the fact that the man whose arm was around me was the man I wanted to be with.

I couldn't waste any more time. I needed to act. I wasn't guaranteed anything in this life—least of all time.

I turned in toward Cole, and he wrapped his other arm around me. I breathed him in, feeling comfort in his unexpected tenderness and that fresh, clean scent of the shower gel I'd taken the time to memorize our first morning in the hotel together.

His lips pressed against my temple, and that little motion made me feel about a million times better. Just knowing I had someone who cared about me helped me feel like I was going to get through this without being a total mess.

His arms tightened around me, and his lips moved close to my ear. "Lucy," he whispered, his breath tickling my ear, "I know we need to figure things out, but let's put that on hold. You take what you need right now. I'll still be here when you're ready."

I wanted to cry for ten different reasons, but mostly because I didn't want to put this on hold. We didn't have time to put it on hold. I wanted to figure it out now because I didn't know if I'd have tomorrow. If I stopped right now to look back at my life, could I say I was happy with the way it turned out?

My suitcase came by on the belt, and Cole grabbed it for me. We made our way outside to the warm California air, and Cole ushered me to a car that was waiting for us with a sign labeled "Benson."

I texted my mom to let her know we were on our way. John had replied to my earlier text. *Your mom has more details. Kaylee is stable and Kevin is in surgery.*

Between the fear of heading to the hospital and the confusion in my heart concerning Cole, I felt a sense of doom in the pit of my stomach.

Cole's hand tightened in mine as we pulled onto the street of the hospital. We were getting close, and that meant our time together was coming to an end.

For now.

"I can't hold you the way I want to," he said, leaning in and pressing a gentle kiss to my lips, "but I'll be here however you need me to be. I'll sit back and let your husband comfort you. I'll let you be with your family. I'll drop you off and go home, or I'll go in with you and stay by your side. I care about you, and I've been fighting how I feel because you're married and you're my employee. But I'm done fighting it."

I allowed his words to embed into my mind and warm me.

We pulled up to the hospital's entrance. "As soon as your sister and your brother-in-law are well again, your husband is going to have the fight of his life on his hands."

I bit my lip to try to keep the heat behind my eyes from forming tears. Somehow he'd said everything I'd needed to hear.

"Do you want me to leave or come with you?"

"Come," I whispered.

He nodded. He opened the door and helped me out, said something to the driver, and we walked into the hospital together.

We stood close to one another, but he didn't hold my hand. We checked in at the front desk and headed up to the floor my mom had sent me over text message.

My mom and dad were in the waiting room with Madi. There was no sign of my husband.

As soon as I walked off of the elevator, Madi ran toward me and wrapped her little arms around my legs. "Auntie Lucy!" she squealed, and I picked her up and swung her around the way I always did when I saw her.

"Hi baby," I said.

"I'm not a baby!" she said, shooting me her sassiest look.

Her energy made it clear that she had no idea what was going on, and her innocence was refreshing.

"How are things going?" I asked my mom. Her eyes edged toward Cole.

"This is my boss," I said, nodding toward Cole. "Cole, this is my mom, Barb, and my dad, Bill."

"Nice to meet you," Cole said, nodding at both of them. "And who is this?" he asked, smiling at Madi.

She nuzzled shyly into my neck. "This is Madison, my niece."

"It's nice to meet you, Madison," he said, grinning at her.

"You too, Mr. Cole."

He chuckled. "Have you ever seen the movie *Frozen*?" he asked.

I looked at him incredulously, and he winked at me.

"That's my favorite!" Madi exclaimed.

"Do you like Elsa or Anna better?"

"Elsa! Elsa! Elsa! I love her hair!"

"So do I. But Anna has all that pretty red hair," he said, and Madi started pushing against me to set her down. She took Cole's hand and led him over to some empty chairs, pulling out a *Frozen* book and handing it to him. "Read," she demanded.

I giggled as I watched Cole start reading the book to my niece. She recited the words along with him, not because she knew how to read it, but because she'd heard the book a hundred different times and had memorized the words. Cole acted impressed.

Watching Cole with my niece made me fall even more for him. He was sexy, smart, a great kisser, *and* good with kids?

My heart was a melty puddle of goo.

My mom pulled me out of earshot of my niece and raised an eyebrow at me.

The infamous eyebrow. A single eyebrow took both my sister and me to our knees when we were younger. It meant we were in a whole lot of trouble.

I didn't need my mom's eyebrow to tell me that I was in serious trouble.

"Is this a bad time to mention your husband?" she asked, her voice soft.

I pressed my lips together before replying. "And where the hell is he?"

"He managed to get you here, didn't he?"

"Can we save this conversation for later? How are Kaylee and Kevin doing?"

She glanced at Madi before replying. "We're waiting for them to move Kaylee to a room. Kevin is out of surgery but not out of the woods yet. We need to wait for the swelling by his brain to go down before we'll know more. His parents are driving from Colorado now."

"Is Kay awake?"

She nodded. "They won't let us back in post-op, but as soon as she gets a room, we can go see her. I'd like to keep Madi away from this as much as possible. Would you be able to take her home with you for a few days?"

"Of course. I'll do whatever I have to."

"Thank you. What's going on with you and your boss?"

"What do you mean?"

She glanced over toward Madi again, but I knew she was looking at Cole. "The way you look at him."

"Mom…" I sighed, giving her the warning to stop the conversation by my tone.

"He's handsome."

"That doesn't mean anything." I picked absently at my nails.

"Be careful, Lucy."

I gave her my best offended look and headed over to play with Cole and Madi.

A nurse came out to speak to my mom and dad, and then my mom let me know they were going in to see Kaylee. I couldn't help but wonder where the hell John was and why the hell he wasn't here where he should have been.

I finally texted him. *I'm at the hospital. Where are you?*

Work. How are they?

I fumed. I'd left a work function to head all the way across the country to be here, and he couldn't leave the office for five minutes?

Kay is stable, but Kev just got out of surgery.

I wanted to ask why he wasn't here, but I couldn't muster the energy. Part of me didn't want him in the same room with Cole anyway, but I couldn't help but feel abandoned by him. It was a no-win situation for him.

I'll be there soon.

I wondered what at work could be more important than family, but maybe he didn't see it that way. They were *my* family, not his, and so maybe he just didn't care that much.

My mom and dad came out to let me know that I could go in. My mom had clearly been crying, but she put on a brave face for Madi. Cole's eyes met mine, and I nodded yes to his silent question.

I needed him to hold my hand through this.

We walked together toward the doors that would take us to the hallway that led to my sister's room, and I had no idea what to expect.

As soon as the doors clicked shut behind us, Cole grabbed my hand. I looked to him gratefully, not sure how he knew exactly what I needed while the man I was married to couldn't even be bothered to be here.

Kaylee was asleep, and she looked like hell. Her face was bruised, swollen, and bandaged, and her arm was in a big cast. She barely looked like my sister. I clutched Cole's hand a little tighter.

I sat on the couch under the window. I figured my sister would be out for a while—she'd just had surgery, after all, but it still felt right to be here.

After a few minutes, a nurse walked in to check on Kaylee. We left her to do her job.

Cole opened the door for me and the two of us headed back to the lobby. Halfway down the hall, Cole grabbed my hand in his again, and then he stopped walking.

He pulled me in for a hug.

"Are you okay?" he whispered.

I nodded, and I felt his lips on my cheek.

He took me so completely by surprise that I didn't even realize what was happening until it was all over. His kiss was so gentle and sweet. It only lasted a few seconds, but it was somehow exactly what I needed after seeing my sister lying helplessly in her hospital bed.

I shifted and caught his lips softly with mine. He pulled away first and rested his forehead against mine for just a moment.

He smiled tightly and stepped away from me. I immediately missed his closeness as a shiver ran down my spine.

"If I can do anything, just ask. You know I have the means to get your sister and her husband the best care. Same with your niece."

I looked to him gratefully. "I appreciate it."

He grabbed my hand and held it down the hallway, all the way until we reached the set of double doors that would take us out to the waiting room.

I saw the back of his head the moment we walked out of those doors. The man I'd married, the one I'd pledged my life and my love to, stood talking to my parents. My stomach twisted in violent knots as soon as I saw him. I felt like I was going to throw up.

What I was doing was wrong. Even if I hadn't actually slept with Cole, I'd still betrayed my husband's trust.

John turned around as if he could sense my presence. His eyes met mine, and they slid over to Cole for just a moment. Something dark flashed through his eyes before they moved back to me.

He walked to me and pressed a kiss to my lips. It was the first time he'd initiated a kiss in…I couldn't remember how long. A month, maybe? I was pretty sure the last time he'd kissed me had been on our last monthly date—an entire month earlier.

He was asserting his spot as my husband in front of my boss. It shouldn't matter. He shouldn't have felt the need to act like a caveman.

I wondered if John could taste the betrayal in my kiss. I wondered if he could taste Cole's breath on my lips.

I wondered if I kissed differently. It had been a long time since I'd kissed someone other than my husband.

"How was New York?" he asked tentatively. He was showing an interest in me for the first time in years, and I was certain it was just for show. He had to act like everything was okay between the two of us in front of my parents and Cole. It was a show we were used to acting, and he was clearly going for the Academy Award.

But it was time for me to do what felt right.

"Fine," I answered, childishly giving him a taste of his own medicine. I didn't bother asking him about his couple of days without me.

He gave me a strange look, but I ignored it. He stepped away from my parents and Madi. "How's Kaylee doing?" he asked.

I lowered my voice so Madi wouldn't overhear. "She looks like hell but she'll be okay."

He shook his head. "Can we go see her?"

Cole cleared his throat, and both John and I turned toward him. "I should, uh, go."

"Yeah," John said. "Probably just family needs to be here for now."

"Don't be rude," I said to John.

I turned to Cole, and I felt John's eyes boring into me. "You're welcome to stay, but we're fine if you need to go. I can't thank you enough for all you've done to get me here."

"Don't thank me. I'm glad you could be with your family. They need you."

His eyes told the rest of the story, the words he couldn't voice. He wanted to stay to be with me, and John's presence only served to prove how much I'd come to rely on Cole.

"I'll walk you out," I said.

John shot me a look. "He's a big boy. He can find his way."

"Your husband's right," Cole said thickly. "I'll make sure your luggage gets back to your apartment. See you Monday." He said goodbye to my parents and Madi, cast one last look in my direction, and headed toward the elevators, taking my heart along with him.

"We're going in," John announced to my parents, avoiding mentioning my sister's name in front of Madi. They nodded and I led him back the way I'd just come from.

As soon as we were on the other side of the double doors, he grabbed my arm.

"What the fuck is going on between you and him?" he hissed.

I'd never seen him so mad. A tiny piece of my heart felt triumphant. It was nice to see some emotion out of him for a change.

"Nothing."

"Why were you in the same hotel room as him?"

"We were forced to stay together, and I'm shocked you tore yourself away from work or the constant screens you're always staring at to give a fuck," I retorted.

"I get paid to look at screens. Do you get paid to sleep with your boss?" He let go of my arm and started walking down the hallway, and all I could do was stare after him, totally hurt by his comment—but not entirely shocked by it.

I power-walked to catch up to him. "You can't just say something like that to me and walk away."

"Oh? But you can stay in the same goddamn hotel room as your boss and that's okay?"

A nurse glared at us from behind her work station.

"John, lower your voice. The room was a mix-up."

He lowered his voice to that same hiss he'd directed toward me earlier. "Some mix-up when you can't be bothered to answer your cell phone but your boss answers the hotel room phone sounding awfully out of breath."

An elderly man in a hospital gown pushing an IV stand on wheels walked past us. I smiled genially at the man before looking back at John, who wouldn't look me in the eye. "It's nice that you finally want to talk, but this isn't the place for this conversation."

John blew out a frustrated sigh. "You're right. I'm sorry. Let's see Kaylee and then we'll go home and figure things out."

"Probably not. We're taking Madi home."

"Dammit," he muttered. I shot him a look, and he backed down. "It's fine. I'm just worked up with some things at the office and I'm worried about Kaylee and Kevin."

I reached down and grabbed his hand out of habit. "I am, too."

He pressed his lips together and then we entered Kaylee's room, hand-in-hand—much like I'd entered the room not twenty minutes earlier…with a different man.

Chapter Fifteen

"Bubblegum and then cookie dough."

"Not vanilla?" I asked.

Madi giggled. "Noooooo! Vanilla is the worst!"

"What if they don't have bubblegum?"

"Then I'll get cookie dough, silly!"

John was silent as he drove us to the ice cream shop at Madi's request. With her parents suffering in the hospital, she deserved some ice cream for dinner. And so did I.

I made small talk with my niece, and she was as bubbly as ever. She knew something was going on, but my parents had done a good job of protecting her from seeing her mom and dad in such horrible shape. Even though Madi was her normal, sweet self, she still missed her parents. It wouldn't be long before she started asking questions.

And she shouldn't eat ice cream for dinner more than one night. I was such a pushover I'd probably let it slide.

We'd just placed our orders when I felt my phone vibrate in my pocket. When I glanced covertly at the screen, I saw I had a new text message from Cole.

My heart skipped a beat and I felt the heat creep up my neck and into my cheeks.

I opened it while John paid, but it was lengthy—too lengthy to read quickly without getting caught. I stuck my phone back in my pocket and searched for some reason to check it.

"I need to run to the little girls' room," I said as we waited for our order.

"We'll grab a table, but if the ice cream comes while you're gone, we can't guarantee yours will be safe," John teased.

"I'm gonna eat it all!" Madi sang.

"You better not, missy!" I mock-hurried to the bathroom. As soon as the door clicked shut, I pulled out my phone.

I miss you. That's crazy. I just saw you a couple of hours ago. I don't know if it's okay to send you this. Delete it if you need to. I never thought I'd get caught in the middle of someone's marriage. I respect marriage. I respect your commitment. But something's broken there if you're interested in me. I'll step back if that's what you need, but when you kiss me, I think what you need is me.

I had no idea how to respond to that.

I read it again, and then a third time. I processed his words. He missed me, and that sent a bolt of excitement through my chest. I contemplated how to respond, and finally I typed out a quick text. *I miss you, too. We need to talk, but I've got Madi tonight. You're right, though. About all of it. What I need isn't what I have anymore.*

I stared at the screen for a few extra seconds, reading my words over and over again. There was so much more I wanted to say, but my husband was waiting for me right on the other side of the bathroom door. I needed to get back out there before anyone became suspicious.

I sent the message, read his one more time, deleted both messages, and stuck my phone in my pocket before heading back to my husband and my niece.

Later that night, after I'd put Madi to bed in our guest room and unpacked my suitcase, I lay in bed with a full stomach and a giant wedge between John and me.

He was doing something on his iPad when I got in bed beside him. Sharing a bed with someone who I realized I didn't really like all that much anymore seemed odd. I turned out my light and pulled the covers over me, flipping away from John without saying anything.

"No reading tonight?" he asked quietly.

"Too tired. Goodnight." I added that last part to give him the hint that I wasn't interested in conversation, but he apparently didn't take the bait.

"What were you really doing in the same hotel room as your boss?"

I rolled my eyes even though he couldn't see my face. "We've been over this."

"Go over it again for me."

"Why do you even care? You haven't even looked in my direction in months, and now you suddenly need every detail?" I still faced away from him as I spoke.

"Because you're my wife, Lucy. That's why."

I sighed as I turned toward him. "There was a mix-up. I booked two rooms, but when we got there, they only had one on the confirmation. The hotel was completely booked, and the closest hotel in New York traffic would've made it a huge hassle to get back and forth to the conference. Cole had a suite with two rooms, so we just shared it."

"And that's all that happened?"

My chest shuddered as my heart skipped a beat.

Adrenaline coursed through my veins.

This was my chance.

He was asking all the right questions. He was suspicious. This was my out—my way to tell him the truth.

But we were in bed after a very taxing day, and Madi was in the room just down the hall. My sister was in the hospital and I didn't even know if my brother-in-law was going to live to see another day, to see his daughter again, to kiss his wife again.

I chickened out.

Maybe all of those things should've pushed me to tell him the truth—after all, life could be cut short when we least expected it. It was far too short to waste time with the things that didn't truly make me happy.

"Yeah. That's it."

He stared at me for a long moment as if trying to determine whether I was telling the truth or lying. I forced my face into a smooth mask, and eventually he nodded and turned back to his screen.

"Goodnight," he said.

I flipped back the other way without responding and closed my eyes, but my mind was suddenly wide awake. I forced my breathing to even out so he'd think I was asleep.

I needed to talk to Cole, but I couldn't do it with John awake beside me. I needed to tell him that I felt the same way he did, that I wanted to be with him. That I wanted to leave my husband.

I needed him to calm the thundering ache between my legs.

I wished it was him beside me in this bed instead of my husband.

I waited for John to finish whatever he was doing. He eventually switched off his bedside lamp, and I waited until I heard his familiar, soft snore. It was the snore I'd listened to hundreds of times because he almost always fell asleep before me.

It always annoyed me, listening to that snore while I tried to fall asleep.

But tonight it was a snore that meant I could get out of bed, grab my phone, and creep quietly to our home office.

It was a snore that gave me a chance to talk to the man who'd recently planted roots in my mind and my heart.

I was suddenly grateful for the snore I'd spent so much time lying beside and resenting.

I closed the door to the office behind me, praying Madi would stay asleep and praying even harder that John would stay asleep.

I didn't turn on the big overhead light in the room. Instead, I flicked on the tiny lamp we kept on the desk. The soft glow set an intimate vibe for the phone call I knew I shouldn't make.

This was one of those calls that could change everything. It was one thing to be tempted because we shared the same hotel room. But now I was going out of my way to make contact with Cole while my husband slept soundly just a few rooms away.

I walked around the desk and sat in the leather chair that I'd insisted we buy back when we'd been decorating the office. I'd always wanted a big, comfy chair behind a huge desk, and I loved how our home office had turned out.

I wondered for one brief moment if I'd end up with this chair after John and I split.

It was that moment I realized I hadn't actually voiced the big "D" word in my head yet. I'd thought about leaving him, or separating, or splitting…but "divorce" was such a serious word.

But it was what I was going to have to do to get to where I wanted to be—where I needed to be.

It was just after eleven, and I wondered if it was too late to call. But this was my one shot to talk to him before Monday, and that was still two whole days away. I'd drive myself mad until then.

I pressed the call button before I lost my nerve.

"Lucy." He answered in a husky growl on the first ring. The sound of my first name rolling off his tongue sent a shockwave of desire through my body.

"Cole," I whispered.

We were both quiet for a few exquisite seconds.

"I miss you," he said quietly, breaking the silence.

My heart raced. "I miss you, too." It was strange how much I did.

"I have a confession."

"What?"

"You know that night I drank too much in New York?" he asked.

"Yeah," I whispered.

"I knew you were sleeping beside me. I acted like I didn't know, like I was too drunk."

"You did?"

"Yeah. And when I forgot to bring clothes in the bathroom with me after my shower? I didn't really forget."

"You wanted to tempt me?"

"Did it work?"

My mouth started watering just remembering what he looked like wearing only a towel. "Oh, it worked."

He chuckled. "I had to take what opportunities I could."

We were both quiet again as we navigated an unfamiliar, intimate conversation for the first time.

"Why are you calling so late?" he asked.

"I needed to hear your voice."

"I'm glad you called."

"Me too."

"I want to kiss you again."

My stomach fluttered in the best way. "I want that, too."

"I need it, Lucy."

"I need it, too, Mr. Benson."

He laughed, and the sound was soothing to my frazzled nerves.

"Any update on your sister or her husband?"

"Not yet. But, as my mother always says, no news is good news."

"It was nice meeting your parents."

"It's funny that I already know your parents."

"My dad definitely approves."

"Oh yeah?"

"He loves you like you're the daughter he never had."

I warmed as I thought about that. I supposed I didn't really need his parents' approval considering our situation, but it still felt nice.

"Well I enjoyed working for him. He's much nicer than my new boss."

That earned me another laugh.

"Is your husband near you?" he asked.

"No. He's sleeping. I'm in our office."

"Where's Madi?"

"She's asleep in our guest room."

"So you're all alone?" he asked, a hint of slyness in his voice.

"Indeed."

"So, Ms. Cleary, tell me about your new boss."

"Well, he's very attractive. He can be a total ass, but recently I saw a different side of him."

"What side is that?"

"The side where he wasn't wearing a shirt. He really needs to reconsider the office dress code."

"Consider it done. I won't wear a shirt, and you should parade around in something short and revealing."

I laughed. "You wish."

"I do. And as long as we're wishing for things, I wish I was there with you."

"What would you do if you were?" The dark and intimate room I was in made me boldly flirtatious.

He paused for a few beats, as if choosing his words carefully. "First I'd slide my hand up under that tank top you sleep in."

I glanced down at my tank top. "How did you—"

"You wore it to bed at the hotel, and every time I looked at you and saw your hard nipples poking through the delicate material, I nearly lost it. Shit, I'm getting hard just thinking about it now."

His words made me ache for him. I slid my hand under the very top he'd mentioned and allowed my own warm hand to gently caress my stomach.

"What would you do with your hand?" I asked quietly.

"I'd feel your skin. Will you feel it for me?"

"I am."

He sucked in a sharp breath. "I want you to feel the soft skin of your flat stomach."

I moaned softly for him.

"Run your hand along your skin up to your gorgeous breasts."

I did as he said.

"Massage your breast and then pinch your nipple."

I moaned again, trying my hardest to remain quiet just in case anyone in my apartment might wake up. His voice in my ear mixed with my own touch intensified the ache between my legs.

"God, your moans are making me so hard." His voice was husky and warm.

"Do something about it." I was trying to whisper, but my voice came out hoarse.

"What should I do?"

"Do something I can't do right now."

"Like what?" he goaded.

"Touch yourself."

"Where?"

I'd never actually had phone sex before. I always thought I'd feel so awkward doing it that I wouldn't enjoy it.

But I supposed when you're doing it with the right person…it just worked.

"Grab your cock in your hand."

"Oh God," he moaned, and I heard some rustling as he presumably took off whatever he was wearing. "Now what?"

"Stroke your hand up and down."

"Slide your hand down into your panties and touch your clit." I did what he said. My panties were soaked.

"I have a confession," I said, feeling bold again in the darkness.

"What?" he asked, his voice strained.

"Sometimes I touch myself and I think of you."

"Oh fuck," he growled. "I'm going to come."

"Stop stroking yourself."

"Get there with me, Lucy. Finger yourself."

I pumped two fingers inside, reveling in his dirty mouth. "It's so wet, Cole. Oh my God. It's never been so wet before."

"Harder."

I started panting as I moved my fingers in and out, in and out, and I heard him resume his stroking over the phone. He groaned, a loud, guttural sound that sent a wave of heat down to my core.

"I'm coming," I whispered. "I'm coming, I'm coming."

"Fuck," he muttered as he came along with me.

We both panted for a few quiet moments of bliss.

"I should go," I finally said, feeling the tiniest twinge of guilt over what I'd just done.

"I want to keep talking."

"I do, too. But this is risky. I shouldn't call you when I'm at home."

"I understand." He sounded disappointed, and I felt the same way.

"Thank you again for everything you did. For flying home with me. For getting me to the hospital. For holding my hand in some of the scariest moments of my life."

"Question," he said.

"What?"

"Can I text you?"

"Yeah. I'll change the passcode to my phone and save your contact as someone else."

"This is wrong," he said. "I don't want you to have to lie."

"I know. I'll make it right, though. I'll talk to him soon."

"Okay. Goodnight, Ms. Cleary."

"Goodnight, Mr. Benson."

I stared down at my phone for a few moments after ending the call. I didn't really accomplish what I wanted to by calling him. I'd wanted to talk, to let him know how I felt, to express the millions of thoughts I was having where he was concerned.

Instead I'd gotten off on one of the best orgasms I'd ever had as I listened to him jerk off over the phone.

"Wake Up Call" by Maroon 5 started playing in my head as I changed *Cole Benson* in my contacts to *Adam Levine*. And then, on second thought, I changed it to a girl's name just to help avoid any suspicion. *April Levine.*

I went to the bathroom, washed my hands, and filled a cup with water. I returned to the bedroom and slid into bed beside my husband, who still snored away, oblivious to the fact that his wife was falling for another man.

Chapter Sixteen

When my phone buzzed a little after six, I picked it up off of my nightstand to see that a text message awaited me from April Levine.

I glanced over at John, who slept soundly beside me.

I entered my new passcode, my heart beating wildly in my chest as I thought about what would happen if John woke up and saw the message.

What would happen, though, really?

I thought about the ramifications of getting caught. It would force the conversation rather than allowing me to waffle and blame other factors. It would force me to be honest when it was easier to live the lie.

It would liberate me from the bonds of an unhappy marriage. It would free me and allow me to be with Cole.

But it would also be throwing away five years of my life. Years that, until recently, I'd been fairly happy. Happy enough, at least.

And, perhaps worst of all, it would cause turmoil for my family—and my family was already going through enough.

I finally clicked on the message.

Last night was fun. You free later tonight?

I chuckled, careful to be silent so as not to wake the man in my bed.

All I wanted was another night on the phone with Cole. It had taken my mind off of the grave situation I found my sister in even if only for a few moments. He'd given me exactly what I needed without even being in the same room as me—things I hadn't been getting from John for a long time.

I'm not free, but for you... I'll make time.

I watched as my message was delivered, and then the three little bubbles signaling that he was typing a response appeared. Those three bubbles made my heart race. They meant he was thinking about me—and thinking about me in the same way I'd been thinking about him for longer than I cared to admit.

I know you're not free, and that's something we're going to need to rectify.

My heart agreed with him, but my brain kept putting Madi first.

I know. Soon. I'll be in touch later.

I'll be waiting patiently. Or not.

I giggled as silently as I could. *Not* was more likely. Cole was one of the least patient people I knew, and he demanded excellence at all times. It was one of the things I hated about him as his employee, but it was also one of the things I respected about him as a businessman.

I crept quietly out of the bed I shared with John, a thick layer of guilt washing over me. I showered and dressed, and then I went out to the kitchen to make pancakes and bacon. John came out of the bedroom, his messy hair and sleepy eyes reminding me of the first time I'd realized I was in love with him.

We'd been together for a few weeks, and one particular morning he'd emerged from my bedroom. I lived with a roommate at the time, and we'd been gossiping rather loudly on the couch. John had been grouchy, and that was the first time I learned he simply wasn't a morning person.

But when our eyes had met across the room, his hair an absolute mess from our romp the night before and drowsiness written all over his face, he smiled at me. My heart twisted and I felt a pang in my chest. It was that moment I first thought he was the person I could spend the rest of my life with.

Another pang hit me in the chest as I watched his sleepy eyes land on me while I stood in the kitchen with a bowl of pancake batter, but this time it meant something else. This time, the pang was because I had to end things with him. The hope for the future I'd felt when I first realized I loved him had been replaced with the feeling that I was living with a stranger.

The guilt I'd started the day with never really left. It was a shadow following me everywhere I went.

It followed me to my parents' house as I dropped off Madi so I could go spend time with my sister.

John was "working" again, whatever that meant. It seemed like he was always working during the big moments lately—and, to be fair, during the small moments, too. I could've used him to lean on as I visited my sister and Kevin, but he'd left just after pancakes to head into the office for a few hours.

I called Cole without even thinking twice as soon as I'd dropped off Madi.

"I thought for sure you'd make me wait until tonight," he answered, and I could tell he was smiling.

I smiled, too. "I'm actually heading to the hospital, but I had a few minutes by myself."

"Why are you by yourself?"

"I dropped Madi off at my parents' house."

"Where's your husband?"

He spat out the "H" word like it was poison.

"He had to go into work."

Cole sighed audibly over the phone. "You shouldn't be alone. I'm dealing with something now, but I can meet you at the hospital in about an hour."

My heart fluttered. "That's not necessary," I said, but I wanted him to come. I wanted to see him.

I wanted him to kiss me.

I wanted him to do the things he'd told me over the phone to do to myself.

"I'm coming anyway."

It was his insistence that I loved. It was the fact that he knew I needed him, and he was going to be there—especially in contrast to the one person who *should* have been there but wasn't.

Just a few days ago, I hated him.

But now that I knew why he'd been such an asshole to me, it made a lot of sense. His defense mechanism to protect his own heart had been to lash out. It had been an immature way of dealing with his feelings, but sometimes men were just immature.

He was a shark in the boardroom. He was smart. He had a ton of money. He was savvy.

So it was forgivable if he was a little emotionally immature. He'd spent a lot of years working hard to show people that he wasn't his father, and seducing his assistant immediately after taking over as CEO was probably poor form.

When I got to the hospital, I asked the nurse about Kevin first. I knew Kaylee would want an update.

"His parents are in with him," the nurse informed me.

"Is he awake?"

She shook her head. "The swelling has gone down a little, but he's still in a medically-induced coma. He's doing a little better, but he isn't out of the woods and the doctor can't assess his long-term prognosis yet."

"Thanks," I said, and I headed toward my sister's room.

Even in sleep, she looked as bad as the day before. I said a prayer for my sister and her husband. I included Madi in that prayer. I just wanted everything to go back to how it had been before I'd left for New York.

That statement wasn't entirely true. I wanted things to go back to normal for my sister and her family.

For me, though? I was ready to forge full steam ahead in my affair with Cole.

Affair.

It was such a dirty word with such negative connotations, and rightly so.

But now that I was actually having one, I saw things in a whole new light.

I settled onto the small couch in the corner of the room, checking my email and playing on my phone while my sister slept. There wasn't much to do but sit around and scroll through my Facebook newsfeed.

When the door opened a short while later, my heart started beating a little faster. It had been less than twenty-four hours since I'd last seen him, but I hoped it was Cole walking through that door.

His eyes were dark and a little stormy, but they softened when they focused on me. I smiled, and his expression completely changed as the corners of his mouth tipped up.

He glanced at my sister, who was still asleep, and then he strode across the room toward me. I stood, and our bodies collided as I clung to him. He held me upright, his arms tight in the strength I didn't have because of the fear that squeezed my heart.

"How's she doing?" he whispered, pulling back but not letting go of me.

"She's been asleep the whole time I've been here." I kept my voice low so as not to wake my sister.

"Can I do anything?"

I shook my head and stepped away from him, guilt pressing on my chest as I thought about my husband. What if he walked in the door and saw me embracing my boss? What if my sister woke and saw us?

"Kevin's parents are here visiting him. The nurse at the desk said he's doing a little better." I sat on the couch, curling my legs under me.

"That's good news." He sat beside me and leaned forward, resting his elbows on his knees and clasping his hands in front of him.

I nodded.

"Are you hungry?" he asked.

I shook my head.

"Can I get you anything?"

I shook my head again. "Thanks for asking."

"I feel helpless."

I reached over and placed my hand on his arm. My fingertips tingled where they met his skin. "Just having you here is all I need."

He turned toward me, his eyes darkening again—but this time with lust.

We were interrupted when the door opened again, and I pulled my hand quickly away from his arm before whoever was at the door entered the room. I did my best to mask the guilt from my face.

A nurse smiled warmly at us. "We just need to run some tests. Can you give us a few minutes?"

I nodded, and the two of us stood.

"We're going to give her another dose of painkillers, so I expect she'll be sleeping for the next three to four hours," the nurse said. "If you've got things to do, now would probably be a good time."

"Thank you. Can you let her know her sister was here and loves her very much?"

The nurse smiled. "Of course."

Cole took my hand in his and tugged me toward the door. Once we were in the waiting room, he said, "So your sister will be sleeping for a few hours, your husband is working, and Madi is with your parents. Interesting."

"Indeed."

"Do you want to hang out here? Or can I steal you away for an hour or two?"

I shrugged. "I suppose I could be swayed to be stolen."

He grinned wickedly at me, and I giggled. He tugged my hand, and we speed-walked toward the parking deck.

Cole led me to his car, a sleek and sexy black Audi S8 Sedan. I'd never actually seen it before because it seemed like he took a car with a driver everywhere he went.

"Nice car," I said.

"I know," he answered with arrogance. He pushed me up against the passenger door, pinning me with his hips. "I wonder what you'd look like spread out on the hood."

A shudder raced through my body at his words. I couldn't form a response as my eyes widened and my tongue tied.

He leaned in and kissed my neck. He dragged his lips up to my ear said in a low voice, "I wonder what it would be like to fuck you in the backseat."

I moaned involuntarily. I had to admit, I wondered that very same thing.

"We can find out later," he said, moving away from me with a grin. He opened the passenger door.

"You're an asshole." I slid into the leather seat.

He shrugged. "I've been called worse." He shut the door and walked around to his side of the car.

I inhaled deeply. His car had that same clean and fresh scent that he always sported, and it drove me wild.

He got in and fired up the engine. The car purred provocatively.

"Where are you taking me?" I asked once we were on the highway.

"Santa Monica."

"For the Ferris Wheel?"

He chuckled but didn't respond.

"The roller coaster?"

He glanced in my direction before his eyes returned to the road. I couldn't help but watch his command of the car with a whole lot of desire.

It probably had less to do with his driving and more to do with the man himself. Pretty much everything he did turned me on.

This was a totally different Cole Benson than I was used to dealing with on a daily basis, and I couldn't help but wonder what life at the office was going to be like now that we'd broken down our barriers. His admission as to why he'd been treating me like crap since the day he started was fresh in my mind. Now that I knew his true feelings, I wondered if he'd still feel the need to be a dick at work to put on a show in front of others or if he'd be a little nicer to me.

I thought about his words when he'd admitted he wanted me on my desk the night of the MTC dinner. So much had happened in the two days since he'd confessed that to me.

He pulled off the highway and wound through some streets until we pulled up in front of a house. He got out of the car, and I followed suit. He tugged my hand and led me toward the garage. I watched as he flipped open a keypad and entered a code, and the garage door opened.

"What are we doing here?" I asked as he twisted the knob to let me into the house.

He didn't answer as he stepped through a laundry room and into the living area. At first glance, I decided the house was both enormous and breathtaking. The open floor plan along with the massive windows made the house appear bright and pristine. It was a dream home—one of those kinds of places I could search on the realtor websites but would never see enough money in my lifetime to be able to afford.

He led me through an expansive kitchen and modern great room. We stopped in front of a sliding glass wall overlooking the beach. He gazed out the glass toward the water, and then he turned around and looked at me.

"I bought it. I closed the day before we left for New York. I'll be in the hotel a while longer because I have some remodeling to do."

I held in my gasp, trying to play it cool. I wanted to ask how he could afford it. A gigantic home right on the beach with all the amenities and upgrades this one had? It had to be in the multi-million dollar range, but I supposed he probably made way more money as the company's CEO than I did as his assistant.

"It's gorgeous, Cole."

"My parents are thrilled." He paused, looking out the window again toward the beach. "I took the CEO position so my father could retire. I never wanted to move back to California, so I just stayed in a hotel at first. But now that I've been here a while, I want to stay."

"Your job wasn't always going to be a permanent thing?"

He shrugged, his eyes moving back to me. "According to my father it was, but I wanted a trial period before I decided for sure."

"And now you've decided for sure?"

He nodded.

"What made you decide?"

He looked back out over the beach as if he was contemplating what to say. I gave him the space he needed to think. Finally, his gaze fell back to me. He shrugged. "Want the rest of the tour?" he asked, changing the subject.

"I'd love it."

He led me around the house, showing me each of the four bedrooms and the office. He paused in the master suite as we both gazed at the space where his bed would eventually be. I broke the tension by walking over to the window. "Nice view from up here," I said.

Cole moved in behind me and wrapped his arms around my waist. "I can't wait to fuck you out on that beach."

"What will it be like?" I asked timidly.

A throaty chuckle escaped his throat. "Remember when you came over the phone?" he asked, his voice husky.

I nodded.

"Like that, only about a hundred times more intense."

"A hundred times?"

"A thousand times."

I imagined it would be, and I wondered not for the first time how many women he'd been with. How experienced he was. I wanted to ask, if nothing else to be prepared when the time came, but I wasn't sure how to broach the subject.

"Are you on the pill?" he asked.

I nodded. I opened my mouth to tell him that John and I didn't want kids for at least another year, but I stopped myself. I didn't want to ruin the moment by mentioning John, but I was also convinced that John and I wouldn't have kids in a year. Not with each other, anyway.

"Are you—" I cut off my sentence, not sure how to ask what I really wanted to ask. "There was the blonde the night of the MTC dinner and a different blonde at the benefit…" I trailed off.

"I'm always careful, if that's what you're asking."

"What if I don't want you to be *careful* with me?" I asked, imagining the feel of his skin moving against mine, nothing between us but sweat.

"I'll be careful if you want me to be, but my physical last month came back completely normal. We need to get back to the hospital, but I want you to know that I think about what it'll be like with you all the time."

I moaned. He felt so good behind me, holding me up literally and, in many ways, figuratively. His lips moved away from my ear to my neck, and I arched back into him. He held me up with his arms around me, and I trembled at his words and his proximity.

I turned around, and his arms tightened around my waist as I wrapped my arms around his neck. He leaned down to kiss me, and I allowed myself to get lost in the moment as his tongue danced slowly against mine and our bodies melded together.

I never wanted to leave. Leaving meant going back to the hospital and facing reality. It meant going home to John instead of staying with the man I really wanted.

But the real world was knocking, and I needed to answer the door.

Chapter Seventeen

As the hospital came into view, guilt started stabbing at my abdomen. What if John was there waiting for me? What if Kaylee woke up? What if my parents were there with Madi, waiting for me to take her for a while? What if Kevin's condition worsened?

A million different worries plagued me, but the old adage that virtually everything we worry about will never actually happen rang true for me this time.

Everything was just as we'd left it only a couple of hours earlier, but Cole's hold over me squeezed just a little tighter.

Once we were back in Kaylee's room, Cole glanced at his phone and then stood. "I hate to leave, but I have a dinner I need to get to."

I stood and grabbed his hand. "Thank you for spending the afternoon with me."

"You shouldn't be alone, Lucy."

"I'm not. My sister's right here." I nodded in her direction.

He narrowed his eyes at me. "You know what I mean."

I nodded, and I appreciated his concern. "I'll be okay."

"Call me tonight."

"I'll try. I had to sneak out of bed last night."

He sighed. "Get caught so we can move forward."

I wanted to ask him what we were moving forward to, but I refrained. It wasn't the time for that conversation.

"Soon. I promise."

He nodded, leaned forward and planted a soft kiss on my lips, and then left.

"How long have I been out?"

I jumped at my sister's voice. "Jesus, Kay. You scared the shit out of me."

"Sorry," she said, wincing. "Any update on Kevin?"

I shook my head. "No news."

"Is good news," she finished my mom's adage.

"Do you need more painkillers?" I asked.

"No. I hate sleeping the day away."

"You need rest."

"You need to explain why that gorgeous boss of yours just kissed you."

I felt my face heat. "You saw that?"

She gave me a pointed look.

"Don't worry about me. Let's get you healthy so you can get out of here."

A nurse walked in to check on my sister, so I was saved from more grilling. I said my goodbyes even though I hadn't spent much time with Kaylee. She reminded me to give her daughter a million kisses, and then I headed out to pick up Madi. I'd promised her a big Saturday night sleepover that included hot chocolate, popcorn, nail polish, and, of course, *Frozen*.

I thought for sure that John would be home by the time we got there, but I was wrong.

"Where's Uncle John?" Madi asked when we walked into the quiet apartment.

"Working, sweetie."

"On a Saturday?"

I nodded and gave her my best apologetic smile.

"Can we call him?"

I would've preferred not to, actually. "Sure." I pulled up his contact information and handed the phone to Madi.

"Hi Uncle John. When are you coming home?"

I watched as she waited patiently for a response, her blonde curls bouncing as she nodded her head as if the fate of the universe depended on this phone call. I chuckled at her dramatics.

"Okay. We're going to start the movie," she said into the phone. "You're gonna miss it."

She waited for his reply. "Okay. Bye!" She handed me the phone. "He wants to talk to you."

"Hey," I said.

"Low blow making Madi call. I thought something was wrong."

"Nothing new. Madi wanted to call. When will you be home?"

"Ask your niece."

I fumed. He didn't have to be such an asshole, and I'd have told him that if she wasn't standing right beside me.

"Isn't that nice. Can't wait until then." I used the fakest, most sugary-sweet sarcastic voice that I could muster, and I hung up the phone.

"You didn't say 'I love you.' Mommy always says that to Daddy when they hang up."

"He knows I do," I lied. "What do you want first? Popcorn or pizza?"

"Pizza!"

I called and placed the order, and then we sat down to watch the movie. I didn't bother asking Madi when John said he'd be coming home.

Just after the pizza arrived and we were introduced to the snowman for the first time in the movie, my phone dinged with a text notification.

I checked the screen, and it said I had a new message from April Levine.

My heart pitter-pattered. He was thinking about me, and that was enough to bring a big, wide smile to my face.

"Is it Uncle John?" Madi asked.

"Uh...no. It's just a friend."

"What's it say?"

"I don't know. I didn't read it yet." I was sure I was blushing. How had a child made me blush?

She turned back to the movie, obviously losing interest in my text, but my curiosity was surely piqued.

I excused myself to the restroom to read the text.

I can't stop thinking about kissing you this afternoon in my new house. I want to press your naked body up against the glass. When can I see you? Monday is too far away.

I grinned like a maniac at his text. I agreed. Monday felt like ages away. I didn't want to wait until then, either, but I wasn't sure when I'd be able to see him. Not with Madi here, and not with John coming home who the hell knew when. I thought quickly.

Up against the glass? I'm in. I need to see you, too. Can you meet tomorrow around ten? I'm dropping Madi off at my parents' in the morning.

I saw the bubbles appear indicating that he was replying to my text, so I waited. *Where?*

There's a Starbucks around the corner from my parents' house. I'll text the address later.

I slipped my phone into my pocket and headed back out to watch the rest of the movie. We started another movie, and five minutes in, Madi fell fast asleep on the couch. I pulled a blanket over her and shut off the movie.

I pulled my phone out of my pocket and texted Cole. *Madi just fell asleep and John isn't home.*

Can you call me?

I headed into the office to make the call. I quietly shut the door behind me and sat in the big, comfy chair.

"Hey," he answered after a few rings.

"Hey."

"How are you?"

"Good. You?"

"Fine. I'm still at this awful dinner, but I said I had to take this call."

"I feel so important."

He chuckled. "Where are you?"

"In the office, in the same chair I was in last night." I toyed with the edge of the desk calendar in front of me.

"The same chair? I wonder if we could produce the same result as the last time you sat in that chair."

My cheeks heated. "I bet we could."

His voice lowered to a sexy rasp. "Are you still wearing jeans and that sexy as fuck tight shirt?"

I giggled. "Yes."

"Why don't you slip your hand under your shirt?"

I did as he requested, my fingertips grazing the skin of my belly and moving up toward my breasts. "Now what?"

"Hold on a second. I'm standing in the lobby of the Hilton." I heard some shuffling, and then he muffled his voice. "Leave your breasts in your bra, but slip your fingers into one of the cups and play with your nipple."

I caressed my hardening nipple, the idea of his public exhibitionism sending an extra thrill to my core. "It's getting hard."

"So am I. Now pinch it."

I did, and I let out a soft moan. I closed my eyes, soaking in the pleasure of my own touch while picturing Cole in a towel from that day in our hotel room.

My peaceful moment of pleasure was shot to hell when the door to the office opened. I whipped my hand out of my shirt, my eyes wide as I was both exposed and caught. My first thought was Madi, but it wasn't Madi who walked through the door.

It was my husband.

"What are you doing in here?" he asked.

"Um, I have to go," I said into the phone. I hung up and looked up at John. I thought quickly, trying my hardest not to appear guilty…which was incredibly hard since I *was* guilty. "I didn't want to wake Madi. She fell asleep while we were watching *Frozen*."

He gave me a strange look like he didn't really believe me. He shouldn't have believed me. Part of me wanted him to probe, but I knew he wouldn't.

He was just making it easy for me.

It was wrong for me to take advantage of him, but I'd justified my reasons enough times in my head. As soon as Kaylee and Kevin were well again, I'd talk to John. But for now, I planned to be a pillar of strength and a shining example of stability for sweet Madi.

"Who was on the phone?"

"My friend April."

"April?"

"I met her in New York." The lie rolled easily off my tongue.

"Any news on Kaylee or Kevin?"

I shook my head. "Everything's the same. Hopefully tomorrow we'll get some good news."

He nodded. "I'm going to change."

"Okay."

He walked out of the room, and I closed my eyes. God, that had been a close call.

I texted "April" to let him know why I'd hung up so abruptly. *John came home. Sorry.*

I didn't get a text back. Either he'd gone back into his dinner or he didn't want to text me again in case John was around. I just hoped we'd be able to meet up in the morning.

Chapter Eighteen

I woke up the next morning when John was just getting out of bed. He peeked over at me before standing up. "Good morning," he said.

"Good morning." I stretched with grogginess. "You been up long?"

He shook his head. "Just woke up."

He paused and looked at me thoughtfully as if he wanted to say something more, but then he stood and started toward the bathroom. I couldn't help but wonder what he wanted to say. Did he want to finally clear the air? Was he going to ask me to be honest with him?

Was I ready to be honest with him?

I got up and checked on Madi, who was just waking up. I helped her out of bed and we got to work on breakfast.

"Smells good in here," John said after he emerged from his shower. He picked up a giggling Madi to swing her around.

"We made bacon," she announced.

"My favorite," John said.

From the outside, surely we looked like a happy little family. But we were two adults in a broken marriage and a child whose parents were suffering.

This was all wrong, and there wasn't much I could immediately do to fix any of it.

After we ate, John announced that he had to go into the office.

"On a Sunday?" I asked.

His gaze lingered on me for a moment, making me feel a bit uncomfortable. "Yep. Sorry."

I shrugged, and he mussed Madi's hair before heading out the door.

"You ready to head to Grammy's house?"

"I want to go home."

I pulled her into my arms. "I know you do, sweetheart. And you will get to go home very soon."

She sighed and rested her head on my shoulder, and my heart broke a little more for my sweet niece.

Immediately after dropping her off, I called Cole. "Are we still on for Starbucks?"

"I'm already at a table waiting for you."

I glanced at the clock. It was only a few minutes after ten. "Sorry I'm running late. I had a hard time leaving Madi."

I knew how he lived for punctuality, but this wasn't business. This was the two of us meeting under personal circumstances, and surely he couldn't fault me for being late considering what was going on with my sister.

Instead of reassuring me that it was no big deal, he said, "What would you like to drink?"

I thought for a moment. "Iced caramel macchiato."

"I'll be waiting here with it." His words were short.

Something was up with him, and I had a feeling it wasn't just because I was running late.

"What's wrong, Cole?"

"I'm next in line. We'll talk when you get here."

He cut off the call, and my heart started pounding. I was terrified that this was the end for us. It couldn't be the end—not when we'd hardly even gotten started.

I sped through town and my tires practically squealed as I turned into a parking space in front of Starbucks. I raced out of my car and through the doors, my heart pounding faster and faster the closer I got to him.

I spotted him the moment I walked through the door. He had an imposing presence, an aura of power and strength and manliness surrounding him.

He wore a suit, and my heart beat wildly in my chest as I stared at the man in a suit in the middle of a busy Starbucks drinking coffee as he tapped away on his phone.

He glanced up when he felt my stare, and our eyes locked across the coffeehouse. He set his phone down.

He held up my drink and smiled, and I heaved out a breath as I made my way to his table.

He handed me the drink—a venti, even though I hadn't specified a size—and I thanked him.

"You look gorgeous this morning," he said.

"I'm sorry I'm late. You sounded angry over the phone."

I opened my straw wrapper and stuck the straw in my drink as his gaze pinned me to my seat.

"I hate talking on the phone in a public place."

"I get it."

"It's good to see you."

"It's good to see you, too."

He leaned across the table to kiss me, but then he thought better of it and sat back down before he actually did it. I took a nervous sip of my drink.

Had it really only been the day before that I'd last seen him? It felt like much longer.

"How was your dinner last night?" I asked cautiously.

"Awful."

"Why?"

He gazed out the window while he spoke. "I was with my parents and some of my dad's old business associates. The meeting consisted of old men talking about the glory days and how today's generation has no work ethic. They spoke like I wasn't part of the exact generation they were criticizing, and frankly, I was offended."

"That sounds awful."

His eyes flicked over to mine. "The one highlight of my evening was when you called."

"And then I basically hung up on you."

He glanced down at the table. "And reminded me that you're not really mine."

I reached across the table and took his hand in mine. "I am, Cole. In the way that really matters, I'm yours."

He shook his head and pulled his hand away. "Dammit, Lucy," he muttered. "No, you're not. In the way that matters, you're not." He lowered his voice and leaned in toward me. "You're wearing a wedding ring that another man gave you. You have someone else to answer to. And until you can be honest with him, I don't think we should keep doing this."

I knew in my heart that he was absolutely right. But that was the same heart that started racing in fear the moment he mentioned we shouldn't keep seeing each other.

I tried to think of something—anything---that would prove to him that it was over with John, that I was just waiting for the right moment to tell him. I didn't know what to do to convince him that I was all in on him.

"I don't love him anymore."

His eyes locked on mine. "How do you feel about me?"

My eyebrows shot up in surprise at his question. Was he asking me if I was in love with him?

Was I in love with him?

I knew I was falling for him. I knew I had a blistering attraction to him. But I hadn't stopped to really figure out exactly what I was feeling.

I was silent as I tried to figure out how to answer, but he read me all wrong.

"That's what I thought," he said, taking a long sip of his coffee and returning his gaze to the window.

I was done trying to categorize how I felt. I let the words spill from my mouth unfiltered. "You can't just judge me for not knowing how to answer that question. You're putting me on the spot. I don't know how I feel about you, Cole. You mix me up. You turn everything upside down. You ignite me and infuriate me. You push me and you create this heated passion within me. I've felt more for you in the past month than I think I ever felt for John." His eyes slid back over to me during my impassioned diatribe. "Sometimes I hate you, but sometimes I think I might love you."

He smiled sadly. "Sometimes I hate you, too. And sometimes I think I might love you, too."

"Then why do you want to end this?"

"I don't. God, I don't. I didn't say that."

"You said we shouldn't be doing this."

"We shouldn't." He lowered his voice. "We shouldn't be having phone sex. We shouldn't be meeting for coffee in secret on a Sunday morning. We shouldn't feel so strongly that we can't seem to stay away from each other. It's wrong." He paused, and my heart raced. "But just because we shouldn't be doing it doesn't mean either one of us can stop."

A wave of relief surged through my chest. "You scared me."

"I do lots of things I shouldn't do."

"I'd like to be one of those things."

He grinned wickedly at me. "You will be."

A tremor of lust darted through me.

As much as I wanted it to happen right then and there, Cole had an afternoon meeting scheduled. We parted ways as he gave me understated kiss on the cheek in front of Starbucks, and I headed to the hospital to visit my sister.

I couldn't help but replay my conversation with Cole. We both knew that what we were doing was wrong, yet we couldn't seem to stop ourselves. And when John kept putting work in front of my family and me, I had a hard time feeling any guilt at all over it.

Chapter Nineteen

Usually I hated Monday mornings with a fiery passion, but I was so excited that I hardly slept at all on Sunday night.

Exhaustion would plague me once my morning caffeine wore off, but excitement was the primary emotion I felt. I couldn't wait to see what awaited me at the office. I'd never been in a secret affair with my boss. This was new territory, and everything inside me was alight with anticipation.

I dressed in a fairly low-cut dress with a green and white chevron pattern. I wore tall white heels that accentuated my calves and made me feel sexy. I spent a little extra time perfecting my hair and make-up. I was dressed and ready to go before John even rolled out of bed. I brewed the coffee and made myself some oatmeal, and then I filled my travel mug and scooted out the door before I had to interact with my dear husband.

I got to the office twenty minutes earlier than normal, and instead of flying through the door right at the last minute to avoid the wrath of Mr. Benson, I walked casually to my desk. He was in his office already. I could hear him rustling around in there, but I wasn't sure of the protocol. I sat at my desk and powered up my computer, and once I logged in, I decided to pop into his office.

I knocked on the doorframe. "Good morning," I said with genuine cheerfulness.

Cole didn't look up in my direction. His eyes were glued to some paperwork on his desk. "I'll need an update on the Genesis Group before nine-thirty. I've got a conference call at ten. Get me the marketing files for GeoTech. We need to fix the underperforming ads. Did Aaron send you the details?"

"I haven't checked my email yet," I said, my voice filled with disappointment.

Cole sighed. "Check it and get back to me ASAP. I also need you to focus on the MTC account. I have a meeting with Lincoln next week and you'll need to be there. He wants some preliminary ideas."

"Where do I start?"

He finally looked up at me. His eyes drifted down to my cleavage and paused for a moment, and I watched as lust splashed momentarily across his face. He shook his head just slightly, and then he looked back down at his paperwork.

"You'll figure it out."

I rolled my eyes since he wasn't looking at me anyway and headed back out to my desk in total defeat.

Why did I even like him?

Sure, he was hot. But he was a complete jerk. I hated him more than I liked him. He treated me like shit, and I deserved better. I was putting everything on the line, and for what?

I couldn't help but wonder: Why did I have to be so attracted to such an asshole?

I pulled up my email and found the details he had requested. I gathered the data he'd need for his conference call. I emailed everything to him, and then I dialed into his office.

"Yes?"

"The items you requested are in your email, Cole."

He hung up on me.

Hung up.

With no reply.

No "thanks." No "that was sure helpful." No "you look sexy in that green and white dress."

Nothing.

Instead, he appeared in front of my desk. His eyes flashed with anger.

Anger?

What the hell did he have to be angry about? I'd just delivered everything he'd asked for. I'd been nothing but pleasant, and he was back to ass-Cole the asshole.

"It's Mr. Benson."

"Excuse me?" I said.

"You are to refer to me as Mr. Benson." His voice was thick with annoyance as he enunciated each word as if I was stupid.

"Yes, sir."

He spun around into his office, and I sat at my desk trying everything in my power not to cry.

It didn't work.

I ran to the restroom to compose myself. This was ridiculous. What the fuck had changed in the course of a few hours that made Cole think he could go backward? What made him think he could treat me like shit after everything that had happened between us the past few days?

I glanced around at the ladies' room. I was alone. It was a fancy restroom for an office. One side had a set of three stalls and sinks, and the other side featured a little sitting area with a couch, a couple of end tables, and some comfy chairs.

I gazed at myself in the mirror as I thought about Cole. I really thought we'd turned a corner both professionally and personally. I thought things would change now that he'd admitted his feelings for me. I thought the whole reason he'd been treating me like crap was because he was hiding his true feelings for me. He'd been overcompensating.

Instead, we were back to square one.

I was just about to collapse on the couch when the door to the ladies' room opened. I wiped at my eyes and sniffled as I expected a *lady* to walk in.

Instead, Cole Benson walked through the door. He gazed at me for a moment, and then he turned the deadbolt to lock us in.

"Stop crying," he commanded.

"I may be your assistant, but you can't order me around."

"That's actually exactly what I can do to my assistant."

"You shouldn't be in here."

"But I am."

"Some people would call that harassment."

"Would you? Am I harassing you?"

I didn't respond. We both knew that I'd crawl across hot coals for him. We both knew that I'd eat the little crumbs he dropped just to be near him.

He strode toward me. "We both know you want me."

"We both know you want me, too, Mr. Benson." I said his name with as much loathing as I could muster. I didn't know where my sass was coming from, but I needed to stand up for myself. I needed to force myself to be strong even though I was so uncharacteristically weak when it came to him.

He pushed me up against the wall and shoved his hips into me. He grabbed a fistful of my hair and tugged my head back before he lowered his head and his lips met my neck. "I do want you," he hissed, his breath warm on my skin. "I can't keep denying myself what I want. What I need." His lips dragged over the skin of my neck to my throat, and I closed my eyes. "I keep thinking that if I treat you like shit, these feelings will just go away. But they won't."

He shoved his hips toward me again, his steel erection pressing into me.

"What are you going to do about it?" I goaded him.

He growled. "I'm going to do what I've wanted to do since the first second I walked into this office and saw you sitting at your desk in your pretty little dress."

He lifted me up by my ass, and I wrapped my legs around his waist. He carried me over to the couch and threw me down. He straddled me, his eyes hot on mine. "No more interruptions."

I shook my head, unable to speak. Fear knotted my stomach, but lust drowned it out as Cole's mouth moved back over mine.

His tongue thrust against mine with careless abandon, his hips bucking wildly against me. His hands were everywhere as they kneaded and squeezed every erogenous zone on my body seemingly at the same time. My moans and his groans were muffled only by our hungry and fiery kiss.

His lips broke from mine as he sat up and pulled down the top of my dress. He yanked the cups of my bra down. His lips found my breast, and I couldn't help the guttural groan that rumbled up from my chest when he bit down on my tight nipple.

As he worked my breast with his mouth, his fingers trailed down my torso. He slid the hem of my dress up, and all I could do was tighten my arms around him as I felt the girlish tickles of being touched in a place that had gone untouched by a man for far too long. His fingers were rough, and he tugged my panties aside before sliding one long finger inside of me.

A wrenching cry escaped me as he drove his finger in and out, his mouth still attached to my breast. My fingers scratched his back. I wanted his shirt off. I wanted to feel his skin against mine.

I craved every sensation at the same time.

I was getting close. It wasn't going to take much.

Every one of my senses lit on fire; the feel of his finger moving in and out of me, the sound of our moans, the smell of his clean and fresh body wash, the sight of him moving over me, the taste of his breath on mine.

Just as I was about to fly over the edge, everything came to a screeching halt.

"What the hell?" I muttered.

His mouth came back over mine, distracting me as one of his hands fumbled with his pants. His mouth didn't leave mine as he reached down to slide my panties back over to the side. And then without warning he plunged into me.

He stretched my body with his as he filled me completely. My mind went blank with the velvety sensation of skin on skin. We fit together like pieces of a puzzle as he moved in and out of me, slowly at first but quickly gaining speed as he drove into my slickness. I quaked with pleasure as he thrust over and over, propelling into me with all the desire and hunger we'd been hiding and denying.

It all happened much too quickly as his body powered into mine with urgency. The lust and desire between us had been pent up for far too long, pushing us both toward our climaxes nearly instantaneously. It was too good, too sweet feeling him move against me, inside me.

He growled a deep and carnal moan, thrusting somehow even harder a few more times before coming into me. His warmth filled me and pushed me into my own quivering bliss as my body shattered under his.

He collapsed on top of me for just a moment, both of us panting to catch our breath.

A sheen of sweat broke out across my forehead, and as I looked down at us and realized we were both still wearing our clothes and we were in a ladies' room, I couldn't help a giggle.

He pulled up off of me and kissed me, and then he grinned down at me. "It's no hotel room in New York City with a view of Times Square, but it's got a lock and it's private."

His comment made me wonder for the first time if *he* had been the one behind the room mix-up in New York. I let it go, too lost in bliss to really comprehend it.

He got up and helped me into a sitting position, and then he tucked himself back into his pants and fastened them. "You deserve better, and you'll get it. I just couldn't stop myself."

"I'm glad you didn't. That was by far the best sex of my life."

His grin widened. "By far?"

I giggled, and then I reached down to pull my bra back up over my breasts and straighten out my dress. "Far and away."

He held out a hand to help me up. "I'm sorry I was a dick earlier. We're at the office, and I don't know how I'm supposed to treat you."

"Like a human being?"

"I know. I just…we can't get caught. For both of our sakes."

"Then why did you follow me into the ladies' room?"

"I told you. I couldn't stop myself."

"I guess until we figure this out, just keep treating me the way you do. That way no one will be suspicious. But following me into the restroom isn't a good way to keep this under wraps."

"You're right. We shouldn't do this again. Not in here. But just know that any time I'm acting like an ass, it's my way of telling you how much I care about you." He chuckled.

"Right. I'll remember that. And I'll try not to call you bad names in my head."

He narrowed his eyes at me. I laughed and then headed to the mirror to try to tame my sexed-up hair while he peeked out the door to make sure the coast was clear before going back to his office.

Back at my desk a short while later, I opened the files for the MTC account and set to work. I immediately ran into about fifteen different questions. This was new territory for me. While I'd done many different tasks for the company, I'd never taken on an account by myself.

I made a list of my questions as I reviewed the files so I could ask everything at once, and then I dialed into Cole's office.

"Yes?" he answered. His tone was much more pleasant than earlier, but I still thought he could've said a simple "Hello."

"Do you have time to meet about MTC?"

He paused and shuffled some papers. "I can fit you in at lunch."

I giggled.

"Stop," he demanded. He lowered and softened his voice. "Your laugh does things to me."

"My apologies, sir."

I hung up and couldn't help my huge grin. I was lucky that I worked in a semi-private area, because if I worked around other people, they would've thought I was nuts with the way I was smiling. I forced my smile off of my face just in case someone should happen to walk by.

When lunchtime rolled around, I knocked on Cole's door.

"Yes?"

I pushed the door open. "Are you ready for me, sir?"

"Shut the door."

I did as he requested, and he strode across his expansive office toward me. He pushed me against the door roughly and his mouth crashed down to mine. I stood in surprise for a brief moment before my lips molded to his.

"Sorry," he said, pulling back. "When you act all obedient, it really turns me on."

I was in a bit of a daze after the way he kissed me. "Well, then. Anything else I can do for you, sir?"

He grinned as he casually leaned his arm above me against the door and gazed down at me. "You better stop. We don't have time for what I want to do to you, and you have work to do."

I ducked under his arm. "You're right. I have about a million questions and if you need this information by next week, we need to get started." I sat in the chair where I always sat when I was in his office, but this time, everything was different.

This time, I knew how he felt about me.

This time, I'd cheated on my husband.

Officially.

Sex with Cole in the ladies' room hadn't been my classiest moment, but it had certainly been one of my most pleasurable.

There were no boundaries between us any longer. I couldn't be sure where and when it would happen again; all I knew was that it was going to happen again.

And I hoped it would be soon.

Like soon as in maybe after he answered the questions I had about the MTC account.

But that, unfortunately, wasn't the case.

Instead, we went over everything I needed to know, and then a call came in that he had to take. He dismissed me back to my desk (in a somewhat more polite manner than usual), and I got back to work.

He came out of his office a little before three, announcing that he had a meeting. I was disappointed that he was heading out, but I probably had a better chance of getting work done without him in the next room distracting me.

But instead of getting work done, I found myself distracted by thoughts of what we'd done. I hadn't given myself the chance to really process the fact that I'd slept with another man.

A brief fear made my stomach clench. I didn't know much about him, and it was irresponsible of both of us to get so caught up in the moment that we didn't stop for a second to consider the potential consequences.

I'd cheated on my husband.

I suddenly felt like a different person. I wondered if I looked different. Could people tell what I'd done just by looking at me? Would John be able to sense my betrayal?

Cole was still in his meeting when it was time for me to head home, and I'd promised my mom I'd swing by the hospital and pick up Madi for dinner that night. When the two of us arrived home, I was surprised to find John already there.

John smiled at Madi and me when we walked through the door. I couldn't imagine the shock on my face when our eyes met.

Could he tell?

He walked over to us. He pressed a gentle kiss to the top of Madi's head and then, to my surprise, on my lips.

Could he tell from my rigid posture and cold demeanor that I'd slept with another man?

"I was thinking maybe it would be nice for us to spend the evening together. You, me, and Madi."

I had zero interest in hanging out with my husband. But Kaylee had taught me that the first rule of parenthood was to put aside your own desires for the sake of the kid. Madi needed this. She needed us, her aunt and uncle, to show her a stable family while her own was falling apart.

And so, with a heavy heart, I nodded. "That sounds nice."

John surprised me by grilling cheeseburgers, and once again we were the picture of a perfect little family.

But we weren't.

We weren't mommy and daddy doting over our little girl. We weren't the husband and wife in the perfect marriage.

I'd had sex with another man.

Even without Cole in the picture, I wasn't sure where John and I stood anymore. I tried to think back to the last time John had told me he loved me.

I tried to think back to the last time I'd told John I loved him.

Neither memory came to mind.

It was our reality, and we needed some good news at the hospital so I could sit him down and have the talk I'd been avoiding.

We ate dinner, and shortly afterward, my phone rang. I'd just finished polishing Madi's nails while John read her a story. *April Levine* flashed across my screen. I glanced at Madi, who was blowing on her nails, and John, who was engrossed in some tale about going to the dentist.

"I need to take this," I said, and I got up and rushed toward the office.

"Hey," I answered quietly once the door was shut behind me.

"Hey." His voice was quiet, too.

"What's up?"

"Did I catch you at a bad time?"

I didn't know how to answer that. Was there ever a good time for him to call me when I was in the home I shared with another man? "It's okay. Madi's engrossed in a book about the dentist, so I've got a few minutes."

"I'm sorry."

"For what?"

"For calling you at home. This can wait until tomorrow."

"Stop. It's fine. What's going on?"

"I might need to meet with a client in New York next week. I was just thinking maybe you could come, too, and we could have that night in the hotel overlooking Times Square that we missed out on the first time."

My mind and heart raced. Could I do it?

Physically, yes. Every last part of me ached to be with him.

But *should* I do it?

Aside from the obvious reason why I shouldn't, I had to consider my family. They needed me.

"Next week?" I asked, buying time to try to figure this out.

"I just need to go for one night, but we could turn it into two or three nights. Just you and me, Lucy."

God, I wanted it.

I didn't want to go into work and find his office empty. I wanted to be by his side instead, in his arms, in his bed.

But I couldn't leave, not when Kaylee was in the hospital and Kevin's future was so uncertain. I finally told Cole that with a heavy sigh.

"I understand," he said, disappointment evident in his voice. "Maybe next time."

"If Kay gets out before you leave, maybe we could make it work."

"It's okay. Get back to your niece."

"Yes, sir."

He chuckled softly. "Today was…" he trailed off.

"The best," I finished, thinking back to his body moving hotly over mine. Tingles raced up my spine just at the thought of what we'd done.

"The best," he echoed. "Goodnight, Ms. Cleary."

"Goodnight, Mr. Benson."

I stared at the phone for a few seconds, and then I gazed toward the door as I thought about what waited for me just on the other side.

Chapter Twenty

"What's on the agenda for today?" I asked Cole the next morning. He looked painfully beautiful in another suit as he sat behind his walnut desk. His gaze fell on me, and my heart beat a little faster.

"I need you to pull together a focus group for MTC. I emailed you the details. Send me a draft of your ideas by the end of the day. I also need you to review my schedule for the week of the fifteenth. Vince will be in town all week, and I need to fit him in for a dinner. Pick somewhere semi-classy. I don't care where or when. Reservations for six, including yourself."

When I got back to my desk, I got started on the list Cole had rattled off in his office. His tasks kept me busy through the end of the day, and I couldn't help but feel the pull of desire as the clock ticked toward five and people started leaving the office for the day.

I gathered up my stuff to leave and peeked into Cole's office, hoping for a repeat performance of the day before, but he was on the phone.

He looked up at me with raised brows, and then his face smoothed into a smile meant for me. I couldn't help but lean against the doorframe to steady myself. He was so damn handsome that sometimes my knees gave out just looking at him.

And he wanted *me*.

He'd ravished *me* the day before.

He wanted *me* to leave my husband to be with him.

He continued with his call, pointing to the phone and rolling his eyes. I pointed to my watch to indicate the time, and he nodded. He waved as if to tell me to have a good day, and I waved back with a smile.

Disappointment filled me as I rode the elevator down to the first floor. I'd been hoping for a goodbye kiss, at the very least, if not a goodbye shag.

Instead I'd gotten a smile and a wave. On any other day, it would've been enough. I would've been delighted with that.

But today…today I needed more. I craved more. I craved Cole.

I arrived home to an empty apartment as usual. I changed into leggings and my comfiest t-shirt, pulled my hair up into a messy ponytail, and set about mopping the kitchen to work off some of the energy that I'd built up over the course of the day.

I worked up a good sweat, and I'd just finished cleaning the dirty water out of the sink and was wiping my face with a wet paper towel when I heard a knock at my door.

I blew the strands of hair that had come loose from my ponytail out of my face and opened the door without even looking through the peephole.

Big mistake.

Cole stood in front of me in all of his clean and non-sweaty glory. His suit was as crisp as when I first saw him that morning, but his scruff was a little more grown in and his hair was a little messier from a busy day of running his hands through it at the office.

I wanted to jump into his arms. I wanted to run to him and press my lips to his. I wanted him to strip me naked and thrust into me right in the doorway.

But I was a sweaty, disgusting mess, and my husband could walk through that door at any moment. He already had his suspicions, and I couldn't imagine what he'd say if he found Cole in our apartment.

"What are you doing here?" I asked.

He grinned and leaned casually against the doorframe. "I didn't think it was possible."

"What?" I asked, smoothing my hair back in a futile attempt to look somewhat presentable.

"That you could look just as gorgeous casual at home as you do in those sexy outfits you wear to work."

"Shut up," I mumbled, turning from the door and motioning for him to come in.

He chuckled and followed me in, kicking the door shut behind him. He caught up to me and pulled my arm, spinning me around, and then he cupped my neck with one of his big hands.

"Cole, I'm a sweaty mess," I protested.

"You'll be sweatier after I'm done with you," he growled. His mouth crashed hungrily down to mine, and he kissed me like he needed me in order to survive.

His tongue battered fiercely against mine, all of the pent-up desire from our day of sitting ten feet apart separated only by a wall coming to a head. His hand remained on my neck as his other arm twined around my waist, and my arms moved as if by their own accord around his shoulders. I clung to him, never wanting to let him go.

His hand trailed down, and he pulled me closer against him with a firm hand on my ass. He came up for air only for a second to growl, "Fuck, I need you. Now."

I backed away, ready to lead him into my bedroom, but I stopped. "But he might come home at any second."

His eyes were wild with longing and anticipation. "I don't care."

We stared at each other for a few beats, and then I grabbed his hand and led him down the hallway.

At the last second, I cut off into our office. There was nothing ethical about what we were about to do, but it felt even more wrong to take him into the bedroom I shared with John. The bedroom was sacred ground for a husband and wife despite the sins I'd committed.

His hand clutched mine as he looked around the office. I shut the door behind us, and I locked it for good measure. His eyes focused in on the chair.

"Is that where you were sitting when…?" he trailed off.

"When just hearing your voice got me off?" I finished for him, and he smiled lazily, his eyes still hot with lust. "Yes."

"Let's see if I can do it with my cock this time."

His dirty words sent a bolt of need down my spine. I knew he'd be able to get me off with his cock. He had the day before, and my body vibrated with hunger for him. I couldn't wait until he shoved it into me. I couldn't wait until he filled my body again. He was a drug, and I was addicted after one hit.

He led me over to the chair, taking charge in my own home. He unbuckled his belt, unbuttoned his pants, and lowered his zipper, each movement painfully slow as it heightened the ache between my legs.

He sat in the chair, and then he pulled himself out of his pants. I stared, my mouth watering, as he stroked his hand up and down a few times and gazed at me as if inviting me to hop on.

I hadn't had the pleasure of really seeing him the day before. We'd fucked so quickly that it was all over before I'd had the chance to see just exactly how big the cock he'd shoved into me was.

I knelt on the floor in front of him, craving a taste of him. I had no other thought in my mind except pleasing him. I didn't even care if he reciprocated, but I knew he'd never take pleasure without giving it back.

I pushed his hand away and took hold of him, stroking lightly a few times. He leaned back in the chair and closed his eyes, a sexy groan vibrating his chest. I sucked him into my mouth gently at first, and then I gained momentum, picking up speed as his moans goaded me on.

I felt his hand on my shoulder, pushing me away. I looked up at him, our eyes meeting, and he gazed down at me with a raw tenderness I'd never seen from him.

"You're good at that," he said, catching his breath.

I grinned. "Thanks."

"Too good, and I want to fuck you. If you keep doing that, I won't be able to."

"I want you to fuck me."

"Take off your clothes."

I did as instructed as he watched my every move. Heat crept up my neck as I stood exposed before him. I'd never felt more naked, but it wasn't just the absence of clothes. It was his penetrating gaze.

He admired my body with appreciation. "So fucking gorgeous."

I moved closer to him, and he leaned back as I lifted one leg and looped it over his. He helped me get my other leg up, and then he lifted my ass as I braced myself on his shoulders.

He grabbed his thick cock in one hand and then guided himself through my wetness a few times before plunging into me.

We both yelled out at the pleasure of his entrance, and he stilled inside of me for a few beats, his eyes burning into mine. "God, you feel perfect," he said.

"So perfect," I whispered, and then he unleashed the desire that had built between us since the last time we'd been together.

He thrust into me in an unforgiving frenzy, bringing both of us to the precipice before he slowed. He circled his hips, hitting every pleasure point inside of me, and let go of my ass, his fingertips moving to my hips and digging in.

I needed the friction.

I needed more.

I used his shoulders as support as I moved up and down over him, feeling him glide in and out with a pleasure that was almost too much to handle.

"Christ, this is so good," he muttered, his gorgeous face contorting with satisfaction as I watched him. I moved my mouth over his. His tongue immediately thrust against mine, fucking my mouth with his as I continued to maneuver over him.

He was right. It was *so good.*

It was better than I'd ever experienced before, and if I could stay right there for the rest of my life, connected as one with him, I'd die happy.

Cole started to drive upward. He yelled out a string of obscenities, and I matched his cries with my own as we flew headfirst together into our climaxes. I collapsed against him, my head resting on his shoulder and my face turned in toward his neck.

We didn't move for a few heated moments as our cries quieted. I breathed in his scent as my heart rate slowed back to normal, and he simply held me in his arms.

"You should go," I finally murmured, not moving.

He sighed. "I know. But I don't want to."

"He could be home any second." I didn't say his name. We both knew who I was talking about.

"So? Then he'll know."

I sat up. "He can't find out like this."

Cole took my face in his hands and his eyes searched mine. "You're right. But you will tell him, won't you?"

I nodded. I would. "Soon, Cole."

I hated using Madi as an excuse, but I legitimately thought I was doing the right thing.

"Okay," he conceded. His demeanor changed from bliss to sadness.

He clutched me against him, his hand buried in my hair as he held me close. "I hate this, Lucy," he said, his voice full of this intense frustration.

"I do, too. As soon as we get good news on Kay and Kevin, I'll talk to him."

He pulled back and nodded.

"Lucy?" A voice called from the other side of the door. "You home?"

"Oh, fuck." I stiffened, my heart stopping for a second as my husband's voice registered.

I jumped off of Cole and raced to put my sweaty clothes back on. "Fuck," I whispered over and over. He tucked himself back into his pants as if everything was normal, almost like he was moving in slow motion while I sprinted around the room like a maniac.

I scanned the room wildly. The office looked the exact same as it had when we'd walked in, but it wasn't the same.

"Get under the desk," I hissed.

"Are you serious?" he hissed back.

I gave him a wide-eyed pointed look, and he sighed in frustration as he crawled under the desk. I checked to make sure he couldn't be seen from the doorway, and then I took a deep breath and opened the office door.

"In here!" I yelled, and then I stepped out of the office and closed the door behind me, my heart racing violently.

"What were you doing in the office?"

"Just cleaning," I said, hoping he'd buy it. "I just finished mopping."

"That explains the sweat," he said, looking me over.

"Yep, that explains it." My voice came out all shrill and weird.

He gave me a strange look. "Are you okay?"

"Yeah! Great."

"What's for dinner?"

"Whatever. I haven't thought about it."

"I've got some work to do."

"In the office?" Fuck. Not in the office. Fuck. I forced my breathing to even out, but panic was starting to edge in and I wasn't sure how to control it.

"Well, if it's clean…"

I interrupted. "I'm not done in there. I, uh, still need to, um, vacuum. And the desk! I have to dust the desk." I rambled with the first thing that came into my head.

"Fine. I'll work on the couch. I'm just going to go change."

"Sounds great!" My enthusiasm was out of the ordinary, but I couldn't help it.

I was a terrible liar.

I shouldn't be doing this to my husband. I shouldn't be hiding my secret lover under the desk in the office while my husband was on the verge of catching us.

The second John was out of the room, I ran into the office and found Cole crouched under the desk. I felt like a total asshole.

"I'm so sorry," I whispered, grabbing his arm and helping him up from the floor.

He shot me a dirty look.

"I need to get you out of here."

I checked both ways before ushering him toward my front door. I got him out the door and stood in the hallway with him for just a second.

"I just…" He cut himself off. "Never mind. I'll see you tomorrow."

I wanted to know what he was about to say, but he needed to go. He pressed his lips quickly to mine and then disappeared down the hall.

I walked back to the kitchen to put the mop away, and then I went into the office, cleaning the spots I'd told John I needed to.

I stared at the chair where Cole had just fucked me. My body was worn and sated, but guilt pressed heavily down on me.

What we'd just done had been completely amazing, but it had been so stupid, too. We'd come seconds away from getting caught.

I needed to talk to John and I needed to be honest with him. I had to deal with this rather than continue pushing it off with excuses.

I had no idea what to say or how to say it, but I couldn't keep this affair up for much longer.

Chapter Twenty-One

It turns out that I could keep up the affair longer than I thought.

Two weeks after we'd first slept together, guilt pressed on me, but it wasn't strong enough to stop the affair. And when John walked in late each night with a new excuse and a lack of interest in me, the guilt melted easily away.

I was juggling a lot of balls, and one was bound to drop at some point.

Cole couldn't seem to stay away, and I couldn't seem to tell him no. My body constantly ached for him, but it wasn't just the sex. We'd started connecting on a deeper level, too, and that scared me far more than the physical act of sex.

I was actually starting to *like* him. Once I'd successfully chipped away at the wall he'd built between us, I found that the man hiding beneath it was interesting and fun.

Kaylee was still in the hospital, gaining strength every day while her husband continued to battle brain swelling in his medically-induced coma.

Madi bounced between my parents' house and the apartment I shared with John. My mom understood that we were busy with work, and both of my parents were retired, so they offered to take her more often than not. I gave my mother no indication that anything was wrong in my marriage, but I was pretty sure she sensed something was off.

My phone rang Monday just as I was leaving work, and the screen let me know that it was my mother.

No news is good news. Her motto repeated in my head.

She was still at the hospital, and she was calling me.

This was news.

A million thoughts flashed through my head. Kaylee had taken a turn for the worse. Kevin didn't make it. They were both in far worse shape than we thought. Madi was going to have to live without her parents. I was going to have to raise Madi with a man who I didn't even like anymore.

My heart beat in double time and my chest felt heavy. "Is Kaylee alright?" I answered.

"Yes. I have good news. They took Kevin off the meds, and he's awake!"

"Thank God."

"They brought Kay into his room and she sat with him for a while. He woke up when she was telling him how much his little girl needs him."

Tears filled my eyes. "That's the best news."

"He's got a long road to recovery, but he's going to be okay. And Kay's getting released, too!"

"When?" Relief lifted the weight that had been pressing on my shoulders. My sister was getting out, Kevin was awake, and soon I'd be able to tell John everything.

And then I could be with the man who I was starting fall for.

"They're working on the release paperwork now."

"Thank God. Should we bring Madi by to see her?"

"She wants Madi to see her at home. Madi's with me, but could you come get her and bring her to your sister's house?"

"Of course! What time should we bring her?"

"Any time tonight, if you can."

"Done. Around seven o'clock?"

"Perfect. Love you, Lucy."

"I love you, too, Mom. Give Kay and Kevin a kiss from us."

"I will."

I hung up the phone and sighed in relief. I would finally be able to tell John the truth…that things were over between us. I'd finally be free to move forward with Cole.

Or so I thought.

I texted John to let him know that Kay had been released, and he texted back that he wanted to come with me to drop Madi off.

Great. Just what I wanted…an hour alone in the car with my husband.

After I'd picked up Madi from the hospital and John met us for dinner, we drove the hour to Kaylee's house. We waited for my parents to bring Kaylee home, and we were there for the tearful reunion between mother and daughter.

Kaylee looked loads better, although she still sported a cast on her arm and she moved slowly from the pain in her ribs. Much of her bruising was healed and she seemed to be in good spirits.

And then we left. My nerves got the better of me as I knew that this was my moment. This was my chance to be honest with John.

"Can we talk?" he asked once we were on the road again.

"Of course." I'd expected that I was going to be the one to start the conversation, but if he wanted to go first, I wasn't going to stop him.

"I'm sorry I've been at work so much lately. But there's a reason. A good reason, I think. I was going to wait to tell you, but I don't think I should wait any longer."

I studied him as he drove. He was so different from Cole. He was softer. He wasn't commanding. He wasn't rude or domineering.

"I got a promotion at work."

"That's great! Congratulations," I said.

He grinned. "My boss told me at lunch today that they chose me. It's why I've been obsessed with work lately. I know things at home are suffering because of it, but from this moment forward, I'm going to fix that. I'm going to be a better husband."

I opened my mouth to respond, to tell him that more money wasn't going to fix our marriage, but he continued.

"I wanted to keep it a secret because I bought you something. It's something you said you didn't want, but I've always known deep down that you do. It gets here next Tuesday, so keep that night free. I knew that if I logged a lot of hours, I'd be in a better position to get the promotion, and it worked. It all starts here, babe."

I softened at his term of endearment. He hadn't called me "babe" in months, but more importantly, he hadn't quoted our vows in months, either: "It all starts here, babe."

How was I supposed to follow up his speech with what I'd planned to say to him?

He'd essentially just told me that he'd been working so hard because of me. The big division that spanned between us happened so he could make me happy.

Or had it been for a different reason?

I had the sudden terrible thought about the real motivation behind his dedication to work. Had he been working so hard to show the world that he could afford to buy me whatever present was on the way? Or was he really doing it for me?

If he really loved me, wouldn't he have worked harder on showing me that instead of working harder at the office?

A few kind words after months of isolation didn't make everything okay again. It was going to take more than a pronouncement and a gift to fix our marriage.

"Tell me about your new responsibilities."

John chattered away while I zoned out. This certainly threw a wrench in my plan.

I'd do it, and I'd do it soon. But I couldn't take away from his joy and happiness. I couldn't stomp all over his heart when he was so excited, even though it would mean continued time apart from each other.

So I let him go on and on, oblivious to the fact that the person sitting beside him was wholeheartedly thinking about another man.

Chapter Twenty-Two

When the next morning rolled around, I felt like hell.

John had tried to come onto me the night before as a first step on the road of recovering our marriage, but I faked a headache and climbed into bed early.

Part of me thought I should fill Cole in on John's news. I'd wanted to text him the night before to tell him that Kaylee was out of the hospital and Kevin was awake, but John had gotten in bed right after I did.

It hadn't gone unnoticed that the first person I wanted to share good news with was Cole.

I noticed Cole's car in the parking lot—the car he'd shoved me up against in the hospital parking garage. I couldn't help my small smile as I thought about his words from that day.

I arrived at my desk a few minutes early. Cole's door was only pushed halfway closed, and I could hear him talking on the phone. I couldn't make out the words, but just the timber of his voice warmed me. I couldn't wait to see him.

I walked over to his door, my heartrate picking up speed the closer I got to his door.

"Thanks, Lincoln. I'll have Lucy work on the details, and I'll send your ideas along to our other departments."

I froze when I heard my name. I knew it was business-related, but I loved hearing my name roll off his tongue. I loved hearing him talk about me to business associates, and I loved that he trusted me with the account.

He hung up the phone, and I watched as he bent his head to write something down. I knocked on the door, and Cole looked up, his brows knitted. His entire face smoothed into a warm smile when he saw it was me.

"Good morning, Ms. Cleary," he said, his smile widening.

"Good morning, Mr. Benson."

"I'm so sorry I didn't call you last night. I went to dinner with my parents and some of their friends. It ran longer than I expected."

"I have some news."

He raised his eyebrows. "Oh?"

"My sister was released from the hospital and Kevin is awake."

"That's great news." He rose and walked toward me. He stopped and leaned casually against the edge of the desk. He stood there powerfully, all hard lines and pure masculinity in his suit. His eyes were a soft brown as they gazed at me, and I had the sudden urge to hop onto him. He lowered his voice. "Does that mean you're going to talk to John?"

"I will. He, uh…said some things yesterday, and the timing wasn't right."

Cole sighed and looked out the window. He folded his arms across his chest. "I don't want to know."

"I'm sorry."

He turned back toward me, and his eyes were colder than they'd been only seconds earlier. "Can you be honest with me?"

"Of course."

"Are you ever going to tell him?"

I nodded and stepped through the doorway and into his office. "Yes. I am. I promise. I'm just waiting for the right moment."

"You were waiting for your sister to get out of the hospital because of Madi. You were waiting for Kevin to wake up from his coma. Those things have happened, Lucy." His gaze returned to the window, and I felt like I was about two inches tall.

My heart dropped. He was angry—and rightly so. "I know. I'm sorry. I don't know what else to say."

He looked at me again, studying me, and then finally nodded his head almost imperceptibly.

"Aside from MTC, is there anything else you need me to work on today?"

"Actually, yes. Close the door for a second." I did as he instructed, and then he stood from his desk and walked around it. He leaned on the edge. "Now that Kaylee's out, how about that trip we talked about?"

I thought about it. I couldn't really see any reason *not* to go, and it would give me unlimited time with Cole—something both my heart and my body craved.

"To New York?"

He shook his head. "I've got some business in San Diego. I could drive down and get it done in a few hours, or we could go together and stretch it to a few days." His eyes gleamed wickedly.

I couldn't think of anything that sounded more fantastic than Cole, a beach, and the absence of anyone who knew that I was married. "When do we leave?"

He grinned. "I'll forward you the details so you can make arrangements. I have a lot to get done today, but we could leave as early as tomorrow afternoon."

"Yes, sir."

He stood from his leaning position and walked to me. He hauled me firmly against him, and I immediately felt his erection as he thrust his hips toward me. His lips dragged across my neck.

"If we're traveling to San Diego tomorrow, I don't have time to do what I want to do to you right now. But I'm going to spread you out on the bed in the hotel and fuck you until you can't walk straight."

"You can't say shit like that to me and expect me to get back to work."

He chuckled. "If I can work with this raging hard-on, you can work with wet panties."

"How do you know they're wet?" I challenged.

His voice lowered to a raw, sexy whisper. "Because after sleeping with you for the last two weeks, I know your body pretty well."

I couldn't argue there. He kissed me just long enough to make me want him even more, and then he broke away from me and returned to his desk. He tapped a few keys on his computer.

"I hate you," I whined.

"I don't doubt it. Enough shenanigans, Ms. Cleary. Back to work." I let out a long and frustrated sigh before opening his office door. Before I left, he said, "We'll have plenty of time in San Diego."

I turned back. "It'll never be enough."

"I know," he whispered.

I couldn't help the crazy grin that spread across my face as I got to work planning our trip.

I pulled out my phone to text John, trying to come up with the most diplomatic way possible to let him know I was planning to go out of town with the guy he already had his suspicions about.

Need to go to out of town for a few days for work. I read it over a few times before sending it.

His reply came almost immediately. *When and will your boss be there?*

We leave tomorrow and he needs his assistant.

I didn't get a reply from him, but I had a feeling I'd be facing the music when I got home later that night.

I wasn't wrong.

I stayed late to finish work on a few projects since I'd be away from the office for a few days, and John was home already when I walked through the door.

"So another trip with your boss?" he asked without preamble.

"God, John, can I at least set my purse down before you start attacking me?"

"Oh, come on. What's going on between you two?"

He presented me with yet another chance to be honest, but I wasn't ready.

I was terrified to tell him the truth. What if I broke free from him only to realize that Cole and I didn't work in the real world? What if the sex was so good because of the thrill of the secret, the intoxication of the affair?

I'd give myself this time with Cole. I'd selfishly live in this fantasyland for just a few more days, just until I knew for sure that Cole and I could make it work outside of the affair.

I'd use this time away with him to see how it felt, and I'd know my answer once we returned from San Diego.

"It's my fucking job. You of all people should understand that." I dodged his real question by turning it around on him.

He sighed. "You're right. I'm sorry. I know I've been neglecting you lately. I've just been so wrapped up in designing this new software, and I have a huge presentation on Friday."

I was surprised to hear that he had a presentation. He tended to work behind the scenes.

"I hope it goes well."

"Me, too."

He picked his iPad back up and settled into work, and I headed to the closet to pack my bag for my "business" trip.

Chapter Twenty-Three

I slid into Cole's Audi a little after noon to make our way down to San Diego. When I'd left earlier that morning, John had barely mumbled a goodbye. It was better that way, though. I had far less guilt when my husband treated me like an acquaintance than I would if he'd been the loving and attentive man I'd married.

But, then, if he was still loving and attentive, I wondered if Cole would've so easily caught my eye. If I'd been happy in my marriage, would I have strayed?

He set the GPS with the address for Masonite Consultants, the clients he needed to meet with, and we were off.

"Tell me about the best road trip you took as a kid," he said, tuning into the country music station and rolling down his window.

I hadn't pegged him for a country music fan, but it somehow made him more endearing. It turned him from this untouchable, wealthy mogul into a regular guy.

"God, we took road trips practically every summer. But when I was ten, my parents rented an RV and we took a road trip from Santa Clarita all the way to Florida. We did the beach and Disney. We spent over two weeks in that RV."

"That's a hell of a drive."

"You know, there were times I wanted to pull my sister's hair out, and there were times the RV felt smaller than this car, but I wouldn't trade those memories for anything. What about you?"

"We did the Grand Canyon one year. It's really the only road trip we ever took. My dad was always working, so it was rare that we took actual vacations that didn't involve work in some capacity. Even that one was just one night in Williams on the way to Phoenix for business."

I studied him as he focused on the road, and I could see a hint of sadness wash over him. My heart squeezed for Cole's childhood. I'd never thought about what life might be like for the kid of the CEO of a major company, especially when Jack had been building it up from the ground. Cole may have grown up with the sorts of privileges I'd never known, but he probably missed out on some of the big things, too.

"Is that where you learned your work ethic?"

"Something like that," he said.

"Well, where would you want to road trip to?"

"Your Florida trip sounds fun."

"It was."

"When I have kids someday, I want to make sure I take them to all the places I didn't get to see when I was a kid. I don't want to work the way my dad did."

I sensed that Cole held a lot of resentment toward his father, which seemed odd considering the kind Jack I knew. But I knew him toward the end of his career. I didn't know him as the father who worked through my childhood, and I didn't know him as the man who had pressured me into the position of CEO of his company.

"Did your mom work?"

He shook his head. "No. She stayed home and when I was young and she volunteered at my elementary school."

"Are you close with her?"

He nodded. "Very."

I couldn't help my smile. I'd have never guessed the sexy and demanding Cole was a mama's boy.

We reminisced about our respective childhoods, laughing together and singing along with Florida Georgia Line when

Cole's favorite song came on. The two hours to San Diego passed in the blink of an eye.

When Cole pulled into a parking spot at Masonite Consultants, he grabbed my arm before I had the chance to get out of the car. He leaned in close to me.

"Welcome to San Diego," he said, his voice deep and gritty. "In a few hours, you're all mine for the next three days."

His lips pressed firmly to mine for a brief kiss, and then he pulled away from me and opened his door. I sat in my seat breathlessly for a few seconds, trying to pull myself together for this meeting before three days of Cole.

I took meticulous notes as Cole spoke with the president of Masonite. I did my best not to focus on his plush lips, the lips I knew would be dragging across my skin later. I tried my hardest to ignore the ache between my legs that I knew Cole would satisfy over and over.

The minutes dragged.

The harder I tried not to think about what Cole was going to do to me over the next three days, the more the images of his naked body loomed in my mind.

Finally, after what felt like absolute days but was really only four hours later, we slid back into the Audi and headed toward the hotel. I'd booked us an oceanfront villa that featured a private balcony, and my imagination worked overtime as I thought about all the different ways Cole could make love to me in that villa.

We checked in, and Cole smirked when the clerk handed two keys over to us. As we followed the bellhop with our luggage toward our villa, I couldn't help but ask the question I'd only thought once before.

"Did you have something to do with the hotel mix-up in New York?"

His eyes cut quickly over to mine. "What do you mean?" he asked cautiously.

"I mean did you cancel my room?"

I could see the wheels turning in his mind, and finally he looked at me sheepishly and shrugged. "I had to take what opening I could."

I didn't know whether to laugh or punch him. "Damn. You put on quite the act like it was all my fault."

"I'm sorry." He had the decency to actually look apologetic, and he gave me one of those looks with those brown eyes that melted my heart.

It was my turn to smirk. "You know how I feel about apologies, Mr. Benson."

He laughed, and then he grabbed my ass. "I'll give you an apology," he muttered close to my ear, and I giggled loudly. The bellhop opened our door and unloaded our luggage. Cole tipped him while I stood at the slider door overlooking the beach. When the door clicked shut behind the bellhop, our time was finally upon us.

Cole's arms slipped around my waist as his body lengthened firmly behind mine. I settled back into him, peace washing over me as I breathed him in while I watched the waves roll in and out from the shore right outside my window.

This shouldn't have been a moment of peace. What lie ahead of us wouldn't be peaceful. It couldn't be. I was sure it would prove to be tumultuous and chaotic, but in this moment, in this hotel villa on the beach in San Diego, the tranquility washed over me as Cole's lips dragged along my neck.

"What should we do first?" he asked, his voice husky and warm.

His hands reached under my shirt and splayed out across my belly. His fingertips gently caressed my skin. I couldn't help my soft whimpers.

"Your call, boss."

He groaned at my choice of words. I knew how much he loved being in control.

One of his big hands moved up to massage my breast while the other dipped down into my panties as he thrust his hips against me. His steel erection dug into my ass, and I arched back into him to feel more of him—all of him. I braced myself by placing my hands on the glass in front of me.

All the sensations at once drove me wild with need as he worked my body—owned my body—with his hands and his mouth. I was completely lost to the world and lost in Cole.

His fingers continued to plummet downward. He plunged one finger into me, and his lips moved close to my ear. "Holy fuck, you're drenched," he moaned, and my only response was a guttural groan as he pulled his finger out slowly and then pushed it back in.

My legs started to shake. It was far too soon for me to cross that bridge, but Cole had such command over my body that I couldn't stop it.

He continued fucking me with his fingers as his other hand assaulted my breast. I reached behind me to feel him, to grab him in my hand, but he pulled his hips back out of my reach. I sighed and allowed myself to give into the pleasure of his hands in and on my body.

He pulled his finger out and barely stroked my clit before I detonated in his arms. His hand squeezed my breast, his lips continued their onslaught on my neck, and his fingers dove back inside of me as my body contracted around him.

I fell back into him, grateful that he was standing behind me to hold me up. He lifted me up in his arms and carried me over to the bed, and I felt more love from him in those few seconds than I'd felt from John in the past three years.

He set me down so I was lying on my back, and then he leaned over and kissed me. "I'm not even close to finished with you, Ms. Cleary," he said.

I smiled lazily. "I need a minute."

"Sixty seconds," he said. "That's all you're getting."

I watched as he loosened his tie. He took it off and set it on a chair. He unbuttoned his shirt. He removed that, too, and set it on the chair with his tie. He pulled his undershirt over his head and tossed it on the floor. My mouth watered as I took in the view of Cole Benson standing before me.

God, he was perfection. Those abs…I wasn't sure when he had time to work out between running a huge company and sleeping with me, but he managed. His broad chest was smooth and inviting. I wanted to lie my head on it and never leave. And that six pack…or was it an eight pack? I counted again, but I lost track as the muscles shimmered and moved as he stalked his way toward me.

His eyes connected with mine when I finally ripped them off of his abdomen.

"Tell me what you want," I said softly.

"You, Lucy. I want you. Any way I can get you."

My heart melted. I sat up from the bed, and he was positioned directly between my legs. I reached immediately in front of me and ran my fingertips over those abs that I couldn't seem to stop ogling. I looked up at him, and his eyes were closed and his neck was corded as he stretched it back.

I unbuckled his belt, unbuttoned his pants, and lowered his zipper. I reached into his pants and pulled him out. He was hard, thick, and heavy across my hand.

I went right to work, first licking down the shaft and then wrapping my lips around him. His moans started soft, but as I picked up speed, moving my head up and down over him, he became louder and throatier. My own body clenched with desire just seeing this controlled and disciplined man fall apart under my touch.

He held my head in place as his fingers tangled into my hair, feral moans and growled curses falling from his lips.

"Fuck," he groaned, and then I felt his liquid heat erupting against the back of my throat. His body shook with gratification. His hand on the back of my head held me still while the last drops of pleasure spilled onto my tongue.

He grunted as he pulled out of my mouth. "You're a naughty girl," he said, and I grinned as I lay back.

He collapsed on the bed beside me and leaned up on one elbow. He reached over and stroked the skin of my stomach absently, his hands meandering up toward my breasts and back down again as we lay together on the bed.

"Give me five minutes and I'll be good to go again."

I giggled. "Five minutes?"

He shrugged sheepishly. "I'm pretty much always ready when it's you."

Heat crept into my cheeks at his compliment.

"You're so sexy right now, all naked and flushed."

"After sitting in the car for two hours and then that thing you just did to me, I'm sure I look like a disaster."

"Just wait."

"For what?"

"Wait until I fuck you."

"Has it been five minutes yet?" I asked, glancing down at his naked body. My body was ready and aching again. It was always ready and aching for Cole. I'd never been as sexually greedy in a relationship as I was with him, but I couldn't seem to get enough.

He glanced down with me, and then our eyes met. "It's semi-ready."

"Then why don't you semi-fuck me?"

"I don't fuck halfway, Ms. Cleary."

"I think you've proven that, Mr. Benson."

He grinned, and then he shifted. He hovered over me and kissed me for a few tender moments before slamming into me.

Chapter Twenty-Four

"I don't ever want to get up from this bed. Ever." Cole's warm voice wrapped around me like a blanket.

My head rested on his chest, and he drew circles absently on the bare skin of my back. I snuggled closer into the man whose arms were wrapped around me after the third time he'd made me come in the few short hours since we'd arrived to the hotel.

"We have to eat sometime," I pointed out.

"Isn't that why room service was invented?"

"God, we're from such different backgrounds."

"Why do you say that?" He tightened his arms around me.

"Room service was for the privileged. I didn't grow up poor, exactly, but we didn't indulge in such luxuries."

"We always ate breakfast in the room together before my father ran off to whatever meeting he had scheduled."

"What did you and your mom do?"

"Whatever tour she'd set up for us. It depended where we were. We'd visit the Shedd Aquarium in Chicago or the British Museum in London or Times Square in New York."

I had a hard time picturing family vacations where my dad ran off to work while the rest of us toured whatever city we were in. It didn't sound like much of a vacation if one of the family members was absent.

"Why did you move to New York?"

He stiffened for just a moment. "I knew my father wanted me to work for the company, but I wanted to step out of his shadow and prove myself in a place where he wouldn't be hovering over me all the time. I asked if I could work in a different office than him, and when the opening came to run the office in New York, I jumped at it."

"Did you like living there?"

"Yes and no. Part of me loved it, and it will always be the first place where I really learned to figure things out on my own. But it was difficult living across the country from my mom."

"Not your dad?"

"My dad, too," he conceded. "Of course I love both my parents. I've just always wished my dad had spent more time attending my high school baseball games and less time working, you know?"

I didn't know, actually. My dad was the dad who attended every single one of my softball games. When I'd gotten a small part in the fall play my senior year, he and my mom both attended every performance. I'd been supported by a loving set of parents my entire life, so it was hard to imagine a life where that wasn't the case.

Jack was a good and kind man. I couldn't imagine that he worked because he preferred it over his son. He probably had to do it—maybe even to give Cole a wider variety of opportunities and a more comfortable life.

But maybe no one had ever explained that to Cole, and maybe Cole couldn't see the forest for the trees himself.

As we lay naked together on the bed, I found Cole baring more than just his skin. He was letting me in, and I had the feeling that these weren't admissions he shared with just anyone. Somehow I'd earned his trust, and that thought alone pulled at my heartstrings and sent a wave of emotion through my chest.

I found myself falling in deeper and deeper with this man, and I had no idea what to do about it.

Our trip to San Diego had been filled with rough sex followed by gentler sex, with bonding and building emotions, and with a whole lot of naked time.

It was everything I needed to help me see that things might really be able to work with Cole.

"What's on the agenda for today?" I asked my boss after I walked into his office the following Tuesday morning.

"Call Dan Sears' secretary at Utica and find out how many will be on the reservation tonight, and then confirm that number with my eight o'clock at Vine." He gave me a wolfish smile and lowered his voice to a deep rumble. "Include yourself on that, too. And be ready to meet afterward to review."

I gave him my most demure smile. "Is that what we're calling it now?"

He chuckled. "You better get to work before I review you all over my desk."

I turned to leave, but before I walked through the door, I threw over my shoulder, "I'm not saying it would be a bad way to start the day, but I'm still a little sore after our trip."

I heard him laugh behind me as I walked to my desk. It was our little inside joke. We'd had so much sex that we were both sore for a day afterward, but the only soreness I felt now was the ache that was always present between my legs whenever Cole was near.

Utica required reservations for two that night, and with Cole and me, that made four. I called Vine to confirm the reservation, and the second I hung up, I realized one big problem.

John had asked me to keep the night free.

I wasn't sure why, and I didn't know what he had planned, but he'd told me he had something for me. I wondered what it could be, but I had to work. Cole needed me for a dinner meeting.

I texted him. *I have a dinner meeting tonight at eight. I'll be home late.*

His response came quickly, which was unusual for him. I supposed it was his way of showing he wanted to mend things between us, but it was too little too late. *Will you be home between work and dinner?*

Not sure. I've got a lot I need to get done today.

I felt bad when I didn't get an immediate reply, but then Cole stepped out of his office and I forgot all about John.

"I have a few things I need you to add to your agenda in the next few days."

I grabbed a sheet of paper and scribbled down his requests. "And in ten minutes, I need you in my office," he said. I looked up from my paper at him. Our eyes locked, and his radiated hunger.

He turned away from me and headed down the hall. I could hear him greeting colleagues as he walked, but I was completely flipped upside down after the way he'd just looked at me.

That was it. All it took was one simple glance full of lust, and I was done.

"Close the door behind you," Cole said ten minutes later. His voice was quiet, and his low timber rumbled through my chest.

I did as he commanded. He strode across the room toward me, his eyes hot on mine the entire time.

When he stood in front of me, his eyes moved from mine. He focused on a lock of my hair and gently fingered it. "You shouldn't wear skirts that short around the office," he said, tucking the lock of hair behind my ear.

"Why not?" I breathed.

His eyes moved back to mine. "Because it makes me want to fuck you. I shouldn't fuck you in my office. I shouldn't be fucking you anywhere at all." He pushed me against the door, pressing his erection into me. "But then I see you in this short little skirt and I just can't help myself. Do you want me to fuck you?"

I nodded, unable to speak as the familiar and delicious ache pulled at my core.

His lips found my neck, and I leaned my head back and closed my eyes while he kissed his way along my collarbone, to my throat, and down into my cleavage. He trailed his lips upward, finally landing on my own.

He cut off our kiss and pulled me away from the door. "Bend over my desk," he said, his voice husky.

I walked over to his desk to do as he asked.

"Turn toward the window."

The cool wood against my cheek contrasted sharply with the heat permeating my body. I focused my gaze over the same view of downtown LA that Cole looked upon every single day from his desk chair.

"That's perfect," he said, coming up behind me. He bucked his hips against mine, and I used the desk as leverage to keep still. His hand trailed up my thigh to my ass. He cupped one cheek in his big hand, and then he trailed his long fingers down to my slit.

He palmed me between my legs, and I let out a soft moan. "Jesus, Lucy."

He pulled my panties down my legs and tossed them on the floor. He slid one finger into me. Everything went black around me except for that singular sensation of his finger driving in and out of me. Whatever was outside that window was gone as I focused every bit of my attention on what he was doing to me.

His other hand came around the front of me and I lifted up slightly. He reached into the top of my shirt and under the cup of my bra to squeeze my nipple, and I couldn't help another involuntary moan. He leaned forward to kiss my neck, his fingers still pumping in and out of me.

And then everything stopped. His hands were off of me, and I was left feeling cold and empty.

I didn't move as I listened to the hot sound of his belt buckle sliding through the metal and then a zipper.

"I'm going to fuck you from behind," he said, and then he rammed into me without further warning.

He filled me completely, and as he growled over me while he pumped in and out, I couldn't help but feel the overwhelming thrill of having sex with my hot boss in his office.

He was aggressive, powering himself deeply into me before pulling almost all the way out. He moved at a fast pace, driving me swiftly toward my peak.

There was so much wrong with what we were doing, yet nothing could stop us. The combination of Cole Benson and this situation that was forbidden in every single way pushed me into ecstasy.

My core tightened, my legs shook, and my body squeezed Cole tightly to me.

Just as I started to come down from my high, Cole grunted and then spilled stormily into me. The sound of his voice, the force of his orgasm, and the feel of his arms tightening around me pushed me into a second climax.

I barely contained myself from screaming through my second orgasm. When I came down, my limbs felt heavy. Too heavy to lift. Too heavy to carry me.

I allowed all of my weight to press onto the desk as Cole pulled out of me. I was completely drained and thoroughly fucked.

I felt his arms lift me up, and he held me upright for a moment. I rested my head on his shoulder and allowed my heavy arms to just hang.

He chuckled. "You okay?"

"Yeah," I said, my voice lazy. "I just need to sit for a few minutes."

He helped me to a chair, and I sat while I regrouped.

"Jeez, Cole," I said. "How are you still standing after that?"

He grinned at me. "You energize me, Lucy. Being with you is so different from anyone else I've ever been with." He bent down to kiss my forehead, and in that moment, I felt protected and loved. "You're incredible."

"You're not too bad yourself."

He raised one eyebrow at me and lowered his voice. "Is that just the multiple orgasms talking?"

My face heated, but I couldn't deny that what he'd just done to me had been pretty incredible.

A knock at his office door interrupted our post-sex recovery.

"Shit," he muttered. He patted down my hair. "You okay?"

I nodded as I pulled my panties back on, smoothed my skirt, and adjusted my shirt. He glanced at me one last time before opening the door.

"Mr. Benson, we have the proofs ready for Mr. Jarvis." Laura from the marketing department peered into the office at me. She paused and looked back and forth between us as if she'd caught us doing something we shouldn't have been doing. My face heated again, and I could tell my neck was turning red. Cole maintained perfect composure as Laura spoke again. "We just need your final approval."

"I'll be down in ten minutes."

"Yes, sir." She gazed up at him with a look of adoration in her eyes. It was similar to the way I looked at him, but I felt like I had a right to now that I'd had sex with him. She hadn't.

Well, to my knowledge she hadn't.

What if she had?

I suddenly wondered how many women in this very office Cole had been with.

"You could have called," he said sternly.

"Yes, sir."

He shut the door and leaned up against it, closing his eyes for the briefest of moments.

I couldn't help my chuckle. "I always thought you just treated me like shit. You got a thing for her, too?"

He gave me a sharp look. "You keep talking like that and I may just have to discipline you."

"Yes, sir." I stood on shaky legs and walked toward the door.

He grinned at me. "Get back to work." He swatted my ass on my way out.

I checked my phone at lunch, and I had a new text from John. The time stamp let me know he'd sent it just after our earlier texts, and it had been sitting on my phone waiting for over three hours. *I was hoping you'd be home tonight. I have something I want to give you, and we need to talk.*

He was right. We did need to talk, but I was pretty sure he wasn't going to like what I had to say.

I thought about what to say in reply. *Sorry, but I'd rather spend time with Cole* seemed inappropriate and cold, but it was the first thought that ran through my mind.

Instead, I replied, *I'm sorry. Busy day at the office. Can we talk tomorrow?*

I didn't have a reply by the time I was done eating. I went back to my desk and tucked my phone away.

I didn't see much of Cole after lunch. He was tied up in a meeting with all the top executives in the company, and I was on my own. I wondered if the meeting was about the Assistant of the Year since a glance at my calendar told me that the announcement was scheduled for the next day. I'd been so preoccupied with hiding my affair with Cole that it had snuck right up on me.

I finished Cole's checklist and got to work on some new ideas for the MTC account, and before I knew it, the clock ticked past five o'clock.

I worked right through it, lost in brainstorming fresh ideas. I didn't even realize the time until Cole interrupted my train of thought by clearing his throat.

I scribbled one last thought down and then looked up at him.

"I appreciate your dedication, but you don't have to work this late. We need to leave for dinner in less than an hour, so if you need to run home, now's the time."

I set down my pen and smiled up at my boss. "I don't need to go home. In fact, I thought I'd just hang out here and get some more ideas down for MTC while I'm on a roll."

"Great enthusiasm for the project. Clearly you were the right choice for the account." He glanced around, and once he realized we were completely alone in the office, he lowered his voice. "I've got something in my office that you can show the same enthusiasm for."

I laughed. "Oh, do you?"

He nodded. "Follow me."

I stood and stretched, thinking that one more romp before dinner didn't sound so bad.

Even though the office was empty, I appreciated Cole's discretion. As soon as I was through the doorway, he kicked the door shut and then pushed my body against it. His mouth crashed down aggressively to mine, and it was the passion and fervor he exhibited for me that completely turned me on in a way no other man had ever managed before him.

His tongue pushed past the seam of my lips, dancing hungrily against my own. A deep moan rumbled involuntarily out of me as he assailed my mouth with his. The ever-present ache in my core intensified as he tightened his hold on me.

He was going to fuck me again, and I was ready for him.

He pushed off the door, separating from me. He stared me down as we both panted, and the way he looked at me with so much hunger and lust made me want him even more.

"What was that?" he muttered, and it was only then that I realized he hadn't stopped because he'd been about to toss me on his desk and he'd wanted to switch positions. He'd stopped because he'd heard something.

And I'd been so caught up in his kiss that I didn't even hear whatever it was that made him stop.

"What was what?" I asked stupidly, not bothering to whisper.

"Someone's out there," he said.

I glanced at the clock. "The cleaning crew?"

He shook his head. "They don't start for another half hour."

"Well, why don't we just go out there?"

"Your hot little moans aren't exactly quiet. Go in my private bathroom and wait there. I'll check it out."

"I can go see who it is. Isn't that my job as your assistant?"

"Your job is to do what I tell you. I can't let our relationship get out. Not when you're married and the Assistant of the Year is being announced tomorrow."

My heart raced and my eyes widened. "Is it me?"

He narrowed his eyes at me. "Now isn't the time. Get in the goddamn bathroom before I carry you in there."

I raised my eyebrows and couldn't help my smile. "Carry me in there?"

"Go," he snarled. He meant business, so I scurried into his bathroom. I kept the door cracked open so I could listen to his conversation with whoever was out there.

He opened the door. "Can I help y—" He was interrupted.

"Where's Lucy?"

Fuck.

John's voice was clear as day, and I pressed myself to the wall a little tighter as my heart raced in fear.

It wasn't supposed to be like this. We couldn't get caught. I needed to talk to John, to tell him that I was leaving him. He wasn't supposed to find us about to screw on Cole's desk. This was all wrong.

God, what if he found me? My heart raced even faster as I held my breath.

"It's not my job to keep track of your wife," Cole said irritably.

"She said she had to work late. Her car is in the parking lot. So where is she?"

"How the hell should I know? We're meeting here at seven and we have a dinner with clients at eight."

"Who's in your office?" John demanded.

"None of your business. Now get the fuck out of my building."

"It's my business when you're screwing my wife."

"Excuse me? I haven't touched your wife." Cole's indignation was award-worthy, and his easy ability to lie was more than a tad concerning.

Silence followed Cole's declaration, and I imagined John trying to stare Cole down in the quiet.

But Cole would never back down. Cole Benson didn't lose, especially not on his home turf. He didn't withdraw. He didn't give up. It just wasn't in his DNA.

I heard John sigh, and then I heard a soft thud, retreating footsteps, and the elevator doors. My heart rate slowed back to normal the further John moved from our corner of the building.

"Jesus Christ, Lucy. You need to talk to him. I can't keep doing this."

I emerged from my hiding place and found Cole sitting in one of the chairs that faced his desk. He rubbed the bridge of his nose as if he had a sudden headache.

"I'm sorry."

He glared at me. "Don't apologize. Fix it. Be honest. I don't want to be in the middle of this shit. This is why I stayed the hell away from you."

I felt tears prick behind my eyes, and then one cascaded down my cheek. I wiped it away.

I wanted Cole to offer me some comfort. That had been close for both of us, and the adrenaline that had rushed through me was gone now, leaving me crashing to the ground.

Instead, he was angry. And he had every right to be. "You don't have the right to cry right now."

"I know I don't. This is my fault, and I'm going to fix it."

"When, Lucy? When the fuck are you going to fix it?"

"I don't know," I whispered.

"Just go. I need some time."

I stared at the back of his head for a minute, wanting nothing more than to run to him and hold him in my arms.

And then I walked out of his office toward my desk.

My breath caught as I spotted the item that had made the thudding noise before John had left.

A black velvet box sat on my desk, and the second I spotted it, guilt knotted my stomach.

I knew exactly what it was before I picked it up and opened it. I stared at it for a long time.

I should've known the second John said he had something for me, the second he said it was something he knew I'd always wanted.

I flipped open the top of the box, and my heart broke.

John was a good man. Everything he'd done had been for me, and I'd been blind to it, lost in my own selfish thoughts that he was choosing work over me when he'd been putting me first all along.

He deserved better than me.

He deserved a faithful woman who would always put him first. When we'd said our vows to each other, I thought I was that person. I'd worked hard to be that person, and I probably would've kept being her if Cole Benson hadn't stepped foot into my life.

It was too late now. I'd navigated a course that I couldn't return from. I'd strayed too far from my husband and from our marriage, and I deserved every cut and crack that slashed my heart.

I pulled the gorgeous ring out of the box. A princess cut diamond gleamed against the black velvet. I thought back to the day John had asked me what my dream ring would be, way back before we'd even gotten engaged. It matched the exact ring I'd told him—a pipe dream, really. It wasn't something I'd ever *really* wanted.

I remembered telling him that a strong marriage with the right person was more important than a huge ring.

I checked for the inscription, knowing what it was going to say before I read it. Sure enough, it predictably matched the words John had said in the car a week earlier, the ones that were from our vows. *It all starts here, babe.*

He thought that a ring was going to fix our marriage. He thought that it was what I wanted. He'd ironically sacrificed us so I could have a tangible sign of our marriage—something I'd never really even wanted.

Cole stepped out of his office as I stared at the ring pinched between my forefinger and thumb.

He gazed at me wordlessly for a few beats. I looked up at him. His eyes were focused on the ring I held.

His eyes finally moved up to mine. "We need to go." His voice was firm, and his face held not a hint of emotion.

I wished I could read him. I wished I knew what he was thinking.

I set the ring back in the cushioned box and put the box in my purse before following Cole toward the elevators so we could head to our dinner.

Chapter Twenty-Five

Silence blanketed our elevator ride down to the first floor. He continued his silent treatment as we exited the building, got in the back of the car, and drove to the restaurant. Just before we pulled up in front of the restaurant, he finally spoke.

"Dan's contract is up in a few weeks and he's shopping around. We need to seal him into a new agreement. Schmooze his wife while I handle the business." He didn't look at me while he spoke, instead focusing on his phone.

I wanted to ask if I should expect the frigid silent treatment to continue, but I bit my tongue.

It felt an awful lot like we were back to where we used to be—back before New York, when everything between us changed so drastically.

I hated that he was treating me with such indifference when I'd experienced the detonation of passion between us.

I wanted us to go into this dinner meeting as a united team ready to conquer Utica and then go home together to make love.

Cole focused his attention on Dan, and I was once again relegated to the position of lowly assistant. As I listened to Dan's wife, Lauren, discuss some new shoe store in her nasally intonation, I couldn't help but think what awaited me after this dinner. I had to go back to the office with Cole, and after that, I had to go home to John. I had no idea what to expect out of either situation.

I started drafting my lie to John in my head. He'd want to know where I'd been when he'd shown up at the office, and I needed to make sure I had my story straight.

Or maybe…

It was time to finally tell him the truth. It was time to end the charade.

I realized after a glass of wine as I tuned out Lauren that the deeply rooted issue in my heart was that I just didn't want to hurt John. I hated that I'd betrayed him the way I had.

I hated it…but I didn't *regret* it.

And that was the root of the issue. I didn't want to mend things with John. I wanted to be with Cole.

If he still wanted me.

Somewhere between the main course and dessert, I finally committed to telling John. It had to be that night when I got home.

The interminable dinner finally ended a little after eleven. While Cole didn't talk to me on the way back to the office, at least his meeting with Dan had gone well. He was busy on his phone the entire car ride back.

When we pulled up at the curb and got out of the car, I finally broke the silence. "Do you need me to come up so we can review?"

He shook his head. "I got it all down. We can review in the morning. You should go home to your husband."

"I'm going to talk to him. Tonight."

He glanced at the clock on his phone, and then his eyes met mine. "It's late."

"I know. But I want to be with you, Cole. I'll do whatever it takes."

He nodded and looked away from me. "I've heard it before." And then he turned and headed into the building as I stood on the sidewalk staring after him.

No hug. No kiss. No comfort. But I didn't deserve those things. I'd let Cole down one too many times, but tonight would be the last time.

I rehearsed in my head what I wanted to say to John, but how did you end a marriage? What were the right words to say?

"I'm leaving you." Too blunt.

"It's over." That might not be clear enough.

"I'm fucking my boss." Too harsh.

I hoped the right words would just come to me when it was time, because rehearsing wasn't doing me much good.

The closer the car crept toward home, the harder my heart pounded in my chest. My stomach was in knots and my ears buzzed. I pulled into my space and took a few deep breaths before I got out of the car. My legs felt like jelly as I moved toward our front door, and my hands shook as I unlocked it.

And then I was inside, and it was dark. When I got to the bedroom, I found my husband on the bed watching television with the lights off.

"Hey," I said, standing in the doorway.

He flipped off the television, sending the room into complete darkness. Then he flipped on the lamp on his nightstand, and we both blinked in the brightness that filled the room.

He sat up in the bed and leaned against the headboard. "Where were you earlier?"

"When?" I asked, dodging his underlying question. I didn't move from the doorway.

"I came to your office a little after seven and you weren't at your desk. Where were you?"

I cleared my throat and pulled in a deep breath as I tried to calm my racing heart. This was my chance, and I wasn't going to back down this time. "I was there."

His eyes narrowed. "Where?"

"In Cole's bathroom."

He nodded slowly, as if he'd known all along, and then he stood. It was as if he needed the less vulnerable position of standing before asking his next question. "What's going on between the two of you?" His voice took on a hard edge.

"I don't know."

"You don't know?" he asked, his voice rising.

I shook my head.

"But it's something. Right?"

I looked down at the floor and closed my eyes.

"What is it?" he asked.

I shrugged, unsure what I should say.

"Do I want to know? I don't want to know."

He was right. He didn't want to know.

"Whatever it is, Lucy, we'll work through it. We'll figure it out. It's us, babe. We can overcome anything."

"Not this," I whispered.

"Not what?" he asked desperately.

"I'm sorry, John," I said, my voice hoarse as tears filled my eyes.

He looked around the room in shock, his eyes out of focus as he pieced it all together. "No. Lucy, no. Tell me you didn't." His eyes slowly drifted to me. His voice lowered to a hiss and his eyes narrowed. "Are you sleeping with him?"

Admission meant the true end of our relationship.

And for as much as I'd convinced myself that I didn't even like John anymore, he was still my home. He was the man I'd married, and he was all I'd known for the past five years.

Everything was going to change.

Everything.

And that wasn't really something I'd thought about when I'd given into the passion I felt for Cole. Was passion enough to build a relationship on? Was passion a solid foundation?

I wasn't sure it was, and I was pretty sure that starting a relationship without really being free to do so wasn't the best place to begin, either.

But my silence was as good as an admission of guilt, and that meant that nothing would ever be the same again.

I looked away from him. I couldn't lie, but I didn't want to admit the truth, not when I knew how much it would hurt both of us.

"Goddammit!" John yelled in anger. "You're married, and you're fucking your boss. What the fuck is wrong with you?"

The tears spilled over onto my cheeks.

"I'm sorry," I repeated.

He took a deep breath as anger turned into blame. "Was it my fault? Did I push you away?" He stepped closer to me and I took a step backward.

I shook my head. Maybe I'd been feeling neglected, but sleeping with Cole had totally been on me.

"Okay," he said, nodding. He'd morphed into problem-solving John. "Okay. We can work through this. It'll take time for me to trust you again, but you're my wife."

"That's not what I want," I said, forcing courage I didn't feel into my tone.

He ignored me and moved closer, his lips moving toward mine.

"John, listen to me." I set both hands on his chest and pushed him away. "That's not what I want. You're not what I want. Not anymore."

He stared at me for a long moment, the words finally registering. "You don't…?"

I shook my head.

"So that's it. It's over." His voice was flat.

A sob pushed up from my chest. "It's over," I whispered.

He was quiet for a few beats, contemplating my declaration. And then I watched as the anger turned him from the man I'd married into a stranger. "Fuck your fake tears. Give me the ring back and go stay with your boyfriend."

I sighed. "He's not my boyfriend. Can't we talk about this?" My voice was meek. I didn't want to provoke his anger further.

"You're fucking your boss and our marriage is over. So we're pretty much through here."

His words stung, but the pain was something I had coming. I deserved every hateful word John flung at me. I deserved his worst.

I pulled the ring box out of my purse and set it on the dresser.

He deserved space from me, so I went into the closet and packed an overnight bag. John was no longer in the bedroom as I moved from the closet to the bathroom. I grabbed a few toiletries and then walked through the apartment I shared with my husband, not sure where I was going but sure that I was no longer welcome in my own home.

Chapter Twenty-Six

I sat in my car, staring at Cole's phone number.

He was staying at a hotel somewhere in LA. That was all I knew about his residence.

In fact, now that the deed was officially done and my relationship with Cole was out in the open, I realized for the first time how little I actually knew about him. I knew how I felt about him, and I knew how he made me feel. I also knew he could be a royal douchebag and he was moody and unpredictable.

Would he even want me to come over? Was I even sure I wanted to see him?

I supposed I could go to my sister's house, but she was an hour away and it was already late. And I wasn't ready to tell my parents about what happened, so I couldn't call them.

I had a few friends I could stay with, but none I felt comfortable calling after eleven at night.

Besides, calling any of my friends would be admitting I'd failed at marriage. I wasn't ready for that to go public, not yet. This was all too fresh.

So really, my only option was Cole. I could go to a hotel, I supposed, but I needed someone. I needed a hug. I needed someone to tell me that everything was going to be okay.

I pressed the call button with shaking hands.

It rang six times and then went to voicemail.

I thought maybe he was still at the office, so I started driving in that direction. I wasn't exactly sure why. My car just sort of led me that way.

I thought I was invincible. I thought I could do whatever I wanted and wouldn't have to face the consequences. I broke wedding vows like they were meaningless. I slept with one man after I'd committed my life to another. In the process, I acted selfishly, doing what felt good instead of what was moral.

I wasn't raised that way. We think of cheaters as horrendous people with tons of issues, but I wasn't like that. I'd simply fallen out of love with one man while I fell in love with another.

Love?

Was I in love with Cole?

It was hard to say, and if I really thought about it, I surmised that it wasn't really love at all.

I was in lust with Cole. I wanted Cole near me all the time. I wanted him inside of me, pumping in and out of me as his strong body hovered over me. I wanted my cheek pressed against the cold wood of his desk while he fucked me from behind.

But did I want to spend the rest of my life with him? Did I want to have children with him? Did I see us growing old together?

They were questions I didn't have the answers to. Not yet, anyway.

But now that John knew the truth, we were free to pursue whatever kind of relationship we wanted.

There might be talk around the office. People might think I was sleeping with the boss to get a raise or the Assistant of the Year bonus. People might presume that it was Cole's fault that my marriage ended. But did I really care what they thought? Did it matter?

As I pulled into my parking spot, I looked around for Cole's car. The gorgeous Audi S8 Sedan sat in the very first spot in the lot.

I got out of the car, my emotions totally mixed as I made my way toward the building. I was drained and tired. I was hurting over the loss of my marriage. Yet I felt this spring of excitement welling up inside of me. Cole and I had real possibilities ahead of us.

There would be no more hiding. No more secrets. No more lies.

I opened the front door. Each step that brought me closer to Cole gave me more and more hope for my future with him. It was scary, to be sure, but he would hold my hand as we took that leap together.

I rode the elevator up, tingles of anticipation dancing down my spine as butterflies took hold of my stomach. Nerves piled on top of my already mixed emotions, and then a sense of giddiness kicked in when the elevator bell rang for our floor.

I stepped off the elevator and headed toward my desk that sat right outside Cole's office. For as much as I'd just lost everything, I housed a whole lot of hope in my heart for my future with Cole.

I walked past my desk to Cole's door, ready to walk in and surprise him. Ready to tell him with excitement that John and I were through, that we could explore whatever this was between us.

When I peered through the door that was wide open for the world to see, my first thought was that my eyes were betraying me—that someone else had gone into Cole's office to have sex in his desk chair. A big joke, screwing someone in the boss's office.

It couldn't be Cole. He wouldn't do that to me. He couldn't be sitting in his chair with his hands cupping the ass of a woman with long blonde hair as she bounced naked on his lap.

It couldn't possibly be Cole in that chair.

But when the woman who straddled the man's lap threw her head back in pleasure and I was able to get a good, clean view of the man in the chair, I could no longer deny it.

Cole Benson was fucking another woman in his office.

Chapter Twenty-Seven

"No," I whispered. "No, no, no." My instinct was to run, and so I ran.

"Fuck!" I vaguely heard Cole behind me as he realized he'd been caught.

Karma was such a mother fucking bitch.

The agony of what I'd just witnessed ripped my heart clean open, but even through the pain, I could still see very coherently that I got exactly what I deserved.

I'd done the exact same thing to John. What made me think that Cole was some stand-up guy who wasn't just using me? I'd known all along what a dick he was, and he'd played on my vulnerability.

The question was *why* he'd done that.

Why had he given me false hope? Why had he preyed on me? Why had he allowed me to ruin my marriage with his lies?

Why was he having sex with some blonde woman in his office?

I was a complete and utter fool.

I ran down the stairs as fast as my legs could carry me, blinded by the tears that poured out of my eyes. A guttural sob rose out of my chest, and I was incapable of stopping it.

I was acting purely on instinct now.

I got into my car and started it. I was in no condition to drive, and I had no idea where I was going, but I had to get the hell away from the man who I had allowed to ruin my life.

I pulled onto the road, tears still blinding me. I knew it was dumb, but I wasn't lucid enough to stop. I didn't want

Cole to run after me and to find me. I couldn't face him, not now and maybe not ever.

Because it was so late, the roads were essentially empty. I pulled into the parking lot of a local bar that looked like it was still open. I gulped in a few deep breaths, and then I got out of the car, headed into the bar, and ordered a shot of tequila. I took it, the liquid burning my throat, and I ordered another one. I took that one and ordered another. By the time the third one slid down my throat, it didn't burn quite as badly.

It was just another poor decision in a long string of them.

I waited for the alcohol to permeate my system. I needed the numbing magic that only tequila could give me. I needed to think about something other than John and Cole and…just *men.*

Some asshole tried to hit on me. "I'd love to buy your fourth," he said.

I glared at him and didn't bother with pleasantries. "I'm not interested."

I was pretty sure he called me a name under his breath, but I was beyond caring. He was right. I was a bitch.

John deserved better than me.

But you know what? I deserved better than Cole.

I'd lost count of how many shots I'd taken, but eventually numbness settled over me. I had no idea how I was going to get home.

Actually, I couldn't go home.

I started giggling.

I couldn't even go to my own damn home. John didn't want me there, and he deserved some space from me after what he'd found out. I was homeless and drunk and single.

I'd have to deal with a whole bunch of shit in the morning, but tonight…

Tonight, I was going to dwell in the numbness. I was going to allow myself this one night to forget about everything.

The bartender shot me a strange look as I giggled by myself on a barstool, but I didn't care. Drunken Lucy found the whole situation highly funny.

I saw some bills hit the counter in front of me, appearing as if raining down from the heavens. As I looked up toward the sky to find the source of the raining money, someone grabbed me roughly around the waist and hauled me off the barstool. The scent of Cole Benson assaulted my senses with a vengeance.

"What the hell do you want?" I slurred.

"You're drunk." Cole gazed at me in surprise. We were moving, but I didn't feel my legs walking.

"What the fuck did you expect?"

I heard someone protest, "Leave her alone!"

"She's with me," Cole said over his shoulder, and then the warm California air hit my face.

"Where are you taking me?" I asked.

Cole didn't answer as he dragged me toward his car. He pushed me into the passenger seat and leaned around me to fasten my seatbelt. I accidentally breathed in his scent as he passed in front of me, and even through the haze of tequila, I felt the pang of heartbreak.

That scent represented lust and possibilities, and both were shot to hell forever where Cole Benson was concerned. He was playing some game, and I couldn't be a pawn anymore.

He walked in front of the car and then got into the driver's seat. He fired up the engine, and every movement seemed to be happening with a blurred shadow following it. I watched in silence as he drove, pushing out the painful memories of the last time we'd been in his car together.

"Who was she?" I spat out bitterly.

"Is this really a conversation you want to have when you're drunk?"

I pursed my lips and looked out the window. Asshole.

I may have muttered the insult aloud. He didn't bother with denial; instead, he remained silent as we drove on toward some unknown destination.

The urge to break the seal, so to speak, suddenly overwhelmed me at about the same time my stomach started to turn on me.

"I have to pee. Or puke."

"If you do either of those things in my car, you'll be cleaning it in the morning."

"Fuck you, Cole Benson."

He smirked. "Can you wait three minutes? We're almost there."

I exhaled noisily in frustration. I couldn't stop my knee from bouncing up and down as I did my best to hold it.

"Where?"

"My hotel."

"Cole, I don't want to go to your hotel."

"Too bad."

"I don't even want to be in the same room as you."

"Too bad."

"I hate you."

"I don't doubt it. You'll get over it."

"God, you're an asshole."

"An asshole who's taking care of your drunk ass, Ms. Cleary. An asshole who's presenting you with a ten thousand dollar check tomorrow, so you may want to drink some water so you're not sporting an epic hangover in the morning."

"A ten thousand dollar check?" I looked over at Cole. "I won?"

"Congratulations, Assistant of the Year." He glanced in my direction with a wry smile.

"Are you serious right now?"

"I am," he said.

Holy shit. I hoped to God I remembered this conversation in the morning.

"And I just want to reiterate that you winning this award has nothing to do with the fact that we've been sleeping together."

I glared at him, unable to think up a witty response. I was certain one would come to me much later. It always did after the fact.

We pulled up in front of the Ritz-Carlton.

"Fucking Ritz," I muttered petulantly. Cole could've stayed anywhere he wanted, and of course he chose a five-star hotel for his extended stay before he settled into a new home. Of course he could afford such a luxury while his now homeless assistant was desperate for the huge bonus offered by the Assistant of the Year award. He probably spent the same amount in a week at the Ritz while I clipped coupons for Greek yogurt and frozen pizza.

My bitterness only reminded me how drunk I actually was. Cole's money had never been an issue for me before. He deserved to spend it however he wanted.

Cole got out of the driver's seat and tossed his keys to the valet before making his way around to my door to help me out.

As much as I wanted to stand on my own two feet, especially to assert my independence after leaving my husband, I actually did need Cole to steady me. The tequila shots I'd taken so quickly that I'd lost count of them were catching up with me.

He snaked his arm around my waist, and I tumbled into him.

As much as I hated his guts, I loved how I felt there in his arms. I loved his scent. I loved his warmth. I loved his strength.

I loved him.

It just took leaving my husband, catching Cole with another woman, drinking too much tequila, and ultimately being rescued by Cole for me to realize it.

The realization didn't mix well with the tequila, unfortunately. I bent over a bush and promptly expelled the poisonous liquid from my system.

I expected Cole to jump back in disgust, but instead he rubbed my back while I vomited. I felt better once I was done, and reality was hitting me hard.

I wiped my mouth with the back of my hand and shot an embarrassed look at Cole.

"You okay?" he asked.

I nodded. I was fine, just totally drained.

He held out his hand to me. "Then let's get you up to bed."

As much as I wanted to protest, the need to use the restroom and then just lie down and go to sleep was far stronger. I took his big, warm hand in mine and allowed him to lead me to the elevator, up to the top floor—of course—and into his hotel room.

Chapter Twenty-Eight

When I woke the next morning, I was epically confused.

I didn't immediately know where I was. I couldn't remember how I got there. And I had very little recollection of the events that transpired the night before.

Most of it was blocked by the intense, splitting throb that knifed through my brain and the nauseating ache in my belly. It only took me a second to realize I was in a hotel room. The drapes did their job blocking out daylight, but I could tell it was morning by the glow of light peeking around the edges. I turned in the bed and found Cole asleep beside me, and the previous night came back in a rush of traumatic and vile recollections.

I'd caught him with another woman.

Was it wrong of me to be supremely offended? Was it wrong of me to feel betrayed when I myself went home to another man every single night?

It didn't feel wrong. It did, however, feel like the bottom level of hell, especially mixed with a still drunken sensation and the beginnings of an epic hangover.

"Shit," I muttered.

Cole turned toward me. "Good morning, sunshine."

I glared at him. "Screw you."

"Oh, my darling, don't you wish that's how we could start the day? Unfortunately, I have a meeting to get to."

The fact that he was so drop-dead gorgeous and completely pulled together seconds after waking up did nothing but piss me right off. I hopped out of bed, ready to point fingers and throw hateful words at him.

But the tequila stopped me cold.

"Fuck!" I yelled.

"I already told you, Ms. Cleary. Not now. I have to prepare for the Assistant of the Year awards ceremony."

"God, I hate you with a burning vengeance."

"That's sweet of you to say. I hope you feel the same way after you use the restroom and find everything you need to get ready for the day thanks to the help of the hotel concierge. We'll be leaving in an hour." He tossed the covers off of himself and stood from the bed. He stretched lazily in nothing but his boxer briefs. I was torn between running toward him to drop kick him or to jump in his arms.

I hated him. I loved him.

I hated that I loved him.

I didn't do any of that, though. Instead, I said, "You think I'm going into work with you today?"

"I think you don't have much of a choice."

He was right. God DAMMIT, he was right.

I was stuck. I needed to go to work to claim my award. I could quit after the check was deposited. There was no way I was going to work with the asshole standing in front of me. I couldn't even look at him without wanting to throw up.

Well, that may have been because of the tequila, but I was blaming him.

Where the fuck did he get off sleeping with another woman?

My anger took hold of me once again. I huffed out some non-response and turned on my heel toward the restroom.

I rolled my eyes childishly as I looked around. He'd thought of everything. Literally not one single detail was left unattended, from a toothbrush and toothpaste to undergarments and a brand new dress with matching heels in my size.

He'd even left a bottle of water and a small bottle of ibuprofen. I greedily sucked down a few pills to help stave off the pounding in my skull.

I should've been appreciative. He was literally saving my ass on potentially the biggest day of my entire career, but instead of appreciation, I felt frustration and hatred.

The words Luke—the random guy who had befriended me at the conference in New York—had said to me on the bench popped suddenly into my mind.

His words replayed over and over as I undressed and got into the shower. They played while I squirted some of Cole's shower gel onto a loofah. He'd left a bottle of girly shower gel, but my hand automatically reached for his instead.

Luke's words continued to play while I scrubbed shampoo through my hair and then rinsed. They played as I toweled off, and they played as I did my make-up, dried my hair, and put on the lovely black and white dress Cole had chosen for me. They played as I slipped my feet into the heels, and they played again when I fastened the earrings and the necklace that were on the counter—the jewelry that, incidentally, matched perfectly with the dress.

Luke's words became a song chanting through my head.

"When you feel so much passion for someone, it's easy for the lines between love and hate to blur."

I stared at myself in the mirror as I tried to piece together my emotions enough to make sense of them.

I knew who I used to be. I used to be Lucy Cleary. Wife of John Cleary. Assistant to the CEO of Benson Industries. A good girl who had turned into a good woman who planned life carefully and worked hard.

But now as I stared at my own reflection, I saw a passionate and confused woman who no longer knew what she wanted. A cheater. An adulterer. A person who acted on impulse and emotion instead of strategy and logic.

I wasn't sure who I was anymore. Maybe I never was that other person. Maybe deep down I was always this immoral person incapable of redemption.

Or maybe the realizations I was having that morning meant that I was more capable of redemption than I thought.

John gave up on me because I'd slept with another man. Was I a complete hypocrite to give up on Cole because he'd slept with another woman? Or was the bigger issue the fact that I didn't know how many women Cole had on the side?

Would I ever be able to trust him? And worse, would he ever be able to trust me?

This is what came from affairs and cheating. John was hurt. I was hurt.

But was Cole hurt?

I didn't have answers, but I did have to get my ass moving before he left without me. My car was still at the bar a few blocks from the office. I'd easily be able to pick it up and head home later that night.

Home. I smiled sadly at the girl in the mirror. I couldn't go home to the apartment I shared with my husband. He deserved some time to himself.

I didn't really have a home anymore. But I did have ten thousand dollars coming to me that would help me to find one.

I'd earmarked the money for so many other things, but it seemed that now I didn't have much choice in how I was going to spend it.

I took a deep breath, forced myself to smile at the girl in the mirror, and headed back out to Cole.

"You're stunning," he said, his eyes scanning me appreciatively from where he sat on a small couch across the room with his laptop perched across his legs. Why did my heart feel like it was breaking in my chest the second my eyes landed on him sitting there in all his achingly handsome glory?

"Thanks," I mumbled, no longer sure how to handle him. My mind jumbled with relentless questions. Was I supposed to allow him to flirt with me? Was I supposed to flirt back?

And why the hell did every nerve in my body seem to light up when his eyes met mine? Why did the ache between my legs intensify the second my ears picked up on the deep timber of his voice?

"Did you find everything you needed in there?" he asked, trying to make conversation as he snapped his laptop closed and set it on the table in front of him.

"I did. Thank you." My words weren't enough to truly thank him for the effort he'd put forth to make me comfortable that morning, but this situation tossed me headfirst into uncharted territory.

"Your car is at the office and your keys are on your desk."

He really had actually thought of everything.

"Thank you."

"Can we talk before we go?" he hedged, his eyes on me.

I shrugged and looked out the window. "It's your hotel room."

"Sit." The command in his voice had me sitting on the chair across from him. "I'm sorry for what you saw last night."

He was sorry for *what I saw*? He wasn't sorry for what he did?

He continued before I had a chance to open my mouth to respond. "I turned to a friend who…let's just say she makes herself available whenever I call. It was wrong of me and I apologize."

Well shit.

I had to remember when I got to the office to mark down this as the first day in history that Cole Benson actually admitted to doing something wrong. I was about to interject a sarcastic comment along those lines when his next words stopped me cold in my tracks.

"I'm going to say this, and I don't want you to respond. I don't want you to interrupt. I don't want you to stop me. I want you to think about my words today, and at the end of the day, we can talk. But after I say this, we are going to leave separately, and my words are going to hang in the air between us. I've ordered a car for you so we don't show up at work together. I have an out of office meeting this morning, and I'll be in a little after ten. The awards ceremony is at eleven. Do you have any questions?"

I shook my head, floored at the actual amount of thought he'd put into his speech and curious as to what the hell he was about to say.

He stood and faced the window rather than me. He was quiet for a brief moment, and then he took a deep breath, turned toward me, and spoke the words that would linger in my mind for the rest of the day—if not much, much longer than that.

"Lucy, I like you. A lot. I more than *like* you, if I'm being honest. I don't know what this is. I don't know what I'm feeling, but I know it's powerful. And that doesn't happen to me. I don't get involved in committed relationships because—are you ready for this?—because the last time I was in one, she cheated on me. It broke my fucking heart and turned me into a cold bastard who decided that calling a random blonde whose name I wouldn't remember in the morning was easier than having actual feelings for someone."

He stopped for a moment to pick up his laptop and set it in his bag. I wanted to interject, to respond, to say something—anything—but I couldn't, because I promised I wouldn't.

I could feel my heart breaking all over again, and I was powerless to fix any of it.

He picked up his bag and started for the door. He rested his fingers on the handle and turned back to me.

"So if you think I betrayed you because I slept with Heidi last night, you're wrong. I didn't betray you, and I don't owe you anything—including an explanation. But here it is: I was lashing out because I'm sick of your game. We can't label this as exclusive because you are *married*. You're stringing me along. You've always got an excuse why you can't talk to your husband, and I fucking hate being the third wheel in your marriage. I know what it's like to be in John's shoes, and that's why I stayed the hell away from you until I couldn't anymore. There are two losers in this, Lucy, and neither one is you. So make your decision, think it through, choose wisely, man the fuck up, and be honest."

With that, he opened the door and walked out.

It clicked shut behind him with a hollowness that resounded loudly in my heart.

I stared at the door he'd disappeared through for a good three minutes, his words fresh in my mind. I finally drew in a breath, grabbed my purse, and headed down for the car Cole had called to take me to work.

Chapter Twenty-Nine

Cole was usually already in his office by the time I got to work, so it was strange to get in before him. I sat at my desk and powered on my computer, hoping to be able to concentrate on work.

I checked my phone while I waited for my computer. In the haze of my hangover, getting ready in record time, and being seriously put in my place by Cole, I hadn't even thought to look at it to see if John had tried to call.

He hadn't. I wasn't surprised.

He was hurt, and I didn't blame him. I'd been the one to hurt him, and it was only fair for me to leave it up to him to make contact. I supposed I'd need to stop home at some point in the short term, if nothing else to get some of my things. Cole had been nice enough to provide what I needed that morning, but I couldn't rely on him.

In the long term, I'd need to move out of the apartment I shared with John. We'd need to talk, to separate our things, to move forward with our divorce.

But all of that could wait for a bit. Our marriage was over, but John deserved the time to process my confession from the night before.

When my computer was finally on and I'd pulled up my email, I found one from John. It had been sent a little after two in the morning. My heart raced and tears heated my eyes the second I saw his name. I clicked it immediately and began to read.

Lucy,

I don't want to talk to you. I don't want to see you. I'm going to talk to apartment management today to see if we can break our lease. I'm looking into a divorce lawyer. You keep what's yours. I don't want any of it anyway. Come get what you want, but please don't be at the apartment after 7:00 tonight.

John

I read it through three times, looking for hints into his mental state, but other than the fact that he clearly hated me, he was pretty straightforward.

I swiped at a tear that had escaped from my eye and forced myself to focus on work, but it was largely futile. I gathered data for the MTC account, but I couldn't move forward with any of my ideas until I met with Cole.

I hated depending on the men in my life, and it seemed like a vicious cycle. First I depended on John to help me with my family, and then I depended on Cole to take care of me the night before and now with the project.

I needed independence.

It was that realization that made me think perhaps my very best option was to get as far away from Cole as I could.

I needed time to move forward in order to heal. I needed to be on my own for a while. I needed to reconnect with Lucy—not the wife, not the cheater, not the assistant, not the confused woman. Just Lucy.

It was time to just be on my own for a while.

The thought of being away from Cole ripped my heart in half.

It was a sad realization to have on the day I was going to be named Assistant of the Year, but I couldn't see any other way. I knew what I had to do.

I shook my head to clear it and then drafted the email I'd been thinking about all morning. I wasn't sure if I'd actually send it, but I had it there for insurance.

I chickened out of bringing my questions to Cole and chose to email him about the MTC account. It would be easier to handle it over email than to have to meet face-to-face, especially with everything hanging in the air. I couldn't let our personal relationship affect my work. It wasn't professional, and it certainly wasn't how the Assistant of the Year should act.

When Cole got in a little after ten, he kept his head down as he walked toward his office. I didn't bother to look up from my computer anyway.

I didn't know what I was going to say to him at the end of the day, if anything. He'd told me to make a decision.

I thought about that beautiful beach house he'd bought. We could share it. We could play house and make love and look toward our future together.

There was so much about Cole I was sure I loved, and there were probably equal parts that I hated. I knew we had a crazy and intense passion I'd never felt for anyone before him.

But if I was going to be in a relationship with someone, it couldn't start with betrayal on top of betrayal. Passion wasn't enough to sustain a relationship.

We both needed to be free and clear to begin a relationship built on an honest and trustworthy foundation, and we didn't have that—not if I was still married, and not if he was sleeping with Heidi.

My office phone rang. "Hello?" I answered.

"Send out a staff-wide memo from me that the Assistant of the Year will be named in thirty minutes in Training Room A. Mark it high importance."

"Yes, sir."

I felt stupid drafting an invitation to the entire staff for an awards ceremony that honored me, but at least I wasn't signing my name to it.

When Cole headed to the training room a few minutes later to get ready for the ceremony, he kept his head down. I pretended not to look up at him, but I couldn't help it. He was achingly beautiful in his navy suit. His hair was a mess, and I wanted to run my fingers through it to smooth it down. He hadn't shaved, and I could still feel his sexy scruff scratching the sensitive skin by my mouth when he kissed me.

I missed him already, and I hadn't even left him yet.

But I was going to. I didn't have a choice. Cole had this way of sliding right past my better judgment, and if my goal was truly to get to know myself again, to be an independent woman who could get by without leaning on the men around her, then I needed to cut him out of my life.

I closed my eyes when I felt the stinging. I wouldn't cry.

I headed over five minutes before the ceremony was set to begin. Training Room A was the room where the majority of staff development took place. It was set up like a lecture room with a small stage in the front and rows of seats facing it. The room could hold over a hundred people, and it was already filling up with coworkers eager to take a short break from their work to grab some of the refreshments at the back of the room and watch one of their own receive a nice bonus.

Three chairs were set up at the front of the room, and two of them were occupied by the other ladies who I was up against for the award—Mary and Jasmine.

I looked around the crowded room. My nerves calmed the moment I spotted Cole. He was talking to the managers of several departments, and his eyes flickered in my direction. I stood rooted to my spot for a moment, thinking about everything that had happened in a relatively short time. My heart ached as I stared at him.

This was going to be so much harder than I thought.

He turned back to his colleagues, and my legs somehow carried me to the chair waiting for me at the front of the room. Mary and Jasmine were making small talk, and they included me in their conversation. But I couldn't concentrate.

Not when I knew what I had to do.

Cole made his way to the podium just a few feet away from the three of us. I closed my eyes briefly as a hint of his scent floated through the air toward me.

I'd never forget it.

All of our coworkers took their seats, and then Cole began to speak.

"As you know, the Assistant of the Year ceremony was instated by my father several years ago. It was his idea to attach a rather attractive bonus to the award as a way to thank those who really keep our company afloat. I can't say I disagree with my father, but I, along with several other managers, have decided to completely restructure the award this year."

A few murmurs rose up from the crowd, and my heart started pounding with anxiety. Since he'd spilled the beans the night before that I was the winner of the award, I'd been counting on the bonus. Ten thousand dollars was everything to me, especially since John deserved the apartment and I had nowhere to live.

But they'd restructured the award?

"This year's nominees are all very deserving. Mary Banuelos, assistant to Brandon Jeffries, has been with Benson Industries for nine years. Mr. Jeffries has described her as a valuable asset to the entire company, not just to the marketing division. Jasmine Capone, assistant to Kenneth Newlon, has been here for five years. Mr. Newlon has said that the HR department wouldn't run without her. In fact, he told us that she took a well-deserved vacation last year, and the entire department was in complete disarray until she returned." The group who had gathered reacted with a laugh.

He was lighter somehow. He'd always been so professional, but he was cracking jokes and making the crowd laugh. I had to wonder if it had something to do with waking up next to me that morning. I brushed the ridiculously arrogant thought away.

I knew he was going to say a little something about me next, and nerves knotted my stomach. "And finally, Lucy Cleary has been the assistant to the CEO for six years. First she worked with my father, and now with me, and I can honestly say that without her, my transition into CEO of this company wouldn't have been so smooth. She keeps the entire company up and running on a daily basis, and I've just piled more work on top of her after one of our newest acquisitions personally requested her."

He turned back to look at me with a bright smile that just about killed what was left of my soul.

He glanced at Mary and Jasmine, too, but that smile was just for me.

"After much deliberation, the managers and I have arrived at this year's recipient." My heart pounded wildly. "But first, let me explain the restructure."

Jasmine twitched nervously beside me, as did Mary beside her.

"The ten thousand dollar bonus attached to this award certainly makes it high stakes, and in my talks with all of the managers, we agree that all assistants are valuable to this company. All assistants deserve something extra for the long hours they put in. And so, for the first time ever, just like their higher-ups already do, all assistants will be receiving bonuses this year. The structure will depend on the number of years the assistant has been employed with Benson Industries."

The crowd cheered.

"The three ladies sitting behind me, though, will receive a bigger bonus. Benson had its best quarter ever, and I strongly feel that rewarding our own will lead us to even better quarters in the future. We discussed the qualifications of each nominee at length, and while they're all deserving, only one of them can be named Assistant of the Year. There isn't a second place or a third place, so both of the runners-up will receive a five thousand dollar bonus."

Another cheer rose up from the crowd. Cole's speech was definitely winning him fans. He was just steps away from physically throwing money out at his underlings, and they were eating it up.

Mary, Jasmine, and I all looked at each other with shock. That meant that the lowest amount we could possibly leave with was five thousand dollars.

"Our winner will receive the ten thousand dollars that has always been associated with this award, but in addition to that, she will receive two additional weeks of paid vacation per year and a ten percent raise."

Holy shit. I thought the ten thousand was a generous reward, but this…this was unexpected.

This also threw a bit of a wrench into my plans.

"And now I'd like to announce our winner. I can't say enough about what a professional and qualified recipient we have this year. She's dedicated. She's skilled. She's extraordinary, and I'm a lucky, lucky man that I get to call her my assistant. Congratulations, Lucy Cleary."

My coworkers in the crowd cheered for me, and I stood from my chair, feigning shock by putting my hand over my mouth. Truthfully, I was a bit shocked at the additions to the award, but he'd already told me I was the winner.

The money was important. The extra vacation time was excellent. The raise was fantastic. Hearing my name was wonderful, but the compliments that came out of his mouth regarding my performance meant so much more to me. Especially after the way he'd treated me the first month we'd worked together.

Cole came over to me with a big smile and shook my hand. He yanked on my hand and pulled me into a brief, work-appropriate hug.

I had to admit that being in his arms felt all sorts of right. I breathed him in, wanting this moment to last forever. I sighed contentedly, wishing with everything inside of me that he'd never let me go.

But he did. We were on a stage in front of all the people who worked for him, after all.

I took a deep breath and made my way to the microphone. "Thank you," I started. I turned back to Cole, who stood a few feet behind me. He nodded encouragingly. "I really can't thank you enough for this award. I loved working with your father for so many years, and I've learned so much from you since you took over. We've had our ups and downs, but it's been a pleasure working with you."

I stepped away from the microphone, not sure what else I was supposed to say. I stood to the side while Cole stepped back up and told everyone to get back to work, earning himself another laugh from the crowd—and clearly winning all sorts of fans in the process.

The crowd dispersed, and Cole stood in front of Mary, Jasmine, and me. "Your bonus will be in your next check. HR was notified of the bonuses and the payment has already been processed. Congratulations, ladies. You all deserve it." Mary and Jasmine gushed over him for a moment, and I hung back just a bit.

He turned to leave, glanced at his watch, and turned back to me. "Ms. Cleary, I need to meet with you over lunch in an hour."

I nodded, and then he left. I mingled with a few of my coworkers who congratulated me, but my mind was on my lunch meeting with Cole. He'd said we would talk at the end of the day, so this had to be work-related, not personal.

The resident historian, Rebecca, took my photo to put in the next company newsletter.

And then it was all over.

I headed back to my desk ten grand richer. I didn't really suppose it was going to make me work any harder since I already considered myself a hard worker, but I was definitely grateful for it.

I checked my messages, sent the email I'd drafted earlier that morning, and then headed to Cole's office for lunch. I knocked on the door.

"Yes?" he called.

I pushed the door open. "You wanted to see me?"

"Close the door and sit," he said. I did as he requested. He tapped a few more keys on his computer and then turned toward me.

He folded his hands in front of him before his eyes met mine. "I know I said we'd reconvene at the end of the day, but I can't take the waiting. I hate this shit. This is why I don't do relationships."

"I've thought about what you said all morning."

"And?"

"And one thing really stuck out to me."

"What's that?"

"You said I've been stringing you along, but there's something you don't know."

His eyes narrowed.

"I told John last night. I told him everything before I came here to see you."

His eyes lit up. "You did?"

I nodded. "I did. And then I walked in on you with some tramp."

He averted his eyes to the window, his gaze falling over downtown Los Angeles. "I can't change what happened."

"No, you can't. And I can't, either."

"So that's it." He stood and walked around his desk, leaning against it beside me. I knew he wanted me to stand and walk into his arms. "It's over with John, and we can move forward."

"It's not that simple."

He folded his arms across his chest. "Of course it is."

I shook my head. "No, it's not. John isn't what I want, and you *are* what I want, but I can't just jump from one man to the next."

"So we'll take our time."

"No, Cole. You don't get it." I stood up and walked over to the window.

I was going to miss this view.

"Then explain it to me. Help me to understand." His voice took on an edge of anxiety, and it shredded the remains of my already broken heart.

I turned back to Cole. "I need to be on my own. I can't be in a relationship that started on a lie."

"What we have didn't start on a lie." He was arguing, looking for a loophole. But my mind was made up.

"Well then it isn't right for me to start something that could grow into something potentially very serious while I'm still married."

"Then we wait. Divorces can't take that long, can they?"

"Six months minimum in California."

He glanced away from me, somehow sealing in my mind that I'd made the right decision. He digested the idea of waiting six months for me. He knew if he was going to do that, there'd be no more random blondes that he could screw in his desk chair. He'd be committed to a memory until I was free to be with him, and I was sure that wasn't how he envisioned his future.

He drew in a long breath before looking at me again. "Lucy, what are you saying?"

"Mr. Benson, thank you for the opportunity to work with you. Thank you for the Assistant of the Year bonus. Thank you for giving me a chance with MTC, and thank you for trusting me with confidential files and trusted information." His eyes grew wide with horror as I spoke. He knew where I was going with this, and my voice shook as I got to the words that I knew would break both of our hearts. "Thank you for everything. I quit."

I turned and walked toward his door. I felt his eyes on me the entire way, but I couldn't seem to stop my shaking legs from taking me to my desk, where I grabbed my purse out of my bottom drawer, logged off my computer for the last time, and headed toward the elevator.

Chapter Thirty

I sat in my car with no real plan, staring at the steering wheel in a daze. I half expected Cole to come after me. I wasn't sure if I wanted him to or if I just wanted him to leave me alone.

That's a lie.

I wanted him to chase me down and fight for me. I wanted it with every fiber of my being.

But I knew he wouldn't. He'd been pretty clear that morning. He was done playing games. I had no idea what sort of mess I'd left behind. He'd been honest with his feelings for me, and I'd still walked.

What was done was done. I'd acted impulsively for too long, and it was time to get a plan together and move on with my life.

The events of the past twelve hours hadn't quite hit me yet, but I had a feeling that once they did, the emotions would be overwhelming.

I called Kaylee while I sat numbly in the parking lot.

"Hey, Luce." Her voice was tired.

"You need some help with that little girl?" I asked, faking enthusiasm.

"Sure, I could use some help. Don't you have to work?"

"It's a long story."

"Come on over." I knew my sister. She'd never come out and ask for help directly. She'd only take it if it was offered. And I was out of a job and essentially homeless.

I was hoping she'd be interested in a mutually beneficial arrangement. Maybe she'd let me stay with them to help out with Madi while she focused on helping her husband on his road to recovery.

"I'll be there in a couple of hours."

I started the car and glanced up toward Cole's office window. I couldn't see in with the bright sunlight, but I imagined him standing in his window watching me. I imagined our eyes met for one last long glance, and I imagined the pain in his matching the pain in mine.

I tore my gaze from the window and touched my fingers to my lips. I imagined it meant I was giving him a secret kiss, and I closed my eyes for a brief moment before taking a deep breath and heading toward my apartment.

Once I got "home," I packed my suitcase with as many clothes as I could fit. It was early-afternoon, so I had all the time I wanted, really—but I didn't dawdle.

After I brought my clothes and bags to my car, I went back in to leave a note for John. Before I wrote the note, I looked around the apartment that I'd decorated with my husband. I took a moment in each room, allowing the memories to wash over me.

As much as I'd felt neglected recently—and for much of our marriage—it hadn't always been that way. As I walked through the family room, I heard our shared laughter at our favorite sitcom. In the kitchen, I smelled John's burnt toast the morning after we'd moved into this apartment. Down the hallway, I saw us making love up against the wall one night when we hadn't made it to the bedroom—the night we'd gotten engaged.

When I walked into the office, though, I remembered sitting in the chair, cheating on my husband as I listened to the voice of another man guide me to climax.

When I walked into the bedroom, the memory that hit me was the night before.

This wasn't how I ever imagined it.

I always thought marriage was once and forever, but that was before I married the wrong man.

Hindsight makes everything so much easier. It was easy to look back and say he'd been wrong for me, but I hadn't seen the signs when we'd been dating. I hadn't expected to one day wake up and realize that I didn't love him anymore.

I hadn't expected to fall so hard for another man.

And I never expected to fall into an affair.

It just wasn't me. It wasn't my character. It wasn't what I knew and it wasn't where I came from.

Yet I'd done it.

Everyone makes mistakes, but I couldn't look at my time with Cole and call it a *mistake*. That would be a bigger lie than my "happy" marriage had been.

My real mistake had been marrying John. It had been staying with someone when I wasn't happy because I was too complacent to do anything about it.

I walked back through the apartment, realizing that except for my clothes and a few pictures, there wasn't really anything I wanted. Even the desk chair that I'd so desperately had to have just seemed tainted now.

I pulled the paper and pen from the drawer in the kitchen and started writing.

John,

I stopped by to get my clothes. If there's anything here you want, you can have it. I'll be back next week sometime to get the rest of my things. If there's anything you don't want me to take, just mark it.

I know you don't want to talk to me, and I understand. I'm sorry I hurt you. I'm sorry for the way things turned out. I'm sorry I wasn't a better wife to you. You deserve better than me, and I hope you find it.

I'll miss you.

Lucy

I read my note over before leaving it on the counter. I wanted to apologize for cheating on him, but it was a sticky situation. I wasn't sorry I slept with Cole, but I was sorry that John had gotten hurt because of it.

I drove to my sister's house in complete silence. I was so lost in my thoughts that I hadn't even realized I never turned on the radio.

Instead, I thought about all that had transpired over the past few weeks. I thought back to Cole's first day as my boss, to our New York trip, to Cole's softer side that emerged so rarely.

I thought about John and the good times we'd had once upon a time.

And I thought a lot about the future. I wasn't sure where I was going or what I'd do, but I was sure that for the first time in a long time, I was free.

"What's going on?" Kaylee asked when she opened the door.

I couldn't help it. I burst into tears.

My sister limped toward me and did her best to pull me into a hug despite her broken ribs and arm. She gasped when she raised her arm.

"Stop," I said through my tears. "I should be the one hugging you."

"Whatever it is, it'll be okay. If Kev and I could survive the accident, you can survive this."

I nodded and forced a shaky breath. "You're right."

We walked into her house and she gingerly lay back on the couch while I collapsed dramatically in her overstuffed armchair.

"Talk to me, Luce."

"I left John last night."

She sat up and winced. "Oh my God. For your boss?"

I shook my head as tears filled my eyes again. "No. I left him, too. And I quit my job."

"Holy shit!"

"I know. I'm homeless, jobless, and manless."

"You're not homeless. You'll stay here with us."

"I thought I could help out with Madi while you go back and forth to the hospital and while you get better yourself. I should've offered before all of this anyway."

"Stop it. You have a life and I get it."

"Kay, I'll pay you rent. I'll pay for my food. I just need a little time to figure this out."

"You take as much time as you need. Don't be ridiculous. You can stay as long as you want rent-free." She smiled brightly, as if that would make it all better.

"Thank you."

"If you can't lean on family when you need them, who can you lean on?"

"How are you feeling?" I asked, changing the subject.

"Nice try. Talk to me. What happened?" I was quiet for a few seconds, trying to figure out where to even start. "Did you sleep with your boss?" she asked before I could form my words.

I nodded.

"Oh my word, this is juicy. Spill it. All of it. Now."

I giggled. I couldn't help it.

She rolled her eyes. "Look, I'm currently a housewife who is toting a child to school in between visits to the hospital. I need something spicy. My soaps and reality television just aren't hitting the raunch factor like they used to."

"Glad I can be of service," I said dryly.

"You know what I mean. Now start at the beginning and leave nothing out."

I started from the day I met Cole and ended with that morning, and she listened attentively and sympathetically.

I was so glad I'd turned to my sister. Anyone else would've given me exactly what I deserved, but not Kaylee. She didn't judge me. She was on my side.

Despite my shortcomings and the complete disaster I'd made of my life, my sister was going to help me figure out where the hell I was supposed to go from here.

When Madi got home from school, she was thrilled that I was going to be staying with them for a while. I was more grateful than ever for a supportive and loving family.

Later that night after we tucked Madi into bed, I checked my personal email. I had a reply to the email I'd sent right before I quit.

Lucy,

Thanks for getting in touch. I'm so sorry about what happened. I can offer you a part-time, work from home position as a contractor. Is that something you'd be interested in? If you are, we can work out specifics in regard to your duties and pay. I know what an asset you were to Benson, and I'd prefer not to let you get away from MTC. Let's talk soon.

L. Mathers

I read his reply twice before I believed the words. Lincoln was offering me a part-time position. It was more than I could've hoped for. I'd explained to him that I was quitting my job because of some personal issues but that I was invested in his company and I still wanted to work with him. I told him I wouldn't be in or around the city but that I could do everything online.

The best-case scenario was him offering me a position to work from home—especially since I knew Cole would potentially show up at MTC's offices. I didn't want to risk running into him.

I'd half expected him to call by now, or maybe to send a text. To try to make some sort of contact with me. I'd be lying if I said I wasn't disappointed that he hadn't fought for me, but it was a selfish and narcissistic thought. I'd been the one to walk out, and my actions had made it pretty clear that I wanted to be left alone.

So if I'd been the one to make this grand decision, why was I the one crying myself to sleep that night as I thought about Cole and all I'd lost in the past twenty-four hours?

Chapter Thirty-One

The first week was the hardest.

That's what I kept telling myself. If I could just make it through that first week, those seven long days, those one hundred sixty-eight hours, I'd be okay.

I forced myself to focus on one task at a time. Get Madi to school while Kaylee drove to the hospital. Take a shower. Feed myself.

Stay off of my phone since I kept staring at it like it might ring.

It didn't. I wasn't sure why I was disappointed every time it didn't ring.

I wasn't sure why I was surprised that Cole didn't put forth any sort of effort to get in touch.

I'd left him. I'd been the one to end things. I'd been the one to quit.

I'd been the stupid one.

I allowed myself to dwell only when I was alone. When I was around my sister and my niece, I put on my brave face.

But when night rolled around and I lay in bed alone, I thought about Cole. My chest heaved with sadness as I wept. My heart physically ached from the wreckage. My stomach hurt. My head hurt.

Everything hurt.

That first week on my own bled slowly into two, and it wasn't any easier when two bled into three.

When one month had passed, the hole in my heart felt bigger than ever.

The whole point of leaving and venturing off on my own was to find myself. Instead, after that first month, I realized that I'd left my entire heart back in Cole's capable hands. And I was having a hard time surviving without that very important piece of myself.

When Madi was at school and Kaylee was visiting her husband, I focused on my new job. Lincoln had met me halfway for dinner one night, and we worked out the details of my contract.

I told him everything. It probably wasn't the most professional way to begin a business relationship, but Lincoln was one of the few people who knew both Cole and me. Besides, he'd brought his wife, Alexis, along, and the two of them had been surprisingly parental.

Neither of them had been surprised that there was something between Cole and me, even though at the time there hadn't been.

I thought back to the night of the MTC dinner. Cole had admitted that he'd wanted me that night after the fact, and I remembered a very steamy elevator ride where everything and nothing had simultaneously changed.

I immersed myself in work and in helping Kaylee. I forced my smile for Madi. I helped make dinner and do the dishes, but it was all mechanical movements used to bury my feelings.

Because if I let myself think about him—even just for a second—I lost another little piece of myself.

In the blur of the first few weeks that I'd been at Kaylee's, I'd received an email from John.

Lucy,

I've researched divorce and we qualify for a Summary Dissolution since we don't own any property or have any kids. It's quick and easy and it's my preference to handle it this way. We both need to fill out paperwork. I'll complete my portion and leave it on the kitchen counter. We'll need to meet at the county courthouse to file the paperwork, and then it's a six month waiting period. The sooner we can take care of this, the better.

John

I read his email three times.

Quick and easy.

Those were two words that definitely didn't describe any part of divorce. Nothing about this was easy. It wasn't like I had Cole just waiting in the wings for me. It wasn't like I had planned this when we'd gotten married.

It just gave me one more thing to cry over.

I emailed him back to set up a time to meet. Three weeks after John had found out that I had been sleeping with my boss, I ventured out of Kaylee's house to complete the paperwork at the apartment John and I once shared. I took the paperwork to meet him at the courthouse.

I glanced around the parking lot for his car, but I didn't see it. I read through the paperwork one more time, and everything looked good. Kaylee had advised me to contact a lawyer, but I was with John on this one. The sooner we could take care of it, the better. I snapped pictures of the pages on my phone so I'd have a copy.

John pulled into the space next to mine, and I realized it was the first time I'd seen him since the night everything changed.

He had sunglasses on, so I couldn't immediately read him. His beard was a little more unkempt than usual.

I got out of my car, and he turned in my direction but didn't acknowledge me. I trailed him as we walked into the courthouse.

He took off his sunglasses, and the dark circles under his bloodshot eyes told me that he hadn't slept in a while. I supposed that's what being cheated on will do to a person.

I felt the stabbing pain of guilt as I stared at him, but I could offer him no comfort. It was no longer my place.

Instead, I handed him the paperwork with my signature. He searched the directory for where we needed to go, and I simply followed a few paces behind. It was the best I could do for something that was so totally my own fault.

Tears pricked my eyes as the clerk accepted our paperwork.

It was done.

We returned to our cars, not a single word spoken to each other in the twenty minutes we were forced to interact.

I wanted to hug him. I wanted to hold him and apologize and tell him how much I missed his friendship. I wanted to go to lunch and talk about everything—about where we went wrong and why I hadn't been the wife we both thought I would be.

But I didn't do any of that. I watched him get into his car. He paused and looked at me as if he might say something, but he didn't. Instead, he slid into the driver's seat and started his car. I was overcome with the feeling that our trip to the courthouse would be the last time I'd see John.

But before he closed his door, he turned toward me again.

"Can we talk?" I finally said across our cars, realizing that I needed to initiate the conversation. John had never been the initiator of any major conversation ever, so why should I expect that to change now?

He nodded behind his sunglasses, turned off his car, and got out.

He glanced down the block and pointed with his chin toward a restaurant up the street. "Want to grab lunch?"

"I'd love to."

We walked side by side, no words passing between us, and entered the restaurant. We remained silent until we were seated and had both perused the menu. Once we placed our orders, I finally broke the awkward tension.

"I'm so sorry, John," I said softly.

His eyes met mine for just a second before he pressed his lips together and looked away. "This sucks."

"I know."

"You think life is going to end up one way…" he trailed off.

I nodded. "I wish I could've been a better wife to you."

He didn't respond, but what was there to say? This was my idea, this chance for conversation, but I realized I had no idea what I actually wanted to say.

He finally took a deep breath. "I have to know how it happened." Some of the anger he'd felt the night he found out had dissipated in the weeks that had passed. His anger had turned into sadness—with maybe a touch of guilt.

"How what happened?" I asked cautiously.

"With Cole." He cleared his throat. "What made you…go to him?"

I shrugged, not sure how to put it into words and really not sure I wanted to talk about it with John. But he deserved to have his questions answered. "It was just this pull. I can't explain it. He had feelings for me and fought them because of you, but then he realized I wasn't happily married."

"Why weren't you happy?"

"Because you were always working. I tried to talk to you about it. I tried to get you to listen to me, to see that we had a problem. I couldn't get through to you."

"So it's my fault?"

I shook my head vigorously. "I accept full responsibility." We could play the blame game all day, but ultimately I was the one who had stepped outside of our marriage.

"How long were you…did you…?"

I blew out a breath. God, this was hard. "We first kissed in New York, but that was all."

I heard John's sharp intake of breath, but I plowed on. He wanted answers, and he deserved them.

"We weren't actually together until right after Kaylee and Kevin's accident. He was there for me when I really needed someone, but you were always at the office."

He nodded and stared down at the table. I let him think that through.

"Are you still with him?"

I shook my head, and he looked surprised. He seemed like he was about to ask more, but he didn't.

"I miss you," he finally said.

"I've missed you for a long time."

"I'm sorry."

"Me, too."

"We had some good times, though. Didn't we?"

I smiled. "We had a lot of good times."

"Remember that trip when we drove to Temecula to pick strawberries?"

I giggled. It was one of my favorite memories. "Select only the firmest, reddest berries," I said, mimicking our tour guide. It had been a long running joke between the two of us.

He allowed a small smile, the first I'd seen on him since before the night he'd found out about Cole and me.

Our meals arrived, and we both focused on our food for a while. We reminisced, and I felt some of the old warmth I'd always felt for John. I realized as we ate that I'd always love him. Our marriage was over—the paperwork we'd just filed would make sure of that—but the bond that we had through marriage would forever tie our hearts together.

The problem, though, and the reason why our marriage ultimately didn't work, was that the bonds that tied my heart to Cole's were far stronger.

We walked back to our cars.

"If there's anything you need at the apartment…" John trailed off.

I nodded. "Thank you."

He sighed. "I wish we could go back and I could listen to you when you tried to talk to me. I wish I hadn't been so wrapped up in work. It's pretty easy to see now that I put all my focus on the wrong damn thing."

"It's always easier to see it after the fact."

"Ain't that the damn truth?" He smiled sadly, and we looked at each other for an awkward moment. Was this where we shook hands? Hugged? In the old days, we would've kissed goodbye.

Not anymore.

We didn't touch. Instead, I offered a small wave. "Thanks for lunch."

He nodded, got into his car, and drove away.

Chapter Thirty-Two

SEVEN MONTHS LATER

"They look gorgeous," I giggled, holding up my drying nails that had been painted by a currently napping five-year-old.

"Oh, they really do. She's getting good at polishing," Kaylee said matter-of-factly.

Kevin walked into the room, glaring at both of us in jest as we laughed loudly. "Shh! Madi's sleeping! What time is her Christmas recital?" he asked for the tenth time.

"Six o'clock," we said in unison, and then we both giggled again.

"And when is she moving out?" he asked, jerking his thumb at me.

"Shut up," I said petulantly.

Kevin was fully healed after a long road of recovery, and they didn't really *need* me around anymore. They hadn't really *needed* me around since Kevin had been released from the hospital nearly six months earlier.

I always worried Kevin's ribbing had some element of truth in it, though Kaylee assured me it didn't. They loved having me around as much as I loved being with them, but it was time to move out of Santa Clarita and head back to the city that had captured my heart in so many ways.

I'd promised myself I'd assert my independence, yet I was relying on my sister and my niece to help redirect my focus from my brokenness. I was ready to be on my own and to pick up the pieces of the life I'd left behind when I'd walked out the doors of Benson Industries all those months earlier.

"This came for you," Kevin said, handing me a manila envelope.

Los Angeles Superior Court was emblazoned in the upper left-hand corner. Kevin went back to work stringing the Christmas tree with lights to surprise Madi when she woke up from her nap.

My first thought as I looked at the return address was that this was going to be my first Christmas without John.

I headed to my bedroom. I needed privacy for this, because I knew what it was the very second I saw the return address.

I tore open the envelope and pulled out the paperwork. I read the words across the top of the first page: *Judgment of Dissolution.*

Tears burned my eyes.

It was final. I was officially divorced. I was part of the awful statistic I'd heard that fifty percent of marriages end in divorce.

People say divorce is never easy, but ours had been.

Going to the courthouse and filing the paperwork had been a simple task.

It was the aftermath that was the hard part.

It was the heartbreak leading up to the moment I received that piece of mail that was the most difficult.

I stared at the paperwork as I allowed the memories I'd blocked since the night John had found out about Cole and me to seep back into my mind.

We'd been mostly happy. We'd met at a bar of all places. I'd gone for a night out with friends and ended up finding the man I'd eventually marry.

Dating John had been one adventure after another, and that excitement was why I'd fallen in love with him. When the excitement stopped, so did the love.

I felt the loss of what we'd once had. I missed John—or maybe the idea of John. I mostly missed what we'd had when we'd been dating, back before the marriage that had ended up being just one huge disappointment.

I missed the feeling of sharing a home with someone who was always there for me. Even when it had gotten difficult—and it had, all those long hours John had put in at work—even then, he'd still been my home. And that was gone now, just a distant memory.

But that sadness and that feeling of loss was nothing compared to how much I missed Cole.

I thought about Cole often. Daily. Hourly. Even now, eight months after the last time I'd seen him, he never left my mind for even a moment.

I thought about what he might be doing. I wondered if he'd moved into his beach house. I wondered how he was coping with his new assistant, whoever that might be.

I hadn't seen him or spoken to him since the day I'd left his office with those final words: "I quit." There had been no communication via text or email, either. I vowed to myself not to stalk his Facebook or his Instagram. It was too hard to see his smiling face, so I didn't allow myself the opportunity.

I'd gotten a surprise in my final paycheck, though. In addition to the ten grand, he'd also cashed out my vacation time, including the two week bonus he'd given me with the award. He was trying to take care of me in his own way, and I appreciated that. I'd written him a thank you note at the time, telling him how grateful I was for the extra money. I didn't send it, though. He deserved to move on.

It still broke my heart when I spotted him on *Page Six* with a new blonde bimbo or when I checked the local business section of the paper and saw how he was thriving without me.

I knew better than anyone the smile could be fake, that he could be putting on a front for the public to maintain his professional persona. He could be smiling on the outside to project to everyone that life was perfect.

Those few instances of seeing his image were all I had to go on, though, and just like always, I had trouble reading his true feelings.

I'd forgiven him in our time apart. We'd never labeled what we had as exclusive, and while it had hurt to see him with another woman, he'd been right when he put me in my place in his hotel room. We hadn't been able to label what we had together because we'd been having an affair. You can't call someone your boyfriend when you've already got a husband.

He was wrong about one thing, though. He'd told me that there were two losers in this—John and him.

But I was the biggest loser of all. I'd managed to kill two important relationships in a matter of a few hours while also leaving my job.

My mind drifted to the email I'd gotten just that morning.

Lincoln Mathers wanted me to move into a full-time position at his office instead of working as an independent consultant from home. I just wasn't sure how to break the news to Madi. Or Kaylee, for that matter.

I'd gone to lunch with Lincoln and his wife a few times since I'd quit working with Cole. Alexis—Lincoln's wife—had become a friend, and I brought Madi with me for a playdate with their two kids—a boy Madi's age and a girl a little younger.

Lincoln's offer was a totally new position for me. I'd be working with the creative team to develop ideas that would then move to Benson Industries for market research and product development.

I'd enjoyed my work as an executive assistant. It had come with excellent perks, decent hours, pleasant meals, surprising bonuses, and, of course, the chance to work closely with the hottest man I'd ever laid eyes on. Plus it was the type of job where I could work my hours and leave my work at the office.

Being part of a creative team meant longer hours, nights and weekends, and bringing work home.

But I'd always wondered whether there was more out there for me than being someone's assistant. As much as I loved working with Cole and his father, I had ambitions of my own. Clearly Cole had recognized that in me when he'd started giving me more responsibility.

The more I thought about it, the fewer reasons I could come up with as to why working longer hours would be a bad thing. Throwing myself into a new position would probably be exactly what I needed, but there was the risk of running into Cole. I wasn't ready to see him again. Maybe I'd never be ready to see him again, especially not if he'd started dating.

I swiped at the tears that had fallen down my cheeks as I folded the divorce paperwork and slid it back into the envelope. I'd file it away, and soon enough it would be nothing but a memory. These were the last tears I'd cry over my broken marriage, but I was sure they weren't the last tears I'd cry over Cole.

I headed toward the kitchen since it was high time for a glass of wine. Kaylee was in there fiddling with a Santa Claus figurine whose long white beard had seen better days.

"You okay?" my sister asked when I filled the wineglass to the very top.

I nodded.

"What was in the letter Kevin gave you?"

I took a long gulp of wine before I answered. I held my glass up in the air and forced a smile. "It's official. I'm divorced."

"Oh, Lucy," Kaylee said. She touched my arm gently. "Congratulations?"

I pressed my lips into a thin smile. "Yes. It's time to celebrate. I'm officially single, and it's time for me to reclaim my life."

"What do you mean?"

"I'm moving out."

"No, Auntie Lucy! You can't!" A sleepy little girl walked into the room and wrapped her arms around my leg. "Walk," she commanded.

I made a big show of pretending like I couldn't move my leg, and she giggled like she always did with our little game.

"You don't have to," Kaylee said.

I mouthed the word "later" to her and nodded down at Madi. We'd talk later when we weren't around a five-year-old. But my mind was made up, and if the past year had taught me anything, it was that I was one stubborn bitch. Once I got an idea in my head, there was no swaying me from the course.

"Kevin!" Kaylee yelled.

He appeared in the doorway. "Yes, wife?"

"We're taking two cars to the recital, okay?"

He shrugged, used to submitting to his wife's demands. "Okay. Why?"

"Lucy has some celebrating to do, so I'm going to take her out."

"Kay, you don't have to do that," I protested.

She glared at me. “Nonsense. I’m your sister and you need this.” I couldn’t argue with that. She lowered her voice. “Besides, we need to talk.”

I chugged my wine, and then it was time to get ready for the recital.

Chapter Thirty-Three

I was less tipsy than I should've been considering I'd drank half a bottle of wine. It was probably poor form to attend an elementary school Christmas recital after drinking, but I couldn't change what was done.

I got up to use the restroom in the middle of the second grade rendition of "Jingle Bells" and again during the fifth grade's performance of "Santa Claus is Coming to Town." But I didn't miss a second of sweet Madi's class singing "Rudolph the Red Nosed Reindeer."

Once the seemingly everlasting show was over, we congratulated Madi (Kaylee even gave her a bouquet), and then Kevin and Madi headed home while I sat in Kaylee's front seat.

"Where to?" she asked.

"This was your idea. Take me wherever you want."

She chuckled. "You know what? It's been a long-ass time since we hit the scene in LA."

"Let's just go somewhere close," I said, suddenly panicked at the thought of going into the city.

I wasn't ready to go back. I wasn't ready for all that the city represented.

"You told me to take you wherever I want, so sit back and hush up."

It was one of those nights where I realized my sister was stubborn like me, and I didn't like her—or myself—all that much sometimes.

An hour later, she tossed her keys to the valet as we got out at a bar we frequented when we were in our early twenties. In fact, I remembered going there for my twenty-first birthday. Or didn't remember, as the case may be.

But that was over seven years earlier. I was closer to thirty now, newly divorced and feeling my age as I watched the young twenty-somethings walk up to the bouncer in their tight, short dresses. I glanced down at my jeans and sweater and then eyed my sister, who was dressed similar to me.

"We're not dressed for this," I complained.

"Who gives a fuck? We look hotter than those skanks," she said, gesturing with her chin toward a group of girls.

"One drink. Then we leave."

"I didn't drive an hour to the city for one drink. We're getting wasted tonight, babe. I booked us a hotel room and everything."

"You can't just kidnap me and force me to stay in LA for the night."

"Can't I?" Her eyes gleamed wickedly as she stared me down.

She had a point. I had nowhere to go. No job I had to report to.

No man waiting at home for me.

She wasn't giving me much of a choice, so I may as well indulge her. I rolled my eyes and she grinned, knowing right away that I'd conceded before I'd even said a word.

And then she hooked her arm through mine and we walked together into the bar. The bouncer didn't even card us, which made me feel positively geriatric. It was exactly as I remembered it—loud and dark. Lights bounced off every surface, and the large wooden square in the center of the room was filled with ladies showing too much skin and men who'd had too much to drink. It hearkened back to a magical time in my life when I'd had no real cares and very little responsibility other than waking up in time to attend my classes.

I supposed I'd been living a similar existence for the past several months. I didn't have a whole lot of responsibility. Lincoln's flexibility with my schedule had been more than appreciated, and it had allowed me to help with Madi at the drop of a hat.

We walked up to the bar and were largely ignored for a few minutes by the strapping young bartender who sported sleeves of tattoos, a beard, and a man-bun that I was sure the younger ladies liked but I found a bit ridiculous.

The gorgeous bone structure in Cole's face flashed through my mind. He was so…manly, and while he sported some scruff, he was generally clean-cut. He looked like an adult rather than a child playing dress-up.

I sighed as I tried to push him out of my mind.

Man-bun finally looked in our direction, and Kaylee ordered us each a whiskey sour and Alabama slammers. I cast her a look when she ordered shots for us, and she just shrugged her shoulders with feigned innocence.

"What?" she asked once she'd paid for our first round and I gave her a wary look as I held the shot in one hand and the whiskey drink in the other.

"Shots?"

"I thought it would be fun to keep drinking these until we can no longer actually say 'Alabama slammer.'"

I giggled, held up my shot glass and toasted my sister, and then we both tipped our heads back and drank down the sweet liquid.

We worked a little slower on our whiskey sours as we attempted conversation over the loud music and the drunken youngsters shimmying all around us.

"Why are you moving out?" Kaylee asked.

"It's time, Kay. I love living with you and I love helping out with Madi, but it's time. I need to figure out who I am on my own, and I've relied on your hospitality for long enough."

"But where will you go?"

I shrugged. "I got an offer from Lincoln."

Her eyes lit up like they did every time I brought up Lincoln, who Kaylee referred to as the "Silver Fox." "You did?"

"He wants me to come in to discuss the possibility of moving me from part time to full-time. He made it sound sort of like an interview but he also made it sound like I'm guaranteed the position if I'm interested. The interview is a formality, I guess."

"And are you interested?"

I glanced down at the table. "I don't know."

"Because you might run into Cole."

"I'm not ready for that."

"Sweetie, it's been months."

I ran my finger absently along the rim of my glass. "I know." I looked up at my sister. "It's sad and pathetic that I'm still not over him."

"You need another Alabama slammer."

"I need more than an Alabama slammer. I need sex. Maybe I just need a hot night with a stranger to get my mind off of the past. I need to let him go and move on, but I can't stop missing him."

"It's because you're too focused on what you lost. Your head is in the past because you don't have a job or an apartment or something to throw yourself into. Kev and I appreciate all you've done for us, but I knew it wouldn't last forever."

"I don't want to leave you guys, but Kevin's better and you don't need me."

Kaylee reached across the table and squeezed my hand. "We'll always need you, Lucy."

I smiled a bit sadly that this part of my story was coming to an end.

"Hold the table," Kaylee said. "I'll go get us more drinks."

I dug through my purse and handed Kaylee some cash to cover the next round. I pulled out my phone and scrolled aimlessly, and somehow I found myself landing on Cole's Instagram.

I was proud of what a good job I'd done avoiding stalking Cole on social media since I'd quit and walked out of his office. I just had this nagging feeling inside of me to see how he was doing, and of course I found a new photo from earlier that evening.

The caption simply read *Grande Event Charity Gala #givegrande.*

But it was the photograph that caught my eye. Cole looked more handsome than ever, smiling for the camera in a tuxedo. His hair was freshly trimmed, and the scruff that I could still feel against my skin when I closed my eyes was neatly groomed.

His dark eyes crinkled ever so slightly at the corners with a genuine smile for the camera.

But it wasn't just Cole in the photo.

A gorgeous woman with long blonde waves and bright blue eyes wore a smile that matched Cole's. I hadn't seen her before—she was just another blonde from Cole's little black book. She wore a fuchsia dress and lipstick in the exact same shade. She was elegant and tall and a perfect modelesque match for the very dashing and handsome Cole.

I sucked back the rest of my whiskey sour, allowing an ice cube to melt on my tongue in order to savor the flavor while I waited for Kaylee to return. I stared down at the picture. He looked happy. He looked like he had moved on, and I was sitting here all these months later still wishing I was with him. Still pining away.

Hot tears pricked behind my eyes, but I wasn't going to cry. I'd shed enough tears, and this was my own doing anyway.

"What?" Kaylee asked, scaring the shit out of me when she returned with our drinks. She set them down on the table—the same order as the first round.

I slid my phone over to her so she could inspect the picture.

Her eyes met mine, and they were soft and gentle. She slid my phone back to me, and then she slid her Alabama slammer to me. "You need it more than I do."

I slammed both shots and then started on the next whiskey drink.

The alcohol was warm on top of the half bottle of wine I'd guzzled earlier, and I was starting to feel the soft haze of drunkenness.

I'd largely avoided alcohol over the past few months. Being around a five-year-old just didn't seem to call for much drinking other than the occasional glass of wine, and the shots mixed with the whiskey and the wine were hitting my system.

"He looks good, Luce," Kaylee finally said.

"I know," I said miserably. "He looks happy."

"You will, too. Everything takes time. You'll find your happiness."

"Will I? Or did I already have my chance…twice?"

"Everyone deserves happiness. You found it with John, and you found it with Cole. But those didn't work for a reason. They weren't meant to be. You'll find the one that is."

"That's a nice thing to say, but I just don't know anymore."

"Sitting around here drinking your sorrows away isn't going to change anything."

"This was your idea," I reminded her.

She smiled sheepishly. "Actually, it was Kevin's idea."

"Men," I huffed, and she giggled.

"Why don't we just make a fun night out of it? No more wallowing."

"Too late," I said, nodding to the empty shot glasses. "You know I'm not always a fun drunk."

"I remember a few times when I held back your hair."

"Only when I was visiting you in college."

"When you were still in high school?" she asked, and I nodded. We both giggled at the memory, and that led to more ridiculous recollections.

Soon we were laughing so hard that we were both wiping our eyes. Cole (and the gorgeous woman in the photo) was still on my mind, but at least my sister had managed to help me think about something else, even if only for a little bit. And I was grateful for that.

"Let's dance," she said after our next round of drinks. I had to admit that the haze of alcohol was making me antsy, so I nodded and we ditched our table for the dance floor.

Good looking men danced all around us, but most of them either were too young or were dancing with drunken ladies closer to their age. I felt like a cougar as I eyed one guy who had to be barely legal. He was cute, but he didn't hold a candle to the man who had stolen my heart.

Even through the whiskey cloud, even after all these months, there he was, still on my mind.

Sex. A good night of sex with one of these men would most certainly be the cure.

I felt someone's hands at my hips as his body moved in flush against mine. My sister raised her eyebrows and gave me a smile, so I knew he had to be cute. One of his friends started dancing with my sister, and she pushed him off and held up her wedding ring. I watched the denial with amusement.

"You okay?" she mouthed to me. Before I nodded that I was, I turned to look at the man who'd started dancing with me. He was definitely cute with his floppy blonde hair and bright blue eyes that I could see even in the dimness of the bar.

He looked a bit more mature than most of the men around us. His hard body against my backside told me he worked out, and the way he swayed his hips told me he was probably good in bed.

That was all I wanted. Just one night with someone I didn't even know. Just one night to help me forget the past and to see that there was more out there.

I turned back to Kaylee and nodded, and then she went in search of another table while I danced with this mystery hunk.

"You're a great dancer," he yelled smoothly over the music.

"So are you," I said. He was, but I couldn't help comparing him to Cole.

Dancing with some random guy wasn't what I wanted. No random guy could be, because even after all this time, there was still only one man on my mind.

"If you think I'm a good dancer, you should see what I could do in the bedroom."

His age was finally showing. Most men my age or older would never approach a woman and lay that one on her. He was a bit forward, but he was also obviously intoxicated.

I glanced around for Kaylee to see if she'd settled into a table, but the crowd of dancing drunks around us was too thick for me to see through.

He shoved his hips aggressively toward mine.

"What's your name?" I asked, trying to ignore the fact that he was coming on way too strong.

"Cole."

I laughed. "You have got to be kidding me."

He looked mildly annoyed that I was laughing at his name. "Why?"

"That's my ex's name."

"Well then you can call me whatever you want." He ground his hips toward me again.

He thought I was a slam dunk, and while maybe I was since I'd decided I wanted sex with a stranger, I wasn't sure that young blonde Cole was my best option.

He leaned down and ran his lips long my neck, baring his teeth.

"Ouch!" I jumped when he nipped my skin.

He smiled playfully, and it was clear he thought he was doing something to turn me on.

He wasn't.

This wasn't going to work.

"Well, Cole… Is Cole short for something?"

He nodded. "Colton."

"Thank God. Colton, it's been lovely dancing with you, but I should really get back to my sister."

"Or you could just keep dancing with me." He grabbed my hips and pulled me closer to him. I set both of my hands on his chest and pushed, but he didn't budge.

A bit of a panic settled into my chest. The haze from the last shot I'd taken jumbled my thoughts. I thought I'd wanted one night with a stranger, but this stranger was overly aggressive. His arms came around mine, and he pinned them to my side as he managed to place his hands on my ass. He pulled me closer against him as I was trying to push him away, which only served to frighten me.

"Stop, Colton," I said, my voice forceful. He paid no attention to my plea.

"Stop," I repeated, my voice loud and clear.

I looked around again for Kaylee, but we were buried in the middle of the dance floor, loud music pumping all around us as bodies swayed in a blur.

I pushed against him again, but he still didn't move. Instead, his fingers dug painfully into my hips as he kept attempting to pull me closer, and he lowered his head toward my neck again. I pushed his chest as hard as I could as I felt his lips on my neck, sucking and slurping. Sickness burned my stomach as bile rose in my throat.

My heart started beating wildly. Could he hurt me right here in the middle of the dance floor?

"No!" I yelled, hoping someone around me would hear me. Everyone was too caught up in having a good time to realize someone they didn't know might be hurting someone else they didn't know.

This was supposed to be a fun night out with my sister, but this wasn't fun.

No matter how hard I tried to push him away, he didn't move. His arms still had me pinned, so my shoves against his chest were weak compared to his strength.

In my adrenaline-fueled panic, I thought about kneeing him in the nuts and running, but he was holding me so tightly that I couldn't lift my knee to get to him.

When I'd first felt his hard body against mine and assumed he worked out, I'd considered it a bonus. Sexy. Exciting.

But now all that strength just scared me.

He wouldn't stop, and no one was listening to my cries for help.

I had no idea what to do.

One of his hands came up and yanked my hair back so he could continue assaulting my neck, and I yelled out in pain. "Stop!" Once again, my cries were drowned by the loud music.

One second I feared for what this guy could do to me, and the next he was on the floor, holding his face as a ring of drunken dancers who were suddenly interested in what was going on formed around us. Blood poured from Colton's nose as he looked up and behind me.

My heart leapt up to my throat. "What the—?" I yelled in confusion. I turned around to see what he was looking at and found myself looking right into Cole's dark eyes.

My Cole.

Cole Benson.

His eyes were murderous.

He shook his right hand, which had blood all over it, and he averted his eyes from mine as he looked at Colton down on the floor.

"You broke my nose, you motherfucker!" Colton yelled through his blood-covered hands.

The song switched, and a brief moment of quiet fell over the bar between the beats of the new song. Cole knelt down and spoke directly to my would-be assailant. "When a woman tells you no, that's your cue to stop. You're lucky I didn't fucking kill you." He stood, leaving Colton lying on the floor writhing in pain. He turned back to me.

He didn't say a word. His eyes, though…that was a different story.

They said everything he didn't.

"What are you doing here?" I asked.

"Taking care of your drunk ass. Again." He turned to leave, and I grabbed his arm.

"Wait." I wasn't sure what I was going to say. He'd just appeared out of nowhere and attacked a man who was about to attack me. *Thanks* seemed underwhelming.

His eyes burned into mine, and I was transported back to the day I'd walked out of his office. No time had passed between us even though we'd been apart for eight months.

I still felt everything I'd felt the second I left his office. I still wanted to be with him. I still loved him.

And every unsaid word between us still spoke volumes as his eyes darkened.

I'd caught everything I'd needed to see in that one simple glance before his wall came back up.

He still loved me, too.

"Um, thank you for taking care of my drunk ass. Again."

His eyes softened. "You're welcome."

He turned and walked away from me, and I lost him in the sea of people.

My heart felt full, though. Just seeing him again, just knowing that he'd be there to take care of me even when I hadn't seen him or spoken to him in months…that meant everything to me.

I had no idea how he knew I was here or how he found me. I had no idea how he knew I needed to be saved.

But none of that mattered. Maybe all that mattered was that he'd shown up when I'd needed him, and maybe that was enough.

Or maybe I'd never get enough of Cole Benson and I'd regret it for the rest of my life if I didn't go running after him to tell him how much I loved him.

The crowd dispersed once Cole left. His friends pulled Colton up from the floor, and I lost them in the crowd. I walked the perimeter of the bar to find Kaylee, who sat way in the back scrolling through her phone.

"Can we go home? Like right now?" I asked.

"We can go to the hotel. I shouldn't drive."

"Fine. Can we go to the hotel?"

She nodded, and we walked out of the bar and down the block in silence. We checked in and got settled in our room. After I took a shower where I attempted to scrub every last remnant of the evening off my skin under scalding water, she finally spoke. "Do you want to talk about what happened with that hunk of man back there?"

I filled her in, and when I got to the part about Cole, her jaw dropped.

"Lucy! Oh my God. You have to call him. You have to see him. You have to figure this out."

I shook my head. "I thought that, too, at first. But you know what? If he wanted me after all this time, he wouldn't have walked away."

"Don't you think that maybe he was just doing that because he thought that's what you wanted?"

I shook my head. "Cole isn't the type of guy who cares what other people want. He takes what he wants when he wants it."

"He didn't just take you right away when you were married to John."

"No, he didn't. But he also doesn't know I'm divorced. For all he knows, John and I worked things out."

"Don't you want to at least try?"

"I don't know what I want. I'm still under the influence of whiskey, so this might be a better conversation for the morning."

She sighed, wished me goodnight, and turned out the light.

We hadn't shut the curtains, and I stared out the window at some tall building across the street from ours, the lights of the city twinkling in the close distance. Cole was somewhere in this city, the same city as me. Maybe even thinking about me.

Maybe missing me.

And for some reason, that comforting thought lulled me to sleep.

Chapter Thirty-Four

"Good morning, sleepy bear!" My sister's loud voice cut through my magical dream where Cole punched out some drunk asshole and then ravished me properly for the rest of the night.

"Blurgh." It was supposed to be a word, but I wasn't sure which one. My mouth was dry and my words were garbled from whiskey, drama, and sleep. I rolled over and pulled the pillow over my head to block out the sunlight.

"Today's the day you're getting Cole back!" she exclaimed with enthusiasm.

I grabbed the pillow off of my head and threw it in her direction. "You're downright insane."

She giggled. "You missed. And you're hungover."

"That's what happens when you keep shoving your shots at me."

"I told you last night and I stand firmly by it. You needed them more than I did."

"Be that as it may, I kind of hate you this morning."

"You'll get over it." She stood from her bed and stretched. "Let's hit Denny's for a greasy breakfast and then find Cole."

"Let's not hit Denny's and let's not find Cole. Let's just go home."

She walked over and sat on the edge of my bed. "I just want you to be happy, Lucy." Her voice was soft.

"I'm fine."

"No, you're not. I'll admit it was rough when you were with him. But I've never seen you as happy as you were when Cole was standing next to you. You had this glow about you, this radiance. And I haven't seen that since the day you moved in with us."

I sighed. "I was happy with Cole, as brief as it was. But it's in the past. Too much time has passed."

"He showed up when you needed him last night."

"But he left. We've been over this."

She leaned back on the headboard and crossed her feet in front of her. "Why are you fighting this?"

"Why are you pressing this?" I countered. "You don't even know him."

"You're right. But clearly you do, and clearly you still love him."

"What makes you say that?"

"You were nearly attacked last night, Lucy. But you didn't fall apart. You didn't freak out like you should have. Instead, you calmly found me and asked me if we could leave, but that glow was back. That radiance. I knew the second I saw you that something important changed in the ten minutes I left you to dance with that stranger. And when you told me that Cole had shown up, I knew that was why."

"That's ridiculous."

"Is it?"

There was no arguing with Kaylee once she thought she was right, so I didn't answer.

But she'd given me an awful lot to think about.

Thankfully she dropped it and we walked back to the bar to pick up her car. On the ride home, though, the questions started again.

And she wasn't subtle or tactful.

"Tell me again why you aren't hunting down that man and thanking him with your body?"

"Jeez, Kaylee."

"Well?"

I stared out the window and watched the California landscape rush past. The cloudless sky was a clear and vibrant blue, and the mountains hovered out in the distance.

"I can't get my heart broken again," I whispered.

"Isn't he worth the risk?"

I didn't respond to my sister, and she finally turned up the radio and let it go. I knew it was just for the moment and it would be short-lived, but I appreciated the time to think things through on my own without her badgering.

She wanted me to be happy, and I wanted that, too.

But I hadn't known real, true happiness for a long time, and I seemed to be getting by just fine.

***

The house was silent when we arrived home. Madi was at school and Kevin was at work.

I finally called Lincoln.

"Lucy Vance," he boomed warmly.

"Lincoln Mathers." I forced my enthusiasm to match his.

"Come in next week for an interview," he said. "It's just a formality. The job is yours if you want it."

"I need it. I'm ready to get out of my sister's hair."

"That sweet niece of yours is going to miss you."

"I'll miss her, too. How are the kids?"

"Bailee is getting a sassy little mouth on her, and Jackson is climbing everything."

"Sounds about right. How's Alexis?"

"She needs a lunch date with you soon."

"Well when I'm permanently in the city, maybe we can have lunch dates more often."

"She'd love that."

"So would I."

"Email Sierra," he said, referring to his secretary, "to set up a meeting."

"Consider it done, Mr. Mathers."

He chuckled. "See you next week."

Once I had my job prospect lined up, it was time to look for a place to live.

I scoured the internet for an apartment, but there were so many choices that I became both overwhelmed and confused almost immediately.

I emailed an old college friend who was now a realtor. She replied almost immediately, and we exchanged phone numbers and set up a meeting for the same day as my interview at MTC.

I took a deep breath.

I was finally taking my life back.

Chapter Thirty-Five

As I drove toward the city, the prospect of going on a job interview and looking at apartments filled me with excitement.

This was different from the night Kaylee and I went to the bar. This wasn't just for a night of fun.

I wore a brand new dress, I'd polished my nails, and I felt confident and sexy. I listened to Christmas music as I made my way toward the skyscrapers, allowing the catchy jingles to lighten my mood.

This next step terrified me as much as it exhilarated me, but the only way to move forward was to stop hiding at my sister's house and actually take the step.

My GPS got me to the building that housed MTC Industries, and I found a parking deck just around the corner. I parked and walked to the building as I hummed "Silver Bells." I felt a giddiness I hadn't felt in a long time.

It wasn't because I'd seen Cole the week before. And if I kept telling myself that, maybe it would be true.

The receptionist greeted me with a smile.

"Lucy Cle—uh, Vance here to see Mr. Mathers." I still wasn't used to using my maiden name again.

"Of course, Lucy. Have a seat. Lincoln will be right out." She called into Lincoln's office.

"Ms. Vance," Lincoln boomed in a jovial voice a few minutes later. He grinned and gave me a hug. "It's been…what, two days since we spoke?"

I grinned. "Oh, is that all? Feels like at least three."

He chuckled and put his arm around my shoulders as he led me back to his office. Even though I technically worked for the company, I'd never been to the office. I'd been too busy hiding out in Santa Clarita. "Lex wanted to know if you have time for lunch today."

"I'm actually meeting with a realtor to look at apartments, but maybe after that."

"She could go with you, if you want."

"I know she could. I need to do this just for me, though."

He nodded as we turned down another hallway. "Of course you do. I'm so proud of you, Lucy. And I'm excited to get you on board here. We'll miss little Madi, though. Promise you'll still bring her around?"

"Of course I will. I'm sure Kaylee would love to have them out to the house for a pajama party."

We arrived at a closed door with a placard that read *CEO LINCOLN MATHERS*, and Lincoln paused outside of it. "That sounds wonderful. Now are you ready for your interview?"

"So formal. Yes, I'm ready."

He opened the door, and my heart dropped into my stomach before leaping back up into my throat.

This was definitely *not* something I was ready for.

Standing by the windows overlooking the expansive skyline of Los Angeles was none other than Cole Benson.

He stood there in all of his royal beauty, imposing as ever against the backdrop of LA. And he looked just as shocked to see me as I felt in seeing him.

He wore a charcoal suit with a black shirt and tie. His black hair was a mess and the scruff on his chin was perfection. His dark eyes looked tired and a bit haunted, like he hadn't been getting enough sleep.

It was the first time I'd ever been able to read the emotion so clearly on his face. He'd always been so disciplined in hiding his true feelings, but clearly seeing me in the flesh in Lincoln's office had hit him completely off guard.

He looked even more beautiful in person than he'd looked in my memories, and all I wanted to do was run into his arms.

But I didn't. I couldn't. It wasn't my right to anymore.

He started toward me but stopped himself. "Lucy," he whispered.

I cleared my throat. "Cole." My voice shook.

"It's good to see you again, Ms. Cleary." His voice was soft and sincere.

"It's actually Ms. Vance now." My voice continued to shake, as did my hands and knees. I held onto the door frame for support, sure my legs were going to buckle beneath me. He looked at me in wonder at my pronouncement. "And it's good to see you, too."

Lincoln cleared his throat, and both of our heads whipped in his direction. I'd forgotten he was even there. "Cole, when you talk about Lucy in every meeting we have, there's more than a simple professional admiration. I think it's time for you to talk to each other and figure this out."

My eyes darted from Lincoln back to Cole. He'd turned to gaze out the window, but his eyes flicked back to mine.

"I'll leave you two to it," Lincoln said, gently nudging me into his office. He closed the door behind me, leaving Cole and me alone.

We stared at each other for a full ten seconds before either of us spoke, and then we spoke at the same time. "What are you doing here?" we asked the other in unison.

We both laughed nervously. "You first," he said.

"I've been working with Lincoln as an independent consultant. He asked me here today to interview me for a full-time position. You?"

He looked out the window like he always did during our conversations. "He told me he needed to meet with me regarding his account. I thought it was strange since we just met a few days ago."

"I've become close with him and his wife," I said by way of explanation—not that I owed one to Cole.

"They're good people."

"He knows what happened between us."

Cole took a second to digest that information, and then he motioned to the chairs. We both sat even though my natural instinct was to move closer to him and to touch him.

I couldn't believe how strong that instinct was.

It was strange sitting on the same side of the desk as Cole. I was so used to him sitting on the other side, looking down at me, his lowly assistant. As we sat in our chairs, I felt equal to him for maybe the first time since I'd met him. We'd never be equal in the business sense—I'd never aspire to be the CEO of a major company—but at least here we were on equal ground.

"So now he's in the matchmaking business?" Cole asked.

I shrugged. "Maybe he just wanted to give us the chance to talk things out."

He cleared his throat. "Would you have…" He paused, as if searching for the right words. "Would you have gotten in touch if not for Lincoln?"

The truth sounded so harsh, but I'd figured he had moved on by now. I shook my head slowly. "Would you have?"

"Not because I didn't want to," he whispered.

I wasn't ready for this conversation. We'd only been in the same room together for a few minutes. I hadn't expected to see him. I'd expected to go in for an interview for a job I knew was already mine, and instead I was chatting with Cole.

"Thanks for saving me the other night," I blurted.

"It was nothing."

"How'd you know I was there?"

He chuckled mirthlessly. "It was purely coincidental. A friend invited me out for drinks after a fundraiser."

"I'm glad you were there."

"I'm glad I was able to save your drunk ass once again."

We were both quiet for a moment, and all I could think about was what his arms would feel like around me. His familiar scent wafted over toward my nose, and my chest tightened with emotion.

"How's your new assistant?" I asked, changing the subject. I tried to make my voice sunny and bright, but I failed miserably. I wanted to talk about what had happened between us. I wanted to talk about all the months we'd been apart. I wanted to tell him that I was striking out on my own. That I wasn't married anymore. That I was free to begin a relationship now.

I was finally in a place where I understood that everything had happened for a reason. I wasn't meant to spend my life with John, and even though the way I'd gone about destroying what we'd had was harsh, it still got me to where I was supposed to be.

"Fine," he said, answering my question about his assistant. "What have you been up to?"

I wanted more details than *fine*. Was she more efficient than me? Did she work as hard as I did? Did she take notes as good as me? Was she prettier than me? Was he fucking her?

"Well, my divorce is finalized. I've been staying with Kaylee and helping with Madi."

He hid his reaction to my words well. "How's your brother-in-law?"

"Completely recovered. Thanks for asking. I needed a place to live and they needed help with Madi, so it worked out."

"Good. Madi's doing well?"

I nodded. "She's great. She actually asked about you a few times." The words were out of my mouth before I could stop them, which was unfortunate since I was trying to play it cool.

"What did you say?"

"Just that I don't work with you anymore."

"Oh."

His hands rubbed his thighs while I absently fingered the leather armrest of my chair.

"Yeah. It's more complicated than that, I guess, but she's five."

We sat in awkward silence for a few beats, and then I stood and walked toward the door. "Well, it's been great catching up with you. I better go find Lincoln and see about this interview."

I turned the handle and opened the door.

"Lucy, wait," he said, rushing toward me and setting his hand on the door next to me. It shut with a loud click, and Cole Benson was back in my orbit. I turned to face him, my back against the door.

He was close enough that I could smell his body wash and feel his heat. All I had to do was tilt my head back and stand on my tiptoes and our lips would be touching. I could feel his breath against my cheek.

I looked up at him, my eyes round with surprise—and, I was sure, full of lust. He gazed down at me, his eyes full of this tenderness that I'd never seen before.

"She's terrible," he blurted.

I looked up at him in complete confusion.

"My new assistant. She's awful. She's the fourth one I've hired since you left, and not one of them has worked out. Because not one of them even holds a candle to you—to your professionalism, to your efficiency, to your knowledge..." He paused as he gently traced one of his long fingers from my temple, down my cheek, and to my lips, his eyes following the path of his finger. "But most of all to your beauty."

He moved his finger and stared at my lips. His eyes flicked to mine before refocusing on my mouth. "I want to kiss you. It's all I've thought about for two hundred thirty-six days."

"You counted?" I asked in wonder.

He bent his head down closer to me, his eyes on mine. "Each day that has passed has been one more day that I kicked myself for letting you walk away. Each day has been a reminder that I'm alone when I could have had everything. I fucked up, Lucy, and I haven't been able to move on from you. You weren't innocent in this, but I didn't fight hard enough, and I've had to live with that for the past two hundred thirty-six days. But it stops here. Screw the interview you have today with Lincoln. Come work for me again. *Be* with me again. I can't let another day pass without telling you what you mean to me."

I wanted it more than anything.

But even though he was saying the right words and giving me an amazing offer, I needed time to think.

I couldn't make a decision like this when he was so close to me, confusing me with his scent and warmth and sexiness.

"I can't, Cole."

I ducked under his arm and paced around Lincoln's office just to put some space between us.

"Yes, you can. You want a raise? I'll give you a raise. I'll give you better hours. I'll treat you like a woman should be treated. I'll fight for you this time instead of letting you walk out the door."

"Why, Cole? You know what it was like before. Why would you do all that?"

He walked over to the window and leaned his arms down on the windowsill. He stared out at the city. "Because that's what you do when you're in love."

My jaw dropped. "In…in love?"

He turned toward me and nodded slowly. "It didn't take me two hundred thirty-six days to figure that out. I fell in love with you in New York. As stupid as it sounds, it was that night you came in drunk and I was so fucking mad at you for ditching me the night before the presentation." He stalked slowly toward me as he spoke, as if he was the hunter and I was the prey. "I fought my feelings because I had to, and I let you get away because I thought that's what you needed. But you walk in here today and tell me your divorce is finalized? I'm done letting you get away."

He stood in front of me. I hadn't realized I'd been slowly backing up until I was against the desk. I had nowhere else to go, and he knew it. "We're destructive together."

"Passionate." He pressed his body to mine.

I arched back and stiffened. "We hurt other people and we hurt each other."

He set his arms on the desk on either side of me. "We'll stop."

I set my hands on his chest, but I couldn't bring myself to push him away. "I don't know what to say."

"Then say yes. Let's stop this nonsense and finally be together." He leaned forward and pressed his lips to my neck.

I didn't fight him, and speech evaded me as his mouth worked its way up to mine. My only response was a soft moan.

When our lips touched, the fire that ignited inside of me was totally different from before.

Before, our romance had been forbidden. I was doing something wrong and hurting someone else in the process.

But this time, I was clear of all restrictions.

I'd worried that the excitement of having the forbidden was part of what had made my relationship with Cole so fiery. But all that was gone now, and what I found between us was a stronger, brighter, hotter fire.

His mouth opened to mine, and as his tongue started moving against mine, tingles zipped down my spine and the ever-present ache in my core intensified.

My arms automatically went around him as his hands yanked my hips flush against him. He was hard, and I couldn't help but remember exactly what it was like to have him inside me.

Both of us panting.

Both of us moaning.

Both of us tumbling to the brink before free-falling right off of it.

Terror crept in.

What if we tried this again and I lost him?

I couldn't go through what I'd gone through in the past eight months again.

And that was the driving force that pulled my arms from around him and directed them to his chest. I pushed him away, and he looked at me in utter confusion.

"I can't, Cole." I grabbed my purse and ran to the door. I turned out of Lincoln's office, not sure where to go but sure I needed to get out of that room.

"Where's Cole?" Lincoln asked with a grin. He was sitting in one of the chairs in the reception area, shooting the breeze with the receptionist up front when he should've been working in his office.

"In your office. Can we reschedule our interview?"

He stood, concern lighting his face. "What happened?"

"Cole wants to get back together."

He looked confused for a split second. "Of course he does. And so do you. That's why I arranged this meeting today."

"But what about the interview?"

"Sweet girl, there is no interview."

It was my turn to look confused. And then realization dawned.

Lincoln had never intended to interview me. He'd simply concocted a reason to get me to the office so I could make up with Cole.

"Thanks for meddling, but I think I need to get the hell out of here." I was furious with Lincoln. He had no right to step into our lives that way. He had no right to get my hopes up that he might give me a job that could potentially be my ticket to independence.

I spun on my heel and ran out the door, opting for the stairs instead of the elevator. I heard Lincoln yelling my name after me, but I didn't bother to stop. I was too damn angry to talk to him.

Tears blinded me as I ran down the stairs. I slowed on one of the landings, wondering for a split second if I was overreacting. Lincoln might've just had my best interest at heart, but Cole and I needed to find our own way back to each other. Orchestrating some meeting under false pretenses was just as bad as starting a relationship on a lie, which was exactly what had caused me to end things with Cole in the first place.

I continued down the stairs. Why the hell was the office on the twelfth floor? It was just one more item on the list of things that pissed me right the hell off. The tears started falling harder as I rounded the fourth floor, and then my heel slid on a stair and I tumbled down toward the next landing.

I stuck my hand out to stop myself from tumbling further, and then I sat up, the broken heel on my shoe preventing me from standing up for a minute. "Shit," I muttered.

"Shit!" I yelled a little louder when I leaned my weight on my left wrist to help me stand. "Dammit," I muttered, using my right hand to swipe the tears that were streaming down my face as I sat on the landing.

I was one hell of a hot mess.

"Are you okay?" Cole's voice caught up with me before I felt his arms hauling me up from the ground. "Shit. Your wrist is swelling." His arm came around my waist to help me since I couldn't walk on my broken shoe.

"I'm fine," I said, swatting his arm off of me. "Fuck!" I yelled when I'd used my left hand to push him away.

"You're not okay."

"I'll be fine. Just leave me alone."

I started for the next set of stairs, hobbling on my broken heel, but he stopped me by grabbing my hips from behind.

"No." He twirled me around to face him. "The last time I let you walk out of my life, you left me a broken man. I'm not letting you walk out again. Not without a fight, Lucy."

"We're better off apart."

"We never gave it a fair shot."

"Let me go." I tried pushing him away again with just one hand, but it was useless. He was much stronger than me even when I didn't have an injured wrist.

"How bad is your wrist?" he asked, gently taking my hand to inspect it.

"It's fine."

"Stop saying it's fine." His finger came under my chin to force me to look up at him. "How bad?"

"It hurts." I couldn't lie when his eyes were right on mine.

"We're going to urgent care."

"I'm not going to urgent care. Don't be ridiculous."

He closed his eyes in frustration. "You need to get it checked."

"It's fine."

"Oh my God, you're infuriating. I realize you're not my employee anymore and you don't have to listen to me, but will you go to the fucking doctor to get checked out?"

The frustration in his voice convinced me. "Fine."

Shock spread across his handsome face. "Really?"

"Yes, really."

He finally dropped his hands from my waist, and I felt the immediate absence of his touch. Out of nowhere, I was swept off of my feet and into the arms of Cole.

It felt an awful lot like I was in the arms of the man I loved.

I shook the thought out of my head. I didn't know if I still loved him. I couldn't love him. Too much time had passed—or something. I knew there was some reason.

He carried me down the stairs, tossed me into the front seat of his car, and sat with me at urgent care. He carried me back to his car two long hours later with a wrap on my strained—not sprained—wrist, a bottle of mild painkillers in one hand and my shoes in the other. And as each moment passed, the reasons why we were supposed to stay apart drifted further and further from my mind.

But all the reasons why we worked were sure at the forefront of my mind.

Especially the sex.

The sex was right there in the front of my mind.

It may have been the painkillers talking. I'd try to think about things again when I was lucid, but for now, being with Cole felt nice. It felt right.

Something had been missing since the night I'd left John. To be fair, a lot of things were missing, but the only thing that I still missed from that time in my life was Cole.

It wasn't my husband or the home we shared. It wasn't the idea of love. It wasn't marriage.

It was Cole.

"Where to?" he asked.

I yawned. "My car is still by Lincoln's office." I leaned my head against the window. It wasn't a very soft pillow, but my eyes wouldn't stay open.

He fired up his Audi. "We'll get your car tomorrow."

I finally gave up the fight with my eyes and let them stay closed as I spoke. "No, tonight's fine. Kaylee will be expecting me."

"Why don't you text her and let her know that you won't be coming home tonight?"

"Mmm," was the last thing I remembered saying.

Chapter Thirty-Six

A beam of sunlight fell across my eyes, and I woke with a start. I sat up and tried to figure out where the hell I was. I glanced down at the t-shirt I was wearing. It wasn't mine, and I didn't really remember putting it on.

Movement beside me in the bed caused me to gasp.

"Morning," Cole said with a sexy, sleepy smile.

"Where the hell am I?"

"My house." His grin widened. "Construction finally wrapped a couple of weeks ago, but I haven't had time to furnish the guest room." I appreciated the explanation as to why I woke up beside Mr. Benson himself.

"Or purchase blinds, apparently," I said. My eyes adjusted to the brightness, and I couldn't help my stare as my gaze fell to the window. Water rolled tranquilly in and out of the shoreline just steps away from Cole's bedroom window.

He chuckled. "Actually, I purchased them. I'm just waiting on delivery. But I was tired of hotel living, and frankly, window coverings don't bother me."

Anyone on the beach would be able to look in the window and see what was going on if the lighting was right. I had to wonder how many women he'd brought back to this very bed since he'd moved in. It was a bachelor pad to be sure, and he could easily score with whoever he wanted to.

Me included—but I wasn't about to admit that to the devil himself.

"Can I get you some coffee?" he asked.

I nodded. "That'd be great."

He flipped the blanket off and stood from the bed. My mouth watered as I gazed at his naked back down to his boxer-clad ass as he stretched.

My God, he was a fine specimen of a man. His shoulder blades appeared to shimmer in the morning light as I watched each beautiful and smooth muscle flex.

He turned back toward me, opening his mouth as if he was going to speak. But then he caught me totally checking him out with my mouth dropped open. I just hoped to God that I wasn't drooling. He chuckled, closed his mouth, and left the room.

I pulled the sheet up over my face in total embarrassment.

I'd get over it. The man had once screwed me in a ladies' room, for crying out loud.

But it was still embarrassing.

It was hard to believe that all of this could be mine if I would just open myself to the possibility.

I headed into his bathroom and found his toothpaste. I finger brushed my teeth, swished some mouthwash, and ran some cold water over my face. It would have to do. I peeked into Cole's shower and saw a bottle of his shower gel. I picked it up, opened it, and inhaled deeply.

God, I'd missed him.

A flood of memories overwhelmed me. We'd had a lot of good times together. We'd built an emotional bond. We'd started to fall for each other.

Why was I fighting this?

A mental image of blonde Heidi straddling Cole in his desk chair flashed through my mind, and I suddenly remembered why.

He hadn't cheated on me, exactly, and he'd explained himself. Was I harping on the past too much? Wasn't what I had done just as bad?

Why couldn't we just start from scratch?

We couldn't put the past totally behind us. It would always be a part of our story, but the past could remain where it belonged as we started to look toward a future together.

I knew the thought of him with Heidi wouldn't always dominate my mental images. It would take time to erase it from my mind, but considering our circumstances, what he'd done was ultimately a forgivable offense.

I supposed I'd just have to replace the images of Heidi on top of him with images of me on top of him.

Or him on top of me.

Or him behind me.

Or his face between my legs.

I finally emerged from the restroom and found Cole sitting at his kitchen table, his eyes concentrating on his phone and his brow furrowed. Two cups of coffee sat in front of him along with a variety of sweeteners and cream.

It was sure a change of pace to see Cole getting *me* a cup of coffee.

"Can we talk?" I asked softly.

He set his phone down immediately and looked up at me. I appreciated his undivided attention.

My gaze shifted to the packets of sugar and Splenda on the table. "Did you steal those from a restaurant?"

He chuckled. "I'll never tell. I realized I don't know how you take your coffee, so I put out everything."

"I actually like it black."

"Huh. Wouldn't have guessed that."

I sat and took a sip from the steaming mug. "Tastes good."

"I assume you didn't want to chat about coffee this morning. But before we get to that, how are you feeling?"

I held up my wrist. "I'll live."

"Your meds are on the counter. Want me to get you some?"

I shook my head. They had made me so sleepy the night before, and I needed to keep my wits about me for this conversation.

I drew in a deep breath for strength, suddenly nervous. I knew he wanted to be with me, so this shouldn't have been a difficult conversation.

"I thought a lot about what you said yesterday, about not giving up without a fight. I'm terrified, Cole. I'm terrified of you and what you could do to my heart. It already broke once the first time I left, and it's just now starting to heal. It's fragile, and getting involved with you again could shatter it beyond repair."

"I won't let that happen."

I pursed my lips. "I know you, Mr. Benson. You run hot and cold. You're moody as fuck and you don't give a shit what other people think about it."

He tapped his fingers on the side of his coffee mug. "You only know me as your boss. We've never given a relationship a try."

"You admitted that you don't do relationships," I fired back.

"Doesn't that tell you something, then? That I'm willing to try with you?"

"Why didn't you want to try with Heidi?"

He sighed as he looked out the window. I could tell I'd pressed a button, but this would never work if we didn't get it all out on the table.

He searched for the right words, and finally his eyes landed back on mine. He shrugged and shot me a sad smile. "Because she isn't you. You care for me in a way I've never had before. You're someone who my mom would've been proud to see me with."

"Would've?" I asked, flattered at his words but focused on the one word that stuck out more than the others.

His eyes clouded and he shifted his gaze down to the table. "She passed away last month."

"Oh my God, Cole." I rose from my chair and moved toward him. "I'm so, so sorry." I knelt in front of him and wrapped my arms around his waist.

He shifted and pulled me onto his lap. He cradled me like a child, my arms around his neck and my cheek against his racing heart. "What happened?" I asked.

"Cancer. It was fast."

"Are you okay?"

"I'm handling it."

"How's your dad?"

"About as good as can be expected. He's having a rough time, but it helps that I'm so close. I see him nearly every day."

"I want to go with you today."

"He'd love that."

I wrapped my arms around him a little tighter. "I'm sorry I wasn't there for you when it happened."

"You couldn't have known. We'd been apart for months, and even if we hadn't been, we weren't in a relationship."

"I know, but still…"

"Look," he said, pulling back to look me in the eye, "the only thing I can do is use it as a learning experience. My mom was the nicest, most thoughtful person I've ever known. She taught me that every day is a gift, and nothing proved that more than when she was with me one day and gone the next."

He paused, and I let those words sink in. "The moment I saw you at that bar, it all came rushing back. I didn't expect to see you at Lincoln's office, but when I did, I realized what a hole you'd left in my life when you'd gone. Not just at work, but personally. I haven't been the same. Each day just blurs into the next. I feel like I'm living my life but not really experiencing it, you know? And that's no way to live. But seeing you again…seeing you was my answer. You're my answer."

"Then let's live again."

He raised his eyebrows in surprise. "You…you would do that? With me?"

"I'd like to try. I'd like to at least go on a date and see where it goes."

"Go on a date? I was more thinking along the lines of you moving in here with me and taking your old job back."

"Whoa whoa whoa," I said, holding up my hands. "Just hold your horses. We need to take things slowly."

He laughed, and I stood, backing away from him slowly. He hopped out of his chair and charged toward me. I kept backing up, and he kept moving right along with me.

And then I was out of room, up against a wall with nowhere to go. He pinned me there with his hips.

"I really want to make love to you," he said, his lips finding that one spot on my neck that drove me wild with lust for him.

I set my hands on his chest, but I didn't push him away. "And one day, you will. But first, you need to take me on a date. You need to prove that you're ready to commit to just one woman."

"You want proof?" he growled.

I nodded, and his lips trailed up to mine. He kissed me softly, lingering with his mouth closed over mine for a moment.

"Here's your proof, Ms. Vance." I smiled at his use of my maiden name. "I haven't been with anyone since the night you walked in on Heidi and me."

This time I did push him away. "Shut up."

"I swear. I'm done with meaningless relationships. I'm done with the late night booty calls and one night stands. I decided the next time I'm with a woman, it will be with somebody I love. There's only one woman I've ever fallen for in my entire life, and she's standing right in front of me. I love you, Lucy. I've loved you for a long time, and now we can actually give this a real try."

"I love you, too, Cole." The words were out of my mouth before I could stop them. I'd been debating my true feelings for too long. In the moment, the words slipped out unplanned.

It was from the heart rather than from my dumb, overthinking brain, and that was how I knew it was true.

His eyes lit up with shock, and then his mouth crashed down to mine.

Everything turned right in the world as his lips worked against mine and his tongue battered my mouth. One of his arms snaked around my waist to haul me as close as possible to him while his other hand gripped my hair. He was somehow brutal and gentle and rough and tender all at once, and the shards of my shattered heart started to piece back into place once again.

Chapter Thirty-Seven

"Mr. Benson, your three o'clock is here."

I smirked at Julian.

"Send her in."

Cole laughed as I walked into his office. "You don't have to make an appointment, you know."

"I know, but I shouldn't get special treatment just because I'm your girlfriend."

He pressed his lips softly to mine, and I pulled back. "Excuse me, sir, but this isn't a personal call. I actually have a few questions about the Hinkley account for my four o'clock meeting."

His hand found the back of my head. "It can wait." He pressed his lips to mine again, but this time there was nothing soft about it.

I allowed myself an unrestrained moment. I wrapped one arm around him—the other was holding my iPad—and let my fingers wander down to his firm ass. I squeezed hard, and he whimpered.

I giggled. "I'll give you more of that later, but for real, I need your help."

He sighed, kissed me once more, and returned to his desk. I sat across from him in the seat I'd occupied so many times, but this time I sat there as a project manager instead of as an assistant.

It was hard to believe that just two months earlier, I'd been shacking up with my sister while I tried to "find" myself. Turns out someone else had been holding onto the biggest piece of who I was, and I wasn't complete until my heart clicked back into place with Cole's.

Everything had happened so fast. One day Cole had proposed a new position for me at Benson Industries, along with a raise and a standing offer to move in with him, and the next day it was a done deal.

It was next to impossible to find a good apartment at a fair price close to the office, and I'd been staying with Cole anyway.

He'd gone with me to look at several apartments, but compared to his gorgeous beach house, nothing fit. Waking up in Cole's arms morning after morning and taking long walks on the beach evening after evening had spoiled me. Not a single dumpy apartment could compare, and so eventually I stopped looking.

I still assisted Cole from time to time, but typically only for dinner meetings or out of town engagements. He had a new assistant now, Julian, and since Julian was a man who preferred the company of other men, I had little room for concern that Cole would hook up with his new assistant.

I trusted him completely, anyway. He'd more than proven to me that I was the only woman in his life who mattered. He was a changed man in many ways. He was still the Cole I loved, but he had a new lease on life. He lived every day like it could be his last, and he never wasted an opportunity to show me what I meant to him.

"Is that all?" he asked once I'd finished all my questions, and I nodded. He glanced at the clock. "You've got thirty minutes until your meeting."

"Then you've got about fifteen to pleasure me."

He started unbuckling his belt. "Come here," he commanded, always the boss in charge. I did as requested and stopped in front of him. "I know you said fifteen, but I may need twenty."

With that, his hand trailed up my skirt. He found what he was looking for, and I let out a moan when he pushed my panties aside and inserted one of those deliciously long fingers. He let out a low growl. "Jesus, Lucy. You're soaked." He pulled out his finger and I frowned.

"I'm always wet for you, Cole. You should know that by now."

He grinned up at me and then focused on unbuttoning his pants. He stroked himself a few times, and the sight of the attractive and nearly unattainable CEO of Benson Industries stroking himself in his desk chair was a beautiful sight.

"Get on," he said.

Even though we'd been together hundreds of times in this very office in the two months since we'd officially gotten back together, we hadn't had sex in his desk chair. It had brought back too many memories of the time we'd been apart.

But it was time to replace those sad memories with some new memories of our own.

"Just to be clear, has this chair been disinfected since—"

He cut me off with a whine. "Aw shit, woman. Do you have to bring that up now?"

"I'm just saying."

He rolled his eyes. "Yes, it has. And for both of our sakes and the sake of this," he motioned toward his steel erection, "I'm not going to let that question ruin the moment. Now get on because we're wasting time."

All I could do was laugh. He was right, of course. I'd never tell him that, but he was always right.

I straddled him, and he wasted no time before he thrust up into me. I braced myself on his shoulders.

The feel of our bodies connecting was different now than it had been before.

I'd been so worried that the reason the sex was so good between us was because it had been forbidden, but now that we were free to be together, I found that wasn't the case at all. The sex seemed to get inexplicably better and better each time as my love for Cole grew deeper and deeper.

I glanced at his handsome face. His eyes were closed and his lips were twisted in pleasure as he pumped up into me. His eyes opened, and his lips turned up at the corners in a sexy, secret smile reserved just for me.

"God, I love you," he said, and those words with all their sincerity and passion from those plush lips were my undoing as I fell into a frenzied release.

When my body stopped tightening over and over around him, he pushed up hard into me a few more times before letting go himself.

As we clung to each other in our post-orgasmic bliss, I whispered into his chest, "I love you, too."

I worried I'd always wonder if the cost of hurting one man was worth the happiness I had now. Did I deserve Cole after what we'd done?

I wasn't sure if I'd ever know the answer to that, but I looked forward to the road ahead.

THE END

ACKNOWLEDGMENTS

First and foremost, thank you to my husband. Thank you for your unending support and your belief in me. Thank you for reading contemporary romance books when I know they aren't your preferred genre. Thank you for talking plot and characters with me and for offering advice and guidance. Thank you for being an amazing daddy to sweet Mason. Thank you for working hard so I can write and stay home to be a mom. Thank you for believing me when I say I'm making up all the details about the emotions involved in cheating and divorce. I couldn't do this without you.

Thank you to my beta readers: Matt, Susan, Cathy, Pauline, Jen, Anna, Wendy, Kelly, Diane, Johnnie-Marie, and Nikki. I appreciate the time you took to read my book and give me honest and critical feedback. And of course, thank you to Lisa Suzanne's Darlings for being an awesome group of readers. And a special thank you to Anna Nicole Ureta for suggesting *Conflicted* as the title for this book!

In addition to all of the amazing blogs who tirelessly review and promote my books, I also have to give a huge thanks to Give Me Books for running the Release Day Blitz and to The Hype PR for handling the cover reveal. Thank you also to Amy from Q Design for the gorgeous cover.

Finally, thank YOU for reading this book! There are so many things to do in the few hours that each day offers, and I'm honored that you took time out of your day to spend it with my characters. I'd love if you left a review on Amazon.

XOXO,

Lisa Suzanne

ABOUT THE AUTHOR

Lisa Suzanne is a romance author who resides in Arizona with her husband and baby boy. She's a part-time college instructor and former high school English teacher. When she's not cuddling baby Mason, she can be found working on her latest book or watching reruns of *Friends*.

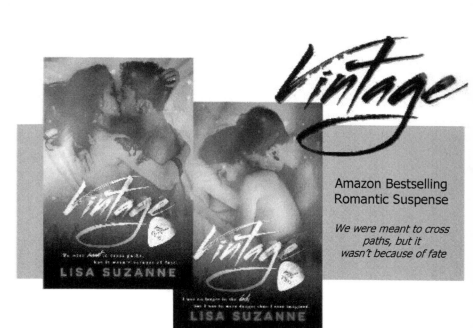

41147551R00210

Made in the USA
Middletown, DE
04 March 2017